THE HERO SHIP

Books by Hank Searls

THE HERO SHIP

THE PILGRIM PROJECT

THE CROWDED SKY

THE BIG X

THE HERO SHIP

by Hank Searls

Copyright © 1969 by Hank Searls.
All rights reserved.
No part of this book may be reproduced without
the permission of the publishers.

Published by The World Publishing Company

AN NAL BOOK
The World Publishing Company
New York and Cleveland

Published by The New American Library, Inc.
in association with The World Publishing Company
2231 West 110th Street, Cleveland, Ohio 44102
Library of Congress Catalog Card No.: 69-10750
Printed in the United States of America

To Captain Walt Schwartz, U.S. Navy,
who died happiest Warrior of all

"To stan' and be still to
the *Birken'ead* drill is
a damn' tough bullet to chew."

Kipling, of troops waiting in formation on the sinking
transport *Birkenhead* while civilians were saved.

CONTENTS

AUTHOR'S NOTE

There was a carrier bombed, like *Shenandoah,* almost in sight of Tokyo Bay. Our own ship, having business elsewhere, churned away with a Task Group and left her drifting and listing, tugging a great plume of smoke toward kamikaze bases in Japan, while burned men and those unburned dropped to the water. The flag and the carrier's air group were transferred by highline to other ships, admirals and pilots being valuable. A few deserters went with them.

Any resemblance between this carrier and *Shenandoah* is intended.

The men are another matter. I knew none of them: admiral, skipper, exec, seamen, or firemen; burned, unburned, heroes, or cowards. The men on *Shenandoah* are a blend of Navy men from many ships and stations and squadrons and each character is fictitious, civilian or military. Any resemblance between them and persons living or dead, while gratifying, is *not* intended.

—Hank Searls

PART ONE

Studbook on a Mustang

CHAPTER ONE

ONE

Her hulk loomed darkly above the Jersey flats, visible from the turnpike for miles. She seemed a feature of terrain, no longer of the sea. Her hull and flight deck were a huge mesa and her island structure a castellated peak. Paint flaked from her plates; her untreated sores ran rust.

He had not intended to see her when he started. Fires of rage long banked within him had flared when Father Epstein phoned from Washington that Admiral Christy Lee was actually up for chief of naval operations. So he had flown east: tanned, graying, but still young enough to attract smiles from stewardesses his daughter's age. He had boarded the jetliner full of resolve, but sipping a martini at thirty thousand feet over the Great Plains he rediscovered a tiny, eternal doubt, a suspicion that hatred might have colored recollection of an instant twenty-three years old. It was not until he landed at National Airport that he decided to visit the ship first, to see if somewhere in her hull, frozen in time for two decades, lay certainty. He rented a car and drove north.

She dwarfed the dock to which they had chained her. For twenty years there had been talk of reprieve: she was to be made a national shrine, her carcass was to be towed to Annapolis, the Navy League was funding her restoration. He had come east once before to launch their good works at a luncheon, speaking over an ice-cream replica with a listing flight deck, but if the league cleared any money it was spent reproducing prints of the Battle of Mobile Bay or the memoirs of a naval surgeon in the War of 1812. She had cost seventy million dollars to build and a thousand dead and wounded to save and last month she had sold to the scrappers for $143,000.

She lay alone; her sisters had left long ago. Some had been drawn and quartered under the wrecker's torches; a few, he guessed, were recommissioned during Korea and slinging jets now toward Vietnam or lying off Cannes or plowing the China Sea.

She seemed as always more solid underfoot than whatever dock she was alongside. On the dark and freezing hangar deck he showed identification and signed the watchman's log: "Ben Casco, Capt., USN (retd.)." The man had a red nose and no handkerchief and didn't recognize the name if he had ever heard it, although it appeared on a bronze plaque six feet from his head. Ben borrowed a flashlight from him and went forward, his footsteps metallic in the vast emptiness. He stepped to the forecastle under the overhang of the flight deck where Chief Catlett, the nucleus of her sickness, had writhed in silent agony rather than allow himself to groan and where the men on the hawser had died for Christy Lee's cowardice, but that was why he was here, to douse the tiny doubt, so he stumbled aft through dark passageways and bunkrooms and messing compartments and galleys. A gutted book of Navy regulations lay in his office, pages scattered. A razor had rusted to the stainless sink in Father Epstein's stateroom. It was as hard to remove the traces of a crew from a ship as a family from a home. Squeezed toothpaste tubes and hidden pinups would ride with her lockers and bulkheads all the way to the blast furnace; it struck him that since matter lived eternally, faint elements of hair and toenails and perhaps a dead seaman's gristle, considering her previous incineration, might appear in some happy family's next-year car.

He found a dimly remembered ladder. He swung down to the brig and paused at the warden's steel desk, poking the light further below at the six stainless-steel cages. In them, under guard of a broiled marine with a Chinese-doll face, three roasted bodies had waited a whole day because there was other work to be done.

He hopped through rainwater in his own unlighted cabin and jabbed light into the captain's, where Mitch's mess steward had died screaming in Tagalog. On the gallery overlooking the vast hangar deck he paused: here, he'd had the charred flesh removed too quickly, perhaps—in GI cans, to the horror of the chaplain, who should have been more concerned with souls and less with corporeal details—and even so the place had oozed death all the way home.

The ship creaked and wailed and a northeasterly straight from Labrador whispered through her vents. But the sweet stench of death was gone. Twenty years of wind had cleared it, where soap and Lysol and hundreds of gallons of water had failed. Now there was only the flattop odor of oil and gasoline, and that smell must have seeped to her marrow, for it had been an eternity since fuel had run in her veins.

He stepped into cutting wind on the flight deck, circled the island structure, and climbed a few rungs of the emergency ladder on the outboard side, hanging over the dock a hundred feet below. He looked up at the five-inch director from which Christy had jumped, trying in his mind to leap backward twenty-three years. He failed. He felt nothing except embarrassment at being there. He dropped quickly back to the deck before some passing yardbird should see him, and then mounted to the bridge where Mitch had died. Still he felt nothing. On the way down he undogged the hatch to flag plot. A bare bulb swung minutely from the overhead. The great plastic plotting board on which they'd tracked the first kamikaze was thick with dust.

His bowels tightened, as they did in any dark and vacant room, but that was all. You were supposed to feel an ache in your heart, and all he sensed was a rumble in his belly.

He signed off in the watchman's book and moved down the gangway. Between dock and hull floated a green industrial scum. Trapped in the center, about where Christy Lee had hit the water, rode a crate: "Jorgensen's Golden Apples."

Lieutenant Commander Christy Lee, Golden Boy. Rotted, always, lieutenant commander then or admiral now, harmless paper-pusher yesterday or chief of naval operations-elect today. Always tarnished to those who knew, perhaps now gray. But forever the All-American, and lucky, lucky, lucky: in sight at long last of the Goal.

He moved off the gangway toward the rented car on the dock. He was foolish to want to rattle a cage locked long ago. The Navy he owed nothing, nor the ship. Twenty-three years ago he had given Justice her chance and she had blown it. To try to goose her into action now was childish. He would get a ticket out of Newark and go home.

He looked up at the great gray shape. The cracked lens of a searchlight glared down at him from the signal bridge. No ghosts, still, but all at once a dim memory: a nameless owl-faced signalman who used to man the light, ordered to a destroyer alongside with a mangled hand, arguing long enough to catch a whistling, jagged engine part dead-center in his face. And Christy Lee floating safely in the wake . . .

The searchlight swung in the wind. Now he felt the anger

rising again, all right, and the stupid doubt recede, and when he turned onto the Jersey turnpike, he drove not to Newark Airport but south, toward Washington.

TWO

He turned from a rain-smeared view of the Capitol dome out Father Epstein's office window. He had spent Korea in the Pentagon consigning helicopter pilots to hell and he hated Washington. He waited, morosely inspecting battered legal tomes and impressionistic Japanese art while Epstein sent his skinny Nisei secretary for the file on Christy Lee. When the girl was gone Ben continued where he had been interrupted. "Well, let's shoot down the son of a bitch."

Father Barney Epstein, proclaimed on a desk plaque in Hebrew, Japanese, and English as an attorney-at-law and the only son of the Rabbi of Tokyo, regarded him over his glasses. His eyes were soft brown, happy because Ben was there; he still wore a thick red moustache but the monk ring of hair around his bald head was almost gone. He offered Ben a cigar, which Ben put away for later. He adjusted the spectacles on the bridge of a noble nose—Cro-Magnin, he called it, claiming an uncle in the department-store family. He put stockinged feet on his desk; he always moored his shoes side by side at the threshold, Japanese-style.

"You said you'd be in yesterday. What happened?"

"I drove up to the ship."

"Why?"

Ben could never admit the doubt, even to Epstein. "Last look," he shrugged.

Epstein accepted it and went to work. "I'll try to set up

lunch with Senator Mosk for tomorrow, just the three of us."
Mosk was Epstein's client, and he was on the Armed Services Committee. The secretary returned with the Lee file and
he told her to get the senator on the phone; he slipped out
three depositions from a long envelope and held up one of
the sheets.

"Japanese original," he said, "we'll leave that in the safe,
for when we need it. Japanese photostat . . . and an English
translation."

"Let me see it," Ben said.

Epstein skidded the translation across the desk. Ben
scanned it. His own hand, he noticed, was trembling. Epstein
watched him narrowly. "I wonder . . . are you really going
through with it—or are you going to pull a Hamlet and
change your mind?"

"When the hell did I ever change my mind?"

"Once," commented Epstein. "Just once."

"Well, I've changed it back."

"Not many people," observed Epstein, licking his cigar,
"get a chance after twenty years."

"There's no statute of limitations," Ben said casually, "on
blackmail."

Epstein's cigar stopped short. He laid it in an ashtray,
never taking his eyes from Ben's. "What's with the 'blackmail'?" he asked carefully.

"That's what it's going to be," Ben told him, bracing for
the storm.

"Character assassination, maybe," Epstein admitted. "The
sword of Damocles falls in the committee. He knows who
dropped it. But by then it's too late. What's the 'blackmail'
bit?"

"Barney," Ben said wearily, "we have to give him a chance
to resign."

Father Epstein dropped his feet from the desk and sat erect. "Like hell we do!"

"We have to," Ben insisted. "He'll resign, he'll drop out of sight, it won't hurt the Navy in the press, it won't hurt the ship."

"The ship's been in mothballs twenty years. She's on her way to the scrappers!"

"I don't want her maligned. Too many widows, too many guys left that have been telling their kids about her."

"Are you really trying to protect the ship?" Epstein demanded. "Or your wife?"

"As you damn well know," Ben said tersely, "my wife can take care of herself. Anyway, I'm the one doing it. My way or not at all."

Epstein rubbed his eyes. "Oh, God! Exactly what *is* your way?"

Ben folded the copy of the deposition and carefully put it in his pocket. "I'm going to show this to him. I'm going to tell him we're turning it over to Senator—what's his name?"

"Mosk," said Father Epstein heavily. "And much as he'd like a crack at a presidential nominee, *any* nominee, you know what he'll say when I tell him you've *warned* Golden Boy?"

Ben shook his head.

"He'll suggest," Father Epstein said, "that I take my 'deposition' and jam it up my ass!"

"It won't be that bad."

Father Epstein got up and began to pace. "Let me tell you something. First, let me paint you a picture of how it ought to be done—how it *has* to be done. O.K.?"

"O.K." Ben agreed reluctantly.

"All right. The committee is sitting in a hearing room. Golden Boy, shining in braid, is ushered in with his four rows of ribbons. No Senate committee has ever turned down a presidential nominee for CNO yet, remember."

"That's right. So he'll resign before it ever happens."

Epstein ignored him. "He enters to silent applause. He takes his seat. The chairman greets him, smiling; the chairman knows nothing. Golden Boy knows nothing. *Nobody* knows nothing, except my client Mosk, an ugly little Jew from the garment district."

Ben nodded. It was very, very tempting.

"One or two questions," Father Epstein went on, "and a call for a voice vote of confirmation, a token. But then Mosk says, 'Admiral, let me ask you something. Have you ever faced a court-martial?' 'No sir.' 'The *prospect* of one?' Confusion, but Golden Boy is fast on his feet. 'Yes sir. I was blown off the USS *Shenandoah* during the war. Or at least'—now he gives it the grin, Ben—'at least the convening authority so found, apparently, since the charges were dropped.' " Epstein flashed a Golden Boy smile, all teeth and level eyes and a firm, firm jaw.

"Spare the histrionics," Ben suggested.

"Then he hits him with a few quotes from the Jap's deposition, and he didn't even know it existed, and he isn't *that* fast on his feet, nobody is, so he comes apart. *But*——"

"Look, Father, it's no use."

"*But*," Epstein went on, knocking his fist on the desk, "you warn him first, you just give him a hint, and he'll limp in on his Purple Heart so loaded with legal aides and fellow admirals and citations and personality that he will clobber the twenty-year-old deposition of Mr. Yokawa, the reluctant kamikaze, which as you know is only the truth and has no legal value whatsoever. Then he will make a treacherous, unpatriotic opportunist out of my ugly little Jew. Worse, he will make a fool of him, senator or not. And my client will know this."

Ben said nothing.

Epstein sat back. "And if he doesn't know it," he concluded, "I'll have to tell him."

"Sorry, Barney," said Ben, "I'm going to see Lee in the morning."

"It won't work! Christ, he's not up for secretary of the Academy Alumni Association! He's up for CNO! He's been shooting for it for thirty years! You think he'll bluff?"

"I hope so."

"You haven't seen him in twenty years! All the time you've been out there trying to sell chopper rides he's been back here practicing jungle warfare. You're a child at this, and you're going to blow our only chance." He moved to the window, looked out, and turned back. "Ben?"

"Yes?"

"He's a murderer."

"Yes."

"He's within reach of a hell of a lot of power."

"So he's vulnerable for the first time."

"He won't quit!"

"If he was yellow then, he's yellow now."

"What do you mean, *if?* You saw him jump!"

The light on Epstein's phone began to flash. Ben found that his head was aching. "I saw him jump," he said softly. "He'll jump again, somehow, and there won't be a lot of crap in the papers, because he'll sidestep it. A conditioned reflex. From football, maybe."

"From football," muttered Epstein, picking up the phone. "Christ!"

While Epstein talked to Senator Mosk, Ben moved idly to a photo hanging, in a splatter of diplomas and plaques from B'nai B'rith, next to Epstein's framed reserve commission. It was an aerial shot of the *Shenandoah*. She was plunging, joyous and virginal, from Puget Sound to open sea. He had seen the picture many times: *Time* magazine had run it with the story of her last fight; he had a clipping at home, somewhere. He had always liked the shot, because it was taken from the precise angle and altitude at which to start your orbit if there were other planes ahead of you to land.

THREE

He had seen her first on her shakedown cruise in 1941, six months before Pearl. After eight years as an enlisted pilot he had been commissioned directly to j.g. and ordered to the newest carrier in the U.S. fleet. With her raw new air group he had broken from cumulus at two thousand feet off the Washington coast and begun to circle her, flying wing on the squadron exec, waiting his turn to land. From the air group's first pass things went wrong, and by sunset she had been tagged as a bad-luck ship, nickname and all, which was a record for ship slandering. To love her over the years took tolerance from the beginning and a certain blind faith, as if she were an erring sister or a daughter bound to improve in time.

From any altitude or angle, she had been beautiful. The afternoon sun, which this far north would hang in the west until taps, had etched her in gold as she plowed from the moss-green narrows of Puget Sound. As he watched she began to take the Pacific swell in ponderous gulps, tossing rose-tinged water port and starboard from her bow, bounding through the strait like a great gray porpoising whale. Whatever she did over the years, whatever they said of her, he would see her in sapphire blue and golden sunlight knifing through sheets of pink-plumed spray.

She had been very different from his last ship, the old *Lexington*. She was almost three football fields long. Officially she weighed twenty-seven thousand tons but that was for foreign consumption: loaded for bear, she would hit closer to forty thousand. Twenty-five hundred men, almost, now that the air group was coming aboard, would live in her. In her fighting top, forty-millimeter gunners rode a hundred and fifty feet above the water; men in steering aft worked thirty feet beneath the surface.

Barbers and cobblers, he knew, had already set up trade in her hull; and butchers and pastry cooks, lawyers and pants pressers, watchmakers and opticians, doctors and male nurses; tailors, typists, storekeepers, accountants, photographers, and auto mechanics for her jeeps. She would have, Ben knew, two or three dentists, a priest, a minister, and possibly a rabbi. At flank speed the whole floating city could move at a respectable pace for a car ashore.

In her magazines, when she was deployed to Pearl next month, would ride enough bombs to destroy half of Tokyo, should war start, and in her tanks sloshed a quarter of a million gallons of high-test aviation gasoline for her planes. Her one hundred aircraft could strike Japan on Monday and Manila, should the Japs be foolish enough to declare war and try to take it, on Tuesday.

Ben's old *Lexington* had been built on a cruiser hull authorized during World War I, when Ben was four. But the *Shenandoah* was new, built keel-up for what she was, a fast fleet carrier, and finished just in time. The United States had only five aircraft carriers, and the British, begging for American help in the North Atlantic and licking their wounds after Dunkirk, had other naval problems than the Pacific.

The air group circled and began a turn into the wind. They were honed sharp by months of field carrier landings

at Sand Point in Seattle, and the flight deck looked so much bigger than what they had qualified on ashore that the greenest ensign in the air group must be facing his first pass calmly.

Mitch Langley, as carrier air-group commander, would land first; a great honor on a new ship. Ben saw him flash with his wingman past the island structure, flick a wing skyward, drop his landing gear, and enter the pattern so low to the water that from Ben's altitude he seemed to be touching the chop. He watched him churn onto imaginary rails, and curve, nose high and stolid, toward the virginal "SH" at the after end of the flight deck. The landing signal officer's paddles were locked rock-steady in the "roger" position: a perfect approach. Suddenly, aghast, Ben watched a blue-jersied handler leap from the starboard catwalk and sprint across the deck. The paddles waved desperately and Mitch clawed for altitude and tucked up his wheels and cleared, so that the first man to get the historic cut and land was not Mitch after all, but his wingman, and then his other wingman missed the cut in the glare of the orange sun and nosed up in the barrier. It took twenty minutes to untangle the plane and wheel it away, and there was a visible gash from the prop in the shining teak deck when they finally did.

Ben sat back in the cockpit with a chill at the pit of his stomach. No one had been hurt, but a wave-off and a barrier crash in the first three landings gave him a strange feeling of doom, as if he had seen a yard workman crushed while the hull slid down the ways.

That night in the wardroom the food was good, as if the ship were trying to make amends. There was even a cake, a tremendous, carrier-type cake, although it had to be served to Mitch's wingman for landing first, instead of Mitch, as planned. But while they were serving it the rhythmic *rattle, bang, shhh . . .* of the catapults stopped, much too soon, and

a steward hurried from a wardroom phone to the senior medical officer. The doctor groaned, shoved back his chair, and left in a rush.

"What happened, boy?" asked the squadron landing signal officer, a potbellied reserve lieutenant from Mississippi called Poopy-Bag because he had got his wings in blimps.

"Plane handler, sir," the Negro answered. "Walked into a prop on the number-two elevator."

Ben felt sick. Poopy-Bag dug at his cake and drawled, "This ship don't know shit from Shinola." He looked up happily. "Shinola!" he said. "The USS *Shinola!*"

Commander Mitch Langley sighed and shook his head. His eyes lost their softness. "That's nice, Poopy-Bag," he said quietly. "That's very, very nice."

It was as close as he ever came to eating out a man in public, and it was lost on Poopy-Bag, who contentedly mouthed his cake. It was too late, anyway, because the name *Shinola* stuck, all the way to Tokyo Bay, and if it had not been that name, someone would have come up with something worse.

Ben awakened the next morning in the JO's bunkroom to find the cats silent and the beat of the screws slowed for fog. There were other aviators aboard, he knew, who would live in her for years without knowing much more than the way from their bunks to the barbershop or the bridge game in the wardroom, but you never knew where a fire or collision might catch you.

He had mastered his first ship, the old battleship *Nevada*, by osmosis, as a native learns the jungle, for he was a seaman apprentice then, liable to be sent to the boatswain's locker for striped paint or the metal shop for a left-handed monkey wrench. He had gradually learned the *Lexington*, too, without really trying, but now he was a kind of plank owner, airedale or not, and he wanted to discover the *Shenandoah* systematically and right. He dressed after breakfast in his oldest khakis. All morning long and half the afternoon he squirmed through manholes and hatches and dogged and un- dogged doors. Everyone, everywhere, seemed to be modify- ing, changing, molding as always on a shakedown cruise.

Emerging from the depths, he wandered through the mess- deck and saw the great, gleaming coffee urns, which could brew five hundred gallons a day. He went past the post office, closed as usual, and the main branch of the three ship's stores, also closed while a soda jerk cleaned mixers and sorted ice-cream scoops behind a chicken-wire screen. He glanced at displays in the case: Zippo lighters, Williams shaving cream, and purple satin pillows inscribed to mother. He poked his head into the ship's laundry. Two lethargic cretins pawed through laundry bags under the sleepy eye of a coxswain; half the machines were shut down already for repair.

"Well, *Mr. Casco!*" Ben tensed. The voice still had the power to chill his guts. His old boot-camp drill instructor, Chief Catlett, stood before him, green eyes beaming with amusement, flashing pearly teeth somehow too small for him. He was tall, tanned, a handsome man, viewed from his right side, until you noticed a strange delicacy of mouth and nose: they, like his teeth, did not quite fit his size or his broad, balding forehead. If you cared to brave the green slitted eyes and look closely at his left side you saw the hideous scar of massive plastic surgery on his lower jaw. He was all cords, sinews, veins, knuckles, and hard head, reputedly in his drill- instructor days powerful and quick enough to knock a man out with a three-inch jab to the heart or cripple him with a knee to the groin.

On his starched khaki shirt glittered a new gold police badge: Chief Master-at-Arms. Ben had not seen Catlett in ten years, but they did not shake hands.

"J.G.!" Catlett grinned, eyeing the silver bars. "I never thought to see the day."

"You're seeing it," said Ben. He waited for Catlett to step aside and moved down the passageway. He noticed that the laundry coxswain on seeing Catlett had decided to try to fix his downed machines and that sweat was pouring from the backs of his two assistants as they began suddenly to manhandle huge bags in 110° heat. The new bars felt very good.

He had felt secure and warm before knowing of Catlett's presence aboard; now, inviolate or not, he was restless and uncomfortable. He moved through the marines' living compartments—immaculate as always, a world of leather and brass, polish and jewelers' rouge, gun oil and slings drumtaut on rifles racked and gleaming. The marines as always had transformed their quarters into a private sanctuary; the globe-and-anchor plaques were everywhere, on office doors and cleaning-gear lockers, and every stenciled sign in red and marine gold. Red-striped trousers hung in their tailor shop, for of course they had to have a separate tailor shop and a presser too for their knife-edge shirts; a file of high-collared blouses hung stiffly in column athwartships. He moved through the dental quarters, all gleaming steel and white enamel, and into sick bay. The senior medical officer stumbled past him. He had a thick black stubble and red eyes. A corpsman told Ben that they had been unable to get the prop victim ashore and a half-hour ago he had died and Ben's high spirits left him. The fog had cleared and the fighters had started carrier landing qualifications again, so he showered and put on his flight jacket. He rode a shining escalator— God, an *escalator*—to the flight deck and climbed to the bridge to watch air ops. He stepped from the island structure and stared at a monkey figure from the old *Nevada*.

Pappy Shea turned, brown eyes starting. He seemed somehow smaller and the eyes had gone watery, but he was still erect and doughty; already, as chief quartermaster, he was lord of the bridge. He grabbed Ben's arm and for a moment Ben thought he was going to embrace him, but he only jabbed the bars on his collar.

"I *heard!* Not from you, you big ape! But Lieutenant, j.g., USN!"

"USN (*T*)," Ben reminded him. The "T" was for "temporary"; he was still a permanent CPO. "What are you doing on a *carrier?*"

"Better than playing acey-deucy in the Pedro Fleet Reserve," Pappy muttered. "She's a good feeder anyway." For Pappy, who would have defended a garbage scow if he were assigned it, it was practically an insult.

Ben liked her already: "She'll be O.K."

"Yeah?" Pappy nodded at the number-two elevator. "I seen that kid get it yesterday. He was a taxi signalman. Hell, Ben, he wasn't as old as you when you came to the *Nevada.* He was walking backward, wiggling his fingers—"

"It happens," Ben said tersely.

"It never happened in the *Nevada,*" Pappy grunted. "Nothing like it, in twenty years. It don't happen on a battleship."

Ben watched the Wildcats trundling to the line. The props thrashed halos of water from the moist air. The green and yellow and red-jersied flight deck men were learning the steps of the old ballet; the launch interval was dropping with each plane, there was constant, raw action below, and when it smoothed out in a week or a month the flight deck would become a three-ring, incredible circus in which every performer from the catapult officer to the tail-hook man sliding like a base runner under the fuselage would know his act so perfectly that you could spend hours gaping down at the show and never want to leave.

"It doesn't happen on a battleship," he told Pappy, "because *nothing* happens on a battleship. She'll be a good ship, Pappy."

"I don't think so," Pappy said softly. "The USS *Shinola. . . .*"

The nickname had already reached the chief's mess. The old *Nevada* had had a nickname too: *No-Go Maru,* from her rickety engines. But Pappy had never used it in the two years Ben had worked for him. "You've never been *on* a carrier," Ben flared. "You don't know the catapult from the number-one wire! How the hell do you know what she's going to be?"

"She's a ship, ain't she? You ever see a woman, in a bar, or on the street, you *know* she's going to end up in a whore-house?"

"Christ," Ben said, "you going to pull that Ancient Mariner crap *here?*"

"Not for long, I hope," Pappy said. "I got in for the *Nevada* again."

They flew carrier qualifications for two weeks and almost lost a fighter jockey on a cold-cat shot off the bow and they did lose a reserve ensign who flew into the ramp when he thought he saw Poopy-Bag give him an early cut; they had two more barrier crashes and a seaman in the 1st division fell off the starboard catwalk at night and was never found; they never knew whether it was suicide or a slippery ladder. But the food remained excellent and the IC room fixed the phone system so at least you could call the chaplain's yeoman for the movie and not end up talking to the exec.

Two fatalities for a two-week cruise made rather sticky odds, and the name *Shinola* turned out to be the kind that the Fleet used cynically, like *No-Go* for the *Nevada*, rather than affectionately, like the *Gray Ghost* or *Fighting Lady;* but when Ben, with his green aviator's bag in hand, went ashore for his last two weeks before they left for Pearl, he looked back at the docked ship and she was just as beautiful as she was from the air, and he didn't care if he had another billet until he retired.

FOUR

His wife was lushly lovely in pregnancy, and contrite since Annapolis. But that week she turned irritable. In Bremerton married officers lived temporarily in a dusty bachelor officers' quarters that must have been built in World War I. It had been converted to married officers' quarters when the reserves began showing up, dragging their families along. The walls were so tissue-thin that, as she said, when an ensign at one end whispered, "Roll over, honey," half the Navy wives on the floor got laid. The bathrooms were communal; men used the second-floor head and women the one on the first floor. She was sick in the mornings and she had to dash down the stairs every dawn. Sporadically they house-hunted. She decided that they were being shunted aside because he was a mustang. "In the commissary, in the housing office—they're supposed to be trying to get us an apartment, aren't they?—and the dispensary. What *I* need is an Academy miniature!"

"That's a lot of crap. Nobody knows who we are, it's all in your mind. What about the reserves? How do they get treated?"

"They've got their own little fraternity; half their wives went to Smith. I wish you'd stayed chief."

"We're not making it on j.g.'s pay," Ben pointed out. "How the hell could we make it again as chief?"

He blamed the bitching on the quarters and her pregnancy and even on the poor, maligned *Shenandoah,* because when he wasn't spending twelve hours a day at Sand Point signing engine logs, he was out qualifying on the ship. He still loved his wife very much; her soft, dirty chuckle stirred him as much as ever. They had one more week to find her an apartment before he left, and for once they had a lead. It was all the way over in Seattle, but that wouldn't matter, because Ben wouldn't be back for six months anyway. He awakened the last Sunday with a vicious hangover and returned from the head with a sour tongue and throbbing eyes.

"Ben, let's not." She was lying in bed smoking, studying him strangely.

"Let's not what?"

"Go see that apartment."

"Honey, you've got to stay *someplace!*"

"I want to go back to San Francisco."

He moved to the window and looked out. The pane was dusty and streaked with the last rain. The screen was gashed. Through the rip he could see the *Shenandoah,* clean and solid and shining in the rain-washed air. He noticed idly that the church pennant had been hoisted with a kink: God help the signal bridge when Pappy came topside and noticed *that.* He ought to phone the officer of the deck himself before the admiral spotted it from the top of the hill. The hell with it; he had his own problems.

"You can't go back. You're all set up in the hospital here."

"I don't want a Navy hospital! If some captain's wife turns up with a splinter in her butt they'll leave me right in the middle of having the baby!"

He reminded her that they couldn't afford to have the baby in a civilian hospital and that her last hospital had been a Navy one and it had saved her life. Keeping his voice low, because he could sense half the floor listening, he pointed out that Bremerton was the ship's home port, and the Navy wouldn't even pay to send her home.

"Then get out!"

"What?"

Reasonably, she said, "You're an officer now. Resign."

He shook his head in disbelief. "You're kidding!"

"You could get a job with an airline! It's time you made a living!"

"Christ, the way things are going, I'll be a lieutenant in three months! They're drafting into the Army! They've called in the Fleet reserve! They got so many feather merchants aboard now it's a wonder we can get under way without tearing every bollard off the dock! You think they'd let me out?"

"You can do *anything* you want to. You always could, even in school."

He wandered to the tiny writing desk and sat down. A red rage swelled in his throat. He couldn't get out, he could prove that, but even if he could, she had no right to ask him to. He fought down an impulse to shift the ground and bring up Annapolis. Hoarsely, without looking at her, he said, "Forget it. You have to stay."

"No."

"You're too far along to drive that far."

"I'll fly down. Or take the train."

"What would we do with the car?"

"Store it, sell it."

"Where would you live?"

"With Mamma."

"No!"

He heard her get up and move behind him. "Why, no?" she asked softly. Then, when he did not answer, she moved around him, put her fingers under his chin, and lifted his face. "*Why*, no?" she asked again, eyes narrow, two bright spots on her cheeks. She looked like Carmen about to stab her lover.

"Take your goddamn hands off my face!" he said, slapping her fingers away. "You're not going."

"Because of your child? You don't want him brought up around my mamma?"

"Or your poor, hardworking daddy?" he asked maliciously. "Do *you?*"

She looked at him and smiled. "You don't understand, do you?" She moved to the window. "The place stinks, do you know that? I mean really, it stinks."

"Seattle won't."

"It's dirty," she said. "The yard, the smell of all that welding, or whatever it is, and the banging and tooting. It's dirty. It smells. It's noisy. I hate it."

"Seattle's quiet."

"I hate the ship, too," she mused.

"You won't see her for another six months."

"Also, I hate the Navy," she murmured. "I hate all the little sailor-boys, and the fat-assed officers."

"You'll get used to them."

"I hate you too," she said softly. "Will I get used to——"

He found himself swinging her around, ready to shake her, to slap the smile from her face, but when he looked into her great amber eyes they were wet. He held her for a long time, and finally she said, "Ben, I don't mean it, I'll stay here, I'll do anything you want . . ." and he knew that she meant *that* and he felt the pressure of her hip on his thigh and kissed her and that of course settled it as it always seemed to; they spent half the day in bed and next morning he put her on the plane for San Francisco. He watched her walk up the ladder, her skirt swinging. He went back to the room in the MOQ and packed.

That evening he got drunk at the officers' club and lost

twenty-five dollars in the slot machines and that night he moved aboard the ship. There was the tiniest, disloyal feeling of relief in sleeping alone for a change, for she had turned in the last months into a tiger in bed, pregnant or not, but six months in the Pacific would recharge his batteries.

It would be almost three years.

CHAPTER TWO

ONE

For the *Shenandoah* pilots who would bumble into the cauldron of Pearl Harbor on December 7 and survive, the days and hours before that Sunday were a kaleidoscope. The Saturday previous was the Army-Navy game, relayed to the *Shenandoah* five hundred miles off Oahu, and Ben, a full lieutenant now, sat sipping coffee in the wardroom to hear it, studying the man he hated, even then, more than he would hate anyone in this life. Golden Boy Lee, tall and wide-shouldered, with slim hips and a firm jaw and a frank, Stover-at-Yale smile, was a very junior ensign who had been aboard only three months, but on this Saturday he commanded the rapt attention of lieutenants and commanders and the admiral's staff and every department head on the ship. About him shone the aura of his last year's glory. He moved a football-shaped magnet on a green steel gridiron complete with little goalposts he had somehow hustled for the broadcast from the metal shop. Occasionally, and modestly, he answered questions from the senior officers: "What now, Christy?" "I think a wide sweep, sir."

He was right, Ben had to admit, most of the time. When he was not, he somehow exuded the feeling that this year's quarterback was, after all, inexperienced. Every Annapolis man not on duty and half the reserves sat tensely in rows of chairs he had set up, cursing and cheering and groaning; Golden Boy had even sent in advance for game programs so that you could follow the names and the numbers.

Ben leafed through the pages at half time: he would later remember that there were almost as many pictures of tanks and ships as of players and that under a bow-on shot of a battlewagon a public-relations caption writer reminded the fan that "despite the claims of air enthusiasts no battleship has yet been sunk by bombs." The picture was of the *Arizona.*

The *Shenandoah* was hammering northeast at the time, carrying a marine squadron of slow, bullheaded Brewster fighters for Midway. The Brewsters were painted wartime gray and their guns were newly boresighted in view of the crisis. They were practically useless, but everyone knew that if the Japs, cut off finally from U.S. oil and scrap and ordered three days ago to "withdraw all forces from China and Indochina," were foolish enough to tangle with the United States they would hit the Asiatic Fleet in the Philippines and there was no use wasting first-line Grumman Wildcats on a squadron of jarhead aviators stranded on an island four thousand miles from Manila.

Navy won, even without Golden Boy, 14–0. Later they would learn that while they had been sitting in the wardroom cheering, the Japanese Pearl Harbor strike force had been pounding toward them less than a thousand miles away. If the *Shenandoah* had continued northeast past Midway, she might well have found herself at night with her three escorting cruisers and five destroyers in the midst of thirty-one Japanese ships, from carriers and battlewagons down to fleet tankers. There would have been no warning, as the Japs were launching no patrols, fearing discovery, and the *Shenandoah* launched none either, fearing nothing. But she sent the marine squadron on to Midway and turned back.

Twelve hundred miles south, heading toward Wake on an identical mission, Admiral Halsey steamed with the other half of the existing U.S. air strength in the central Pacific: the USS *Enterprise*. He was ready for war, and launching patrols. Had the Japanese force turned south, he might well have encountered it, in which case the *Big E* and Halsey would have been lost forever but Pearl Harbor, of course, would have been warned.

The *Shenandoah* steamed back toward Pearl, launching routine training flights; to the south, Admiral Halsey sent off the Wake reinforcements and turned back too. On the Friday after the Army-Navy game Chief Pappy Shea, who after six months had finally got his orders to the battleship *Nevada*, asked Ben if he would fly him in Sunday to Ford Island; he was afraid the *Nevada* would leave Monday on exercises and strand him in the receiving station. Ben spent that Saturday listening to KGMB broadcasting the University of Hawaii-Willamette game; this turned out to be exactly what the Japanese flag communicator, Commander Kanjiro Ono, was listening to as well, to see if the alarm was out. Hawaii won, 20–6, and Ben knew he was missing a wild night in Honolulu.

On Sunday morning, December 7, while both U.S. carriers converged on Pearl, the Japanese strike force was 230 miles northeast of Honolulu. At 0600 the six Japanese carriers swung into the wind. Their crews cheered and cried and waved, and the first of 353 bombers, torpedo planes, and fighter escorts thundered down the pitching flight decks and into the rising sun. At 0750 Army privates George Elliott and Joe Lockard, manning a radar-crammed trailer on Kahuku Point in northern Oahu, spotted a large number of aircraft approaching on their screen. They called the Army interceptor center at Fort Shafter and insisted on speaking directly to the duty officer, an Army pilot named Kermit Tyler. Lieutenant Tyler, who knew that B-17's from California and Halsey's planes were due that day, seemed unimpressed; he decided that their targets were Navy planes and told them not to worry about it. They did worry about it, though; it was the biggest flight either had ever seen and it was closing at 180 knots. They tracked it all the way in to twenty-two miles before they lost it in a dead spot; by that time a truck had arrived to take them to breakfast and they had to lock up the trailer and leave. The lieutenant had been correct: they were Navy planes, only they belonged to the wrong navy, and nobody told the right one.

On the USS *Shenandoah*, two hundred miles northwest of Pearl Harbor, the propellers of six SBD Dauntless dive-bombers ticked over in the morning sun. Ben Casco glanced into his rearview mirror. Pappy Shea was clinging to his arm-rest in the rear cockpit like a monkey in a flying helmet; he hated airplanes; the fact that he was submitting to a catapult shot was a measure of his longing for the *Nevada*. On the port signal halliard the "fox" flag, a red diamond on white, fluttered into view and the ship turned into the wind. The SBD's began to trundle forward, two at a time, passed from one yellow-jersied plane director to another until they were picked up by the signals of the catapult officer. Then, one port and one starboard, each would waddle to the catapult and settle itself over the sling like a fussy duck, brakes locked, while the cat was made fast. The engine would drum and throb and the sound would squeeze the guts of handlers and gun crews and the onlookers twenty feet away in the catwalks over the water; when it seemed that the cylinders must blow apart, the catapult officer would fling his hand to a point and his whole body parallel to the deck, like an adagio dancer. The catapult would fire with a bang and the stocky SBD, seeming always surprised, would bounce down the track, disappear under the overhang of the flight deck, and then, an eternity later, struggle into sight.

Ben launched and joined on the other aircraft in a loose scouting formation. They began to drone toward Oahu. Ben settled back, automatically scanning the glitter below, but thinking really of the next two weeks at Pearl. When they landed, he would get a room at Ford Island BOQ and a shower and a ride into Honolulu. He would have a drink at the Royal Hawaiian, perhaps, watching the surfers mount the great waves surging on Waikiki and ride them endlessly until they were out of sight below the window. He might eat there and check the action—no, not with a pregnant wife. He decided virtuously to return to the BOQ to write a letter to her instead.

Although a lieutenant commander led the flight, Ben cranked the radio to the Ford Island range to check the leader's navigation. Ford Island seemed to be off the air, so he switched channels to KGMB to home in on the Sunday sermons; nothing there either. Thinking that his radio must have blown, he checked the circuit breakers and then tuned to the frequency of the Ford Island tower. The flight leader was calling it: "Ford Island Tower, this is Navy three-five-eight-nine-seven-six, thirty miles northwest, with five. Request straight-in approach." Silence, and then a crazy garbled crackling, and silence again. Ben peered ahead. On the horizon was a great marshmallow cloud which might bring afternoon rain to the Pali, but only served now as an aerial blaze mark to show that Oahu was beneath.

"Fifteen minutes," he told Pappy. Pappy was enjoying the flight now, although he would probably not have admitted it. They droned on for another five minutes until Ben could see the dark-blue coastline between Barbers Point and Diamond Head, backed by the Koolaupoko Range. Squarely in the middle lay Pearl Harbor, like a paper-doll mother scissored out by a child: feet and legs the channel, one ear Ford Island, and one arm holding a squalling infant toward Ewa Marine Airfield. Smoke drifted over the anchorage; odd, to burn cane fields on Sunday. Ben shifted uncomfortably, wishing they could raise the Ford Island Tower.

They began to descend over Barbers Point and Ben noticed a long chain of aircraft skimming Palikea Peak and dropping link by twisting link toward Pearl. The pattern of their runs was strange, even for the Army air corps, and why the Army would pull an exercise on a Sunday morning at 0830 was as inexplicable as the smoke, which he could see now was drifting over the valley of the Halawa almost to Honolulu. His earphones clicked.

"Ben," Pappy reported, "we got visitors abaft our port quarter."

Ben twisted in his seat. Six Army fighters, P-40's, he decided, were winding down an invisible, spiral track in his wake. Well, he had been jumped by Army planes before: Army and Navy pilots delighted in making passes at the rival service's bombers when they figured no brass from Wheeler Field or CINCPACFLT could see them. Ben wished he had a fighter instead of the SBD; in a Wildcat he was pretty sure he could handle any six pilots in the Army air corps; their P-40's were worse dogs, even, than the Navy's Brewster buffaloes. But in the lumbering SBD it was better to stand on his dignity and refuse to play than to try a few half-assed maneuvers, make Pappy airsick, and be shot down anyway by six different zoomies in six different ways.

He was at two thousand feet now, and could see that the cane fires over the central valley were not cane fires at all:

an ammunition ship or something had exploded at Ford Island. The great puffy cumulus cloud, through which morning sun slanted to touch the mountains with scattered patches of apple green, was suddenly pockmarked with black dots; they hung for a moment and then sprouted gray tentacles that writhed in the upper winds.

It was precisely at this moment that he knew: he would wonder all his life whether if he had reacted five seconds sooner things would have been different. Something slotted into place, as if he had lived the moment a dozen times before. He yanked the microphone from its clamp, flicked the radio to emergency in the same motion, pulled up into a laboring wingover.

"Red One, Red One, Red One," he chanted to the flight leader. "We are under attack! This is real! We are under attack!" He did not wait for an answer. The ship, two hundred miles northwest, was steaming into a trap; he hoped she was monitoring the emergency frequency and still in range and that she would believe him. "Mother Carey, Mother Carey! This is Red Six! Pearl Harbor is under attack! Do not acknowledge, do not acknowledge! Pearl Harbor is under attack!"

He jammed his mike back in its clamp. He had done all he could; now he would try to save his own ass, and Pappy Shea's. He dropped his flaps and gear to slow himself down and went to work.

He would live it forever in brightly colored slivers of action: his own squadron mates steaming like airborne battleships toward the center of Ford Island until scattered by their own antiaircraft bursts; a drab-brown fuselage and a wing glaring with a meatball skidding below, fooled by his sudden slowing, and firing anyway in frustration or anger; a glimpse of Pappy in the mirror, trying to unlock the twin thirties without first unlocking the seat, and a howling endless conversation on the intercom: "Unlock the seat!" "Where's the *lock!*" "Drop your left hand!" And then: "They won't fire!" "Charge them, Pappy, *charge* them!" And suddenly he remembered that he had forgotten to charge his own fifties forward, and did. The fighter who had overrun him climbed and settled for another pass. Ben banked and horsed back on the stick; he tightened the turn until he could stand the G's no longer, and when a gray veil began to slide over his eyes, he eased out and looked below, sure that he had spun him out; but he had not, and when he turned to look aft, his bowels tensed. The Jap plane, whatever it was, could incredibly turn inside an SBD. He saw orange flickers dart rhythmically like lights on a pinball machine along the khaki wing; he saw no tracers, no sign that the winks were dangerous; he had an odd inclination, like a hypnotized rabbit, to maintain his altitude and watch. Instead he flung the plane on its back, retracted gear and flaps, pulled straight down and through and into a steep climb. He looked below. The Jap had broken off and was climbing too, for another attack.

He had lost the rest of the flight, now; he was soaking in sweat. Under his yellow life jacket his back stung with salt and the leather padding on his goggles was slimy and he was too busy to push them up to his forehead. There was nowhere to go. He would never make the carrier unless his crazy opponent let him go to trail him; he was sure that he would never make it across the island to Kaneohe or even to hide in the thunderhead; his only salvation seemed to be in the greasy black smoke over Pearl.

It was a shrieking, wild dive, straight down; if there was one thing the Dauntless could do, it was dive. The SBD was overbuilt in every spar, every frame, every longeron; the plane would creak and groan and mourn and wail, but it would hang together if the pilot did. He yelled throughout the descent, to equalize the pressure on his eardrums, hoping that Pappy had heard of the trick. Halfway down, with the oily black smoke everywhere around him, he felt a staccato knocking from aft and smelled cordite; incredulously he realized that Pappy, in the very middle of the dive, had somehow charged his guns.

All at once they burst from under the smoke. Ben sensed a pattern of orange flame and winking muzzles and everywhere great black pyres; then he was pulling out, feeling the plane shudder and fighting a wave of nausea and straining to force the blood back to his dimming eyes. When his vision cleared, he was racing up Battleship Row between Kuahua and Ford Island, staring to starboard at what had been the greatest battle fleet on earth. It was only a glance, but it almost paralyzed him.

Had he not known which ship was moored where, he could never have identified a single battleship. The *Tennessee, Maryland,* and *Pennsylvania* were burning. The *Oklahoma* was turning over like a harpooned whale. The *California* was smoking. The *West Virginia* was awash. The old *Utah* was sinking. The *Arizona,* oozing oil, seemed actually to have been blown apart, Army-Navy game-program or not. Her fighting top canted crazily; she had settled to the bottom and was pouring rivers of oil into the currents and filthy smoke into the general pall. There were cruisers burning and destroyers, and even a seaplane tender and a repair ship.

Ben found himself sobbing in frustration. *Bastards, bastards, bastards! The little yellow bastards!* He banked to starboard, trying to line up with the Ford Island runway. All at once an orange line of tracers reached for him from the fighting top of the *Pennsylvania,* high in dry dock for repairs; he called Ford Island Tower and asked them to have the shooting stopped, but they didn't answer, so he gave up, tucked up his wheels and lurched to port. Ahead he saw a section of three Jap fighters strafing the patrol-plane hangars on Ford. He dove for them, raging. *Bastards, bastards, bastards* . . . He squeezed off a burst at the leader and saw his slugs knock hunks from his cowling, but instead of turning away the Jap climbed toward him trying to ram. In a flash he was by, and Ben had a ludicrous vision of himself sitting last week in the ready room, holding solemnly that when war came the Luftwaffe would be deadly, but the Japs would be sitting ducks.

Pappy's voice came suddenly shrieking over the intercom: "Ben! Look! Look at her!"

He glanced toward the channel mouth by Hospital Point. Threading from the graveyard, churning between a flaming destroyer in a floating dry dock and a shattered dredge, steamed the USS *Nevada*. Her battle ensign fluttered at her after mast, her guns were lashing out at an endless column of diving bombers. Great explosions cratered the pea-green waters around her. She had been hit forward and her forecastle was a furnace. God knew how she had got up steam or pulled away from her dying sisters or what made her think she could get to sea without blocking the channel, but she was belching black smoke, kicking mud astern, and tearing majestically through the harbor with every rpm her tired old *No-Go* shafts could turn. His throat tightened. They might never forget the sight, he realized suddenly, but they had better forget it now.

"Screw the *Nevada!*" he yelled at Pappy. "Check astern!"

It was too late. He caught no more than a glimpse of the plane that jumped them, heard only a series of thumps on the fuselage as if someone were trying to close a car door, and instinctively climbed for the smoke. After that, no matter how he craned he could see no more of Pappy in the rear cockpit, only the guns pointed skyward, and no matter how he yelled into the mike he heard no more either. It was not until he had hedgehopped to Palikea Peak, darting in and out of the Wainae gorges, that the Jap must have run out of ammunition or low on gas or decided it was better to quit than to be scraped off on a saw-toothed ridge. Ben spotted Schofield Barracks and dropped to fifty feet over the valley and flat-hatted all the way to Wheeler Field.

He couldn't contact Wheeler Tower, but he didn't care. He charged the strip, full flaps and gear down; the field was a smoking ruin, with wrecked planes burning everywhere in carefully aligned parking spots. He caught a brief flash of a line of riflemen firing at him from a ditch at the side of the road, a fast image of someone in a wrecked B-17 shooting at him from the top turret, and then he was on the ground with a back-jarring *kapong*, standing on the brakes alternately, fishtailing between tractors, parked planes, and jeeps that strewed the runway to block it.

He stopped. He was halfway out of his cockpit when he heard the screech of tires. A grimy soldier in a skivvy shirt leaped from a jeep driven by a sergeant. In an instant the man was squinting precisely at his belly button over the sights of a Springfield '03. The man's face was twisted and stubbled with dirty iron whiskers, but his eyes shone happily.

"I'm Navy!" Ben screamed. "You goddamn fool, I'm off the *Shenandoah!*"

Almost reluctantly, the man put down the rifle. Ben scrambled along the wing, shoved open the shattered rear canopy, and looked down at Pappy.

He had taken a twenty-seven caliber machinegun slug full

in the head. The cockpit was slimy with blood: blood on the radio, blood on the panel, blood in the bilges and dripping from the handles of the twin thirties. Ben had not realized that there was so much blood in a man, and a small wiry man at that. Numb with shock, he turned to the two Army men, who had backed the jeep under the trailing edge of the wing.

"Bastards," he screamed at them. "Dirty yellow bastards!"

"Cheer up, Lieutenant," the sergeant said. "You ain't seen nothing yet."

The sergeant was right; they had seen nothing yet. In the next months the Japs took Wake, and off Java they sunk the *Langley* and in the Coral Sea Ben's old carrier, the *Lex.* He lost many more friends in the next six months than just Pappy Shea. The *Shenandoah* performed badly and it was not until the Battle of Midway, flying the same stocky SBD he had flown into Pearl, that he avenged Pappy Shea and saved his ship from total disgrace. Every air group but the *Shenandoah*'s had sighted elements of the enemy, but for the *Shinola*'s there had been nothing all day, scouting mission after scouting mission, but whitecaps under the scud below, and the sting of failure and sweat—God it was hot— and the *Shenandoah* fighters above drawing innocent useless contrails across a barren sky, and fuel gauges dropping over an endless sea. On the last patrol they had to turn back with unbloodied hands while they could still get home; on the sinking *Yorktown* and the *Big E* they would be snarling "shit from *Shinola*" again and now she would never live it down. And all at once pure crystal delight, better than a woman: lurking under wispy clouds, four bright yellow flight decks, four glorious yellow flight decks, one burning already, as the *Enterprise* had said, circled by pagoda battlewagons with red disks on their forward turrets, and cruisers and cans. . . .

A quick, hysterical garble of radio calls and then: "Ready, Mac?" to his gunner. "Ready, sir," and over they went. The yellow rectangles grew larger and the white arrow wakes began suddenly to curve and writhe. Flame throbbed from cruiser and battleship turrets and the first red sparks flew up at them, and black puffs bloomed which seemed far too low until you felt the jolt like a curb set across a state highway. His gunner's voice, calling off altitudes methodically and calmly at first, rose at two thousand feet to a plea for mercy, at fifteen hundred to a hysterical screech. The *Hiryu* —and she had been at Pearl—grew large in his sight and began to drift under his prop; he steepened his dive until they were hanging from their belts. He let the yellow platform grow until the sea was gone and there was nothing but flight deck and the ridiculous little Jap superstructure standing to starboard like a lone pine tree in a desert; he could see khaki ants rushing to planes fueled and ready on the fantail and not one Jap fighter, not one, airborne. He had carried it far enough, perhaps too far; he yanked the bomb release and heard the *klung* as his thousand-pound bomb kicked free and knew that even if he never pulled out he had done it, this was Pearl Harbor backward, and he loved it; all through the sickening pullout when he was stone-blind and there was only the feel of the plane around him to tell him that they had not yet hit flight deck or water, he knew he had scored, if it was the last thought he would ever have. He had no way of knowing whether he was on his belly or on his back, but then, gradually, the light returned, a bit at a time, and the puffy gray clouds turned white and the horizon was dead ahead and the whitecaps, which from fifteen thousand feet had looked like new-fallen snow melting on a dark-blue field, were snatching for the tip of his prop.

He banked and looked back. The *Hiryu* glowed cherry-red for an instant. A sheet of orange flame blossomed from her flight deck. Tiny gyrating specks which he would dream of the rest of his life seemed to rise on the column of fire.

The next plane finished her off, but she was Ben's, she was the *Shenandoah's*, and there were pictures from the last plane to prove it. She was their sole victim, and thank Christ they had got *her,* at least. She brought Ben the Air Medal and a spot promotion to lieutenant commander, so that he could take over the *Shenandoah's* fighter squadron, which had for some reason never come down from twenty thousand feet even when Ben and his section had been jumped by a homeless Zero from the ship they had sunk. Then he was back in fighters where he belonged and it was just as well, because after Pappy's death in his rear cockpit and the crazy dive on the *Hiryu* he became bad luck to the whitehats and he could never get a decent gunner again. He got three Zekes in the Mariana Turkey-Shoot and might have been an ace if he hadn't made full commander too soon and if Mitch, who finally got the *Shenandoah* at Ulithi, hadn't made him air officer and finally swung him orders as exec.

Well, fifteen years from boot to exec of a fleet carrier was not bad, especially for an alumnus of the San Diego brig. "A shitty war, Commander," the *Shenandoah's* marine sergeant used to say, "but better than no war at all."

He'd felt that way himself before it started; they all did; the coming conflict was an opportunity and a game. But part of the chauvinism had fled a half-hour after it began when he looked down at Pappy's bloodied corpse, and more of it departed with the swinging, gyrating figures he had left in his wake over the *Hiryu* and the very last of it with the murder of Nagasaki and now there was no long-haired flower-child selling underground papers on Haight Street who disliked the drum and bugle more than he.

He had divorced the Navy when he retired; he never went

to officers' clubs and wouldn't even join the Retired Officers' Association. He felt little for the service anymore, except a sort of cynical satisfaction when the checks arrived in the mail, hardly big enough to pay the rent and maid. Until the call from Father Epstein had stirred him in California, he had not known he would still care enough for the Navy to try to save it from Christy Lee.

TWO

He turned from the photo of the *Shenandoah* on Epstein's office wall as Epstein said good-bye and hung up on his captive senator. "Lunch, tomorrow," he reported. "Two o'clock at the Mayflower Hotel. Just in case," he added bitterly, "Lee doesn't happen to resign after thirty years on the strength of a 'deposition' that isn't worth a nickel."

"O.K., Barney," Ben said wearily. "I'm still going to see him." He turned down an invitation to spend the night with Barney and his wife; he was tired from the drive to New Jersey and wanted to be fresh in the morning when he tackled Lee. He checked into the Marriott Motor Inn within sight of the Pentagon. After dinner he poured himself a nightcap in his room and lit Epstein's cigar to watch the late news. But twin-engine jets howling from the deck of the new *Enterprise* in the South China Sea and supply ships clustered in Camranh Bay reminded him drowsily of another age and the fleet anchorage at Ulithi atoll, and the cockpit of a rattling Catalina flying boat full of Epstein's cigar smoke, enroute from Manila to the *Shenandoah* on the eve of the raid that would end her war.

The Germans had quit in May and the Japanese were cornered in the home islands twelve hundred miles northeast. Below was the greatest congregation of fighting craft the world would ever know. Ben, exec of the *Shenandoah*, throttled back and descended, sweating miserably in the pilot's seat. He banked toward the great steel fortresses floating on a lake of mottled green. All the way back from Manila the western Carolines had baked under thunderheads; beside him the redheaded Jewish lieutenant with the ragged moustache puffed impassively at his cigar, apparently untouched by the heat. But Epstein had never seen Ulithi before and he was not untouched by the fleet that lay below.

"My God, Commander," he exclaimed, above the popping engines, "aren't we a little overgunned?"

"Not for me, Mr. Epstein," said Ben. "Never for me."

Ulithi atoll was a sandy noose of frayed hawser half submerged a thousand miles from land. Its lagoon was a mirror twenty-five miles long in which lay six hundred U.S. carriers, battleships, cruisers, destroyers, tankers, freighters, landing craft, and hospital ships. Strands of the coral rope, awash in the long Pacific swell, made little islets: the largest was Mogmog, a recreation complex with two officers' clubs and a barbed-wire enlisted area for baseball, beer, and gang fights. The natives of the atoll had been moved down the lagoon to Fassarai, it was said, an hour's trip by motor launch from the fleet anchorage and out of reach of any but the highest-ranking sightseers. Ben could see a few outriggers off its coral beach, fishing in the dazzling heat. The plane bounced gently past a thunderhead full of rain. The sun had made a greenhouse of the cockpit; it reeked of sweat and Epstein's cigar and he longed for the shower in his stateroom.

He suggested that the lieutenant, who was not a pilot, move aft. Rear Admiral Hammering Howie Howland, sweating rivers, squirmed into the copilot seat beside him. The admiral took off a soggy baseball cap with an eagle-shit visor and wiped his brow. In the '30's, when he had been navigator on the old *Nevada* and Ben had been a quartermaster-striker, Howland had been squat but trim; he still had the football-player jaw and a cleat-chipped tooth, but now his jowls quivered with the vibrating engines and no matter how he stuck out his jaw when he talked, the shadow of another chin lay below it. He was full of excitement.

"Hot," he smiled. "Let's get her down!"

Ben nodded, hiding a spark of anger. He had borrowed the plane from a patrol squadron at Howland's request to fly him to the Philippines for a conference, for Ben needed the flight time more than the *Shenandoah* needed him. He had hoped to get some help on the stick from the admiral, who God knew needed flight time too, but Hammering Howie had spent most of the trip in consultation with his chief of staff in the waist gunner's compartment, where the slipstream past the thirties made the temperature livable. In Manila Howland had somehow recaptured for the Navy the lieutenant, a Navy air combat intelligence man with brown kindly eyes and a vast suspicion of general and flag officers from two years on MacArthur's staff. The admiral jerked his head aft.

"What do you think of him?"

"I like him."

Howland looked doubtful. "I don't know. Feather merchant. He's a lawyer, too."

What the hell's that got to do with it? Ben thought. He moved his cramped shoulders and locked his straps for the landing. He had jock itch from the Solomons and a headache from the Manila Army-Navy club and he knew that when he returned to his humid stateroom he would find the desk stacked a foot high with dispatches. Howland's flag suite was air-conditioned and so was flag plot and the chief of staff would handle *his* paperwork: he was Jove striking down his new ACI because he didn't like the way he earned a living or the way he wore his hat or more likely, the curve of his Jewish nose. Epstein had learned to hold a course on the way back so that Ben could get a little sleep; it was more than the admiral had offered to do, and the admiral wore wings.

"If you didn't want him, Admiral, why'd you ask for him?"

"Well, he speaks Japanese," the admiral said. "Can you figure that? He's been doing MacArthur's intelligence on kamikazes. I want him to monitor their frequencies up there."

"Up there?"

Hammering Howie winked at him and hit his arm companionably. "Tokyo," he said, and that was all. Ben was cleared top secret and second in command of a forty-thousand-ton capital ship but it was apparently not enough for the details. He shifted uncomfortably, wondering what sort of Jimmy Doolittle strike the staff had come up with now. Whatever it was, it would be full of glory for Hammering Howie Howland.

Howland had grown weekly more bellicose, nonregulation, and brownshoe as the noose on the Empire tightened. Bull Halsey's press releases spoke of Halsey on the Emperor's horse: Hammering Howie wanted to be there to hand him the reins. The admiral had taken to sitting for hours in his big swivel chair on the open bridge, eyes slitted and both jaws grim. He had substituted tiny wings on his baseball cap for the officer's eagle and sent messages to his ships like "OFF THE DECKS OF THIS TASK GROUP FLY THE FINEST PILOTS IN THE WORLD X HIT 'EM AGAIN HARDER." As a pilot, he still didn't know his ass from his aileron, but he had suddenly blossomed as the greatest flying admiral since John H. Towers. He had only been dissuaded from leading the First Formosa Strike by his own chief of staff, who threatened to tell Nimitz, and then Howland had anonymously launched in an F6F for dawn combat air patrol off Okinawa. The fighter section was so nervous with him along that they almost let a Kate full of TNT get through to the group, so he never did it again, but the word got out nevertheless, and the younger pilots took what the admiral's public-relations officer described as "quiet pride" in having as task group commander an admiral who actually flew. He had his eyes, Ben had decided, on another star, and the time was growing short. But when you flew as sloppily as Howland, it took guts to try and his derring-do built a devil-may-care spirit in the air group: he had ensigns and j.g.'s squeezing their hats into fifty-mission droops and soaking their gold chin straps in the officers' head to tarnish them and half the aviators on the ship were wearing nonreg jodhpurs like Howie. It even helped ships' company morale, and morale on the *Shenandoah,* as always, could use all the help it could get. Howland was all right, he guessed. He just hoped, with Army B–29's pounding Tokyo from Saipan and the war already won that the admiral would not lose a half-dozen ships and a couple of thousand men proving that the Navy had won it.

Ben banked gently toward the other PBY's floating like feeding geese in long lines off the beach. Beyond them lay the slabsided carriers of Murderers' Row: *Enterprise,* the new *Lexington, Franklin, Bunker Hill, Hancock, Ticonderoga,* his own *Shenandoah,* and a dozen more besides; farther off loomed the castellated battleships which would this year pound the empire's shores: *North Carolina, Washington, South Dakota, Iowa, Wisconsin,* and the old expendable battleships, too, which would lead the way. The fleet looked strangely open and vulnerable, but the empire had hurled its last bolt at Ulithi months before, when the carrier *Ran-*

dolph, innocently showing movies on her hangar deck, had been hit by a lone kamikaze at night. Now there wasn't a Jap within a thousand miles. It was almost too bad: one scouting report would show Tokyo that trying to stop the fleet below was like fending off a tank with a samurai sword, and perhaps they would throw in the towel. With their goddamn suicide planes they had sunk or damaged four hundred U.S. ships off Okinawa and killed five thousand men; *Shenandoah* had escaped unscathed as always, but maybe she was due and it was too close to the end of the war to get hurt. Tokyo . . . Jesus!

Coming alongside the *Shenandoah* in the admiral's barge, he noticed a gasoline lighter topping off the storage tanks for her planes. He climbed the ladder behind the admiral and saluted the invisible colors aft and the sweating j.g. on watch and squinted past the brass-and-mahogany quarter-deck stage setting into the gloom of the hangar deck.

He knew instantly that the operations order for the Tokyo raid had beaten them back. Long lines of seamen, each carrying a fifty-five-pound AA shell on his shoulder, snaked through the aircraft from the other side, where an ammunition lighter must lay. Ordnancemen trundled one-thousand-pound bombs to ammo hoists for the magazines below. A commissary party stumbled under sacks of flour and rice and sides of beef. A crisscross of carts, tractors, and forklifts rumbled on the steel deck and an anvil chorus rang from the metal shop aft. Above the clanging traffic, draped over the snouts of Corsair fighters or hunched in the cockpits of TBM Avengers, mechs and plane captains worked nonchalantly, each a minor god.

He moved down the ladder to his stateroom. Sure enough, a three-day accumulation of file boards for his signature lay on his desk. The ship's offices never stopped for a mere raid; there were orders to be endorsed, supplies got, ammu--

nition tallies scanned, service-record pages signed. For all
that the yeomanry or the ship's writer or the supply officer
cared, they could be in Brooklyn Navy Yard.

He moved into his bedroom beyond the office. Perry Watkins, his huge Negro steward, was dusting the bookshelf.
Open in his hand was the *Romances of Herman Melville;*
as usual he was reading. "Watkins," said Ben, "you're moving your lips."

The soft brown eyes looked up. On a giant flawless body
was set the head of an African gladiator. His face was pi-
ratical, scarred already at nineteen by a crescent knife cut
from ear to lip and a nose mushroomed with the nightstick
of a frightened Santa Monica cop. He was almost purple in
his blackness, so that the eyes were doubly shocking: gentle
on a field of battle and light brown, almost hazel, in ebony
folds.

"Yes sir," he said. He continued to read but the lips no
longer moved. He noted the page when he was through and
replaced the book on the shelf. "*Typee,* Commander? Is
that a real place?"

"I think so. In the Marquesas, somewhere."

"Near here?"

"No."

Watkins looked disappointed. "How was your trip, Commander?"

"Hot," said Ben. "Finish up later. Take the book with
you."

The Negro shook his head. "Down there? Them mother-
fuckers——"

"Those bastards, yes," Ben said tiredly. "Them mother-
fuckers, no."

"Those bastards most likely steal it," Watkins said,
"them mother-fuckers."

"Get your ass out of here," Ben said. He noticed his shoes

glittering in his locker. "Damn it, I told you. What did you do? Spend all day on them?"

"No sir," Watkins said innocently. "I never touched them mother—those bastards, sir."

He had become Ben's private problem because of shining shoes, or not shining them. He had arrived during yard overhaul in Bremerton in June, a released prisoner in charge of a seventeen-man jailbird draft from Terminal Island Naval Prison. He had been hovering over them like a threatening black cloud; he had them marching down the pierhead like a jarhead drill team instead of a scowling platoon of thieves, deserters, and drunks. Chief Catlett, the master-at-arms, had stared down from the quarterdeck with Ben, his eyes narrowing.

"They screwed us again, Commander. And you better get rid of that jig."

"Why?"

"I bet he was in for assault. Or striking a superior officer. That goo-goo wardroom chief'll never handle him any better than he could Joe Louis. Transfer him somewhere."

"He's done his time, I guess."

Catlett, who knew of his own brig time, who had put him there, really, smiled secretly. Ben turned on his heel and went below. If Catlett would break just once, give him a handle, a solid grasp on the silent contempt, he would be off the ship before he could pack his seabag. But he probably never would. Perhaps it was just as well: in his own way the Cat was irreplaceable, a hardening agent that held the crew together. He inspired fear where the skipper sparked only love and Ben himself, he supposed, furnished the lubricant to make the parts work smoothly.

Catlett was right about Watkins, of course. It had been assault that had put him in Terminal Island, and it almost happened again before the Battle of the Philippine Sea, when Watkins had the Filipino chief backed against the steam table in the wardroom galley and would probably have ended up in prison again had it not been for a task force of Catlett's MAA's.

The huge youngster was headed snarling for the brig when Ben discovered that the Filipino had ordered him to shine a dozen j.o.'s shoes from the bunkroom. The order was illegal; hell, those days were gone forever and besides there was a war going on. Then, having rescued Watkins, Ben felt responsible for him, as if he had saved a Chinaman's life, and had him assigned his own stateroom, which kept him apart from the chief commissary steward except at meals.

Now Ben could see the reflection of half the compartment in the toes of his brown seaboots. "Damn it, Watkins, you don't *have* to shine my shoes!"

"I know that, Commander." The gentle resonant voice was always as surprising as the light-brown eyes.

That night Ben pulled Melville from the shelf and skimmed through *Typee*. His sister Porky had given it to him on his seventeenth birthday, the summer of the Crash; now prose that had seemed sexy was tedious and Kory-Kory and Fayaway the native girl and the vales and groves of Nukuheva bored him. He jammed the book back and wrote his wife, although there had been only one letter from her waiting when the ship had dropped the hook. He removed the tiny shield-and-eagle pinned to his go-to-hell cap and slipped it in for Patty too, because she had been left with her grandmother instead of taken to Bremerton to meet the ship last June and so he had never even seen his own daughter and now she was almost four. There had been another hell of a whispered fight behind the tissue walls of the plywood Bremerton MOQ over *that*. He sealed the envelope

and hit it viciously with his censor stamp and got it into
the mailbox in the passageway quickly, before he made himself mad and tore it up, and the next day he learned of the
rape and there was no time for self-pity before the raid.

CHAPTER THREE

ONE

He sensed the trouble during an informal inspection: he moved through passageways and shops and mess halls and galleys, followed by Catlett, and felt through his pores a secret turmoil aboard the ship. He knew her so well that tiny aberrations stood out like major flaws. He smelled alcohol in band country and Catlett found the coils of a homemade still in a CO_2 fire extinguisher next to the bass drum; Ben confronted Foghorn Bailey, an alcoholic musician-third reputed to have played with Louis Armstrong in Prohibition days. He knew that Foghorn could extract alcohol from raisins, sugar cubes, or the very steel of the hull. Foghorn, reeking, admitted it and Ben took pity on his red eyes and the broken veins in his cheeks and remembered nights on the *Lex* when his clarion taps would float them to sleep, in the '30's before bugle calls came from a turntable below. He told Catlett to deep-six the distillery and forget Foghorn; Catlett shrugged sardonically.

It was not Foghorn's still that bothered Ben, or cigarette butts in a magazine, or unswept sawdust in the carpenter shop; something deeper was wrong. Shifting eyes and blurred glances in the wardroom galley told him finally that it was here; the Negroes were sulking and Mario, chief steward, was scared. The mess treasurer, Harvey Baccus, a gawky ensign right out of the Academy, wouldn't have known if he was having trouble; Ben didn't even ask. Catlett, who had his own senses, murmured, "Something stinks."

"Yes. What?"

The chief shrugged. "I'll find out. No hurry."

"I want to know before we leave on the strike. So get on it."

He found himself continually prodding Catlett. He disliked himself for it, because it was unfair, now that he had all the cards.

"Get on it?" Catlett repeated now, green eyes beaming affably. "Yes, sir."

The tiny note of amusement in his voice seemed finally enough. Ben faced him. "Catlett," he said, "you can't forget San Diego at all, can you?"

"Sir?"

"You heard me. Can you?"

"Why sure, Commander," Catlett smiled, the scars on his chin bone-china white. "Why not, sir? You did your time."

Enough? No, more rope. He told Catlett to secure the ship from inspection and to tell the OOD to expect skippers and CAG's from the task group for a flag conference in the wardroom, and for *Shenandoah* gunnery officers to attend.

"Yes, sir," Catlett said. His eyes were still laughing and the tone was exactly the same. Ben watched him pad down the passageway, corded muscles rippling under khaki, rangy shoulders square. Age had ignored him, despite what the skipper had once said of his shattered jaw; he was as young today as he was as a boot-camp drill instructor, as if he had been frozen for the last fifteen years in a block of ice. A seaman jammed himself tensely against the bulkhead to let him pass; Catlett did not even glance at him.

Ben had been on the ship four years and exec for three months: he should have seen it before. Catlett was no source of strength, but the seat of infection. The signs of discipline aboard *Shenandoah* were braced seamen, hats properly off in a mess line for fear of Catlett's men, never a bare chest topside. But her liberties were notorious: her men were barred from Leyte and last stop at Pearl they had come up with fifteen percent AWOL; on Mogmog he had to double the normal shore patrol for her recreation parties. Catlett had the men under a head of pressure that had to blow, and it blew ashore. Ben had been too blind or too lazy to see it. Well, he couldn't safely tinker with the machinery before the Tokyo raid, but when the strike was over Catlett was through.

TWO

Admiral Hammering Howie Howland removed his pointer from an area on the chart an inch from Tokyo Bay and drew a green-felt curtain over the last map on the tripod in the wardroom lounge. The air-group commanders of his task group, the skippers of his carriers, battleships, cruisers, and tin cans, sat back. Ben had known most of them for years. He and the admiral's new air combat intelligence officer and a few destroyer skippers, perhaps, were the only non-Academy men in the compartment. There was a rattle of coffee cups. The skipper of the *North Carolina*, forgetting that the smoking lamp was out for bomb loading, lit a cigarette. The admiral smiled. "Before my kamikaze expert tries to scare hell out of you, gentlemen, any questions?"

Ben remembered a poem, "The Laws of the Navy," that Christy Lee had taught them, quite seriously, one beery Annapolis evening:

Says the wise: How may I know their purpose?
Then acts without wherefore or why;
Stays the fool but one moment to question,
And the chance of his life passes by.

Ben had a question, why the hell so close to Japan? He was practically certain everyone else had too. He was on the verge of asking when he felt his skipper's hand on his arm. Mitch Langley shook his head. Ben understood: any disapproval must not come from the maligned, notorious *Shinola* but the *Big E* or the *Intrepid* or the *Sara* or another blooded hero ship. It never came: every captain and commander in the wardroom had learned the poem as a plebe and apparently learned it well. There was only a martial mutter of approval and a line of grim, weather-beaten smiles. Oh, shit, he thought, all this rank and not a rumble. His eyes met Barney Epstein's. The new ACI smiled ruefully and pulled down the wardroom movie screen.

"As the admiral says," Epstein began, picking up the pointer, "I'm going to try to scare hell out of you." He hesitated for a moment, then suddenly faced Hammering Howie. "You asked if there were any questions, Admiral. I have a question."

"I asked my *operational commanders*, Mr. Epstein," Hammering Howie said. "Not my own staff. Mr. Epstein, gentlemen, thinks we're going in too close."

There was a restless stirring in the wardroom. In a split second Epstein had leaped the gap between anonymity and notoriety; the moment before, he had been an innocuous

reserve who should probably trim his moustache; suddenly
he was an insubordinate feather merchant you would not
trust as laundry officer of a Landing Craft, Infantry. Jerry
Dalton, a chain-smoking ace who commanded Air Group
Seven, looked up like a terrier guarding a bone. "Mr. Epstein, we appreciate the admiral's philosophy if you don't.
It'll be nice over Tokyo to know the carrier's only twenty
minutes away."

"Under six hundred fathoms of water?" Epstein asked.

"God *damn* it, Epstein," Howland's chief of staff spat,
"let's go!"

"Sorry, Captain. Lights, please?" The wardroom lights
went out and a color slide flicked onto the screen. The effect
was wonderfully apparent: the warrior spirit nose-dived.
"Holy jumping Jesus Christ!" somebody murmured. "What
is it?"

"That, gentlemen," said Epstein amicably, "is the *Ohka-
Eleven*. We feel it's the newest version of the *baka*—or 'fool'
bomb, as we've been calling it, rather prematurely."

Ben stared at the screen. The picture mocked them all. It
was not a bomb at all; it was a Buck Rogers spacecraft
with orange meatballs and sleek stubby wings and tiny
twin rudders on a short tail surface. It looked like some of
the jet aircraft that the Germans had produced in their
eleventh hour, but you expected it of the Luftwaffe. The
Japs had fooled them again.

"Is it *jet?*" he blurted.

"A step beyond," Epstein said, almost proudly. "It's
rocket."

He began to tick off the features with his pointer. It was
twenty-one feet long, with a fourteen-foot wingspan. It was
stuffed with half a ton of TNT fused with a fulminate-of-
mercury detonator; with the doomed pilot it weighed almost

two tons. It was carried under the belly of a twin-engine Betty 22 and the pilot rode in the mother-ship bomb bay until time to climb into his own cockpit.

He flashed on the screen a slide of the cockpit. There was a mutter of surprise. The *baka* bomb was no jerry-built last-minute crate. The instrument panel was simple, but well designed: a compass, altimeter, rate-of-dive indivator, dials for temperature and angle-of-dive. It looked too small for an American pilot but it had excellent visibility. Father Epstein's pointer tapped a switch where the throttle would have been in an aircraft: "Rocket selector switch, gentlemen. Flash Gordon."

He pointed out the one atavistic element, a rudder bar for the feet, as in the days of the Wright Brothers, rather than comfortable footpedals.

"But what difference does it make? Small cockpit, too, but they don't man it until the mother plane has the target on radar, and it's only about a two-minute flight." According to Epstein, who had translated posthumous kamikaze citations in the Philippines, it was a mark of honor if the *baka* pilot could sleep in the mother ship's bomb bay enroute to the target. "Of course if the target's only a hundred miles away, it's a catnap."

Another slide flashed on the screen, this one taken from the pilot's point of view: it was a simple, old-fashioned ring sight, with a post and bead forward. Ben had a distinct image of how a carrier deck would look with the rings enveloping Fly One and the tiny bead on the front sight smack in the middle of the forward elevator.

Nobody shut him up, now. He went on, "His range is fifteen miles from twenty thousand feet. Tell your CAP pilots to get the Betty before the drop: this guy makes six hundred knots and once he's gone there's no use trying, because you won't hit *him*."

"Our *shells* won't hit him," Christy Lee exclaimed. "That's the speed of sound! Our computers won't track that fast!"

"Your computers," Epstein said companionably, "were built to track human beings. When this guy winds a *hachimaki* around his forehead, he's on his way to being a god."

"How many of the goddamn things they *got?*" someone asked from the darkness.

"We don't know, but a task-group CAP off Kyushu intercepted eighteen of them Saturday, still hanging on their mammas, fortunately. The pictures you'll see are of six we found at Kadena Airfield in Okinawa. There were fifty on Okie ready for use on the first day of the invasion: squadron inventories show forty-five MXY–7 *baka* trainers on the home islands, just gliders to use for practice. *Trainers*, they've built! Supply invoices show that the *Ohka–22*, an improved version of what you see here, was given the 721st and 722nd special attack groups at Kanoya, Miyazaki, Oita, Atsugi, and Kamatsu air bases in the home islands. I'll guarantee more than a hundred in Japan right now."

There was a dull silence and then a new slide and another. Ben listened to Epstein speak of suicide tactics: a low-altitude approach under the radar horizon for conventional kamikazes, always the high-altitude run for the *baka*. A feeling of impending doom distracted him; he wondered if the others shared it. There was something wrong on the ship, wrong with the operational plan, wrong with the whole damn campaign. His spirits were sinking by the moment.

The pointer tapped a red leaf on the nose of a *baka*. "Insignia of the Cherry Blossom unit . . . a better aiming point than even the mother plane . . . but don't get too close. . . . Two tons of TNT in the newer models . . ." A head-on shot, a tiny circle with fins and nothing else. "Gentlemen, if you ever see this view, you better make your peace. As to the breed of cat that flies this . . . *baka* pilots are Navy enlisted men or warrants or reserve ensigns . . . but better trained that the conventional kamikaze. . . ." The lights went on.

"Are they doped? Or drunk?" asked Christy Lee.

Epstein put away the pointer. "No. They apparently quit drinking when they're selected. Why?"

"Fear," Christy said. "It's instinctive."

"Oh, they *fear*, according to their staff studies. The kamikaze fears closing his eyes before impact and missing. Or wasting himself on a battleship instead of a carrier, or even missing the forward elevator on a carrier, which is what he's aiming for. He fears getting shot down, and in the Philippines they wouldn't eat for twenty-four hours before a mission for fear of diarrhea. He fears engine trouble in the mother ship—their fuel is lousy and there aren't enough mechs left anymore. Mostly he fears losing the war before he gets to fly his mission."

Epstein drew some Japanese documents from a briefcase and began to translate, smoothly and with great speed. "From a report of Commander Naoshi Arima: 'The lieutenant sobbed when I told him that he had been replaced as flight leader. I told him there would be other chances to die and he seemed visibly to be cheered.' " He read more of the same and stuffed the documents back in the briefcase. "I think from our studies that the special attack force's problem has been too many volunteers and not enough aircraft."

"They're human, though," remarked Mitch Langley, "whether they think they're gods or not. I wonder what motivates them?"

Epstein smiled. "What motivates us?"

"A war, for Christ's sake," growled the admiral. "Besides, they aren't coming back. We are."

"From a hundred miles?" asked Epstein.

"Mr. Epstein, what the hell do *you* want to do?" demanded Howland. "Leave it to the B-29's and go home?"

"The Japanese eat, Admiral, as I said. Starve them."

"We will. This fall." The admiral stood up. "We'll starve them when we land. Rice paddy by rice paddy." He surveyed his commanders. "Any further comment?"

There was no further comment. "Gentlemen," said Hammering Howie, "carry on."

THREE

Ben went ashore to the Mogmog Fleet Officers' Club, a sweaty, thatched oasis smelling of palm fronds and beer. He brought along Josh Lowery, the tall, stooped chief engineer. Josh was a classmate of the skipper's, but he had been navigator of a tin can that had gone on the rocks in the twenties and he would never make captain. He was mild, and pleasant, and never bellyached at water consumption or when he could not blow tubes in a combat zone. He was bent from years of stooping under ventilators; his head was a mass of scars from steam pipes. He was absentminded and casual in dress and never drank too much and could always find the *Shenandoah* officers' launch when it was time to go.

The Mogmog Bar was the focal point of the whole Pacific war now, as the O clubs in Esprit or Manus had been before the war moved on. Here you met everyone you had known during the slogging fight up the southwest Pacific, and many more besides. Instead of shooting craps at a table with the aviators, Ben found himself commanding a two-foot area in the crush at the bar drinking fifteen-cent shots with Josh and

Epstein, who, it turned out, had learned his Japanese in Tokyo, where his father had been an art exporter and the rabbi of the local Jewish congregation. Together, as Josh listened tolerantly, the two lacerated Howland's operation plan. Finally they wove across the dazzling coral to the motor launch. By the time they had snaked over a trade-wind chop through the long lines of warships to the *Shenandoah* Epstein and Ben were practically sober and fast friends.

Ben moved through his office to his stateroom and stripped off his shirt, soaked with brine from the ride back. He inspected his face in the mirror above the stainless-steel sink. He was getting deep, outdoor creases around his eyes, chief-like creases, admiral-like creases. He had thought he was impervious to sun, but his nose was raw-nerve and his ears felt hot and his gray eyes radiated threads of red. He had felt lousy and depressed since Epstein's lecture and there seemed not to have been enough whiskey on Mogmog to help.

He laid out clean clothes. He noted that Melville was missing from his bookcase: Watkins must have changed his mind and taken it below. He stepped into the shower. He wet down, then dutifully, as he had never done as a seaman, turned off the shower in deference to Josh's boilers. He soaped himself and did not turn the water on again until he was ready to rinse—maturity, or the responsibility of rank. He let the cold stream, which was really lukewarm, run on his face until he was revived and finally got dressed and stepped to his office to survey the new crop of dispatch boards. He put his feet on the desk and twisted a bulkhead fan at the itchiest spot on his crotch and began to read the traffic, trying to concentrate over the din of working parties on the hangar deck above.

There was a knock and Catlett came in, a book in his hand. He laid it on the desk, smiling. "We found this in the steward's compartment, Commander. It's got your name on it."

Ben picked it up unbelievingly. It was Melville, fully as thick as the San Francisco telephone directory and torn half across as if it had been ripped by an angry giant. "Son of a *bitch*," he murmured. "Who did this?"

"Who *could* have done it? Now, I got a pretty good grip— I can squeeze beer cans in a ball and Indian-wrestle with most anybody, but *I* couldn't do it."

"Never mind. I know who did it."

"We got some body-beautiful boys work out with weights in the metal shop, but *they* couldn't do it."

"I said never mind! Watkins did it. Where'd he get the booze?"

"Did he have to be drunk?"

"He had to be drunk."

Catlett shrugged. "Mogmog? Beer?"

"No liberty today, no recreation parties," Ben reminded him.

"That's right, only for officers. What about that torpedo juice Foghorn makes? You should have let me take that band room apart, Commander. I bet it was loaded."

"You should have asked. Take it apart."

"Yes, sir. What about Watkins?"

The book itself, when Watkins saw it sober, would be punishment enough. "Get him up here. I'll handle him."

Grimly he set aside the book and took up the dispatches. He read the top one, from an ammunition ship: "INTEND TO MAKE YOUR STARBOARD SIDE AT 1100 TOMORROW AS REQUESTED IN YOUR 12417 ZEBRA." Good—the huge "Tiny Tim" aircraft rockets would arrive in time; no one had ever seen them, but the ordnancemen had been studying up on them for weeks. He initialed the dispatch and took up the next one. "FROM

OFFICER IN CHARGE, FASSARAI ISLAND, ULITHI ATOLL: TO ALL SHIPS PRESENT: REQUEST LIST OF ANY PERSONNEL WHO LANDED FASSARAI NATIVE SETTLEMENT THIS DATE. NEGATIVE REPLIES REQUESTED."

Well, Fassarai was out-of-bounds; some liberty-happy ship was going to catch hell. Ben tore a blank from a pad of dispatch forms and addressed it to the officer in charge, Fassarai atoll; then he printed: "NO PERSONNEL SHENANDOAH ASHORE FASSARAI THIS DATE." He dialed Communications, which sent him a Hawaiian-Chinese radioman-striker named Kwong. Kwong glanced at the outgoing message and hesitated.

"Sir?"

"What's the matter? Reference wrong?"

Kwong changed his mind. "No, sir. We'll get it right out."

Ben started on the next pile, thought for a moment, and called him back. Something was screwy. "Cough it up, Kwong. What's going on?"

Two bright spots of red appeared on his copper cheeks. "Jesus, sir, I hate for us to send this, is all."

"Why? Who got ashore?"

"I don't know, sir. Just scuttlebutt."

"How'd they get there?"

"Jeez, Commander, why ask me?"

Ben took back the dispatch. "If I *don't* know, I have to send this, don't I? And they'll still find out, and how'll that look? The usual 'shit from *Shinola?*' Now, *give!*"

She was Kwong's ship too. "Captain's gig, I heard."

"The *captain's* gig? How much a head?"

"Five bucks."

The captain's coxswain was an overstuffed regular from the Bronx named Rainey. "That goddamned Rainey! I'll have his ass!"

"Yes, sir." Kwong left and Catlett brought Watkins in. The chief might have been able to drop a man with a three-inch punch and fold beer cans between thumb and fore-finger, but he apparently had not attempted to awaken the steward alone. Two MAA's flanked him, and when the Negro had stumbled in, shaking off their hands, Catlett moved to his right side like a policeman interrogating a suspect, so that Watkins would have to shift his feet before a swing.

"Thank you, Chief," said Ben. "I'll talk to him alone."

"Aye-aye, sir," said Catlett doubtfully. He left, and Ben slid Melville across the desk.

"You do this?"

Watkins focused on the book. A drop of spit rolled to his chin. He grunted as if someone had kicked him in the gut. "Oh my God!" he whispered.

"How'd you get so drunk?"

Watkins said nothing, still staring at the volume. "Fog-horn Bailey?" Ben prompted. "In the band locker?" Watkins glanced up quickly, and Ben knew. "O.K. I figured."

"What about the book?" Watkins blurted. He was dead sober now. "Look, I could take it to the printshop. They maybe got glue——"

"Forget the book, Watkins," Ben said wearily, "it's only a book. You wreck anything else?"

"No sir," began Watkins, "not here—"

Ben felt sick. "What do you mean, not *here?*"

Watkins face had gone hard. "I didn't wreck nothing else, sir."

Ben studied the inscrutable features and the veiled eyes and knew. "You went to Fassarai, didn't you?"

The face closed tighter. Ben grated, "You went, all right. The whole damn fleet will know it by tomorrow. 'The *Shinola* did it again.' *Shit!*" Watkins stood behind his mask, and Ben went on. "How many went? What happened there? You chase a native up a tree? Light a fire to the village? Steal a canoe? There's a dispatch, they're looking, they're going to find out. I got to know *now!*" Watkins said nothing. Ben murmured, "I know how you got there, the captain's gig. I even know what it cost. I *know* about Rainey, Watkins, already."

"That mother-fucker!" Watkins lunged for the door. "I'll kill that ofay bastard!"

Ben leaped for his arm. It was like grabbing a wardroom stanchion. "Hold it! *Rainey* didn't tell me!"

"Did he tell you they was nymphos? Did he tell you they was whores? They wanted American babies? Black babies, white babies, no never-mind? Did he tell you they'd fuck for a Hershey bar? He tell you that, Commander? He told *me!*"

"Jesus," breathed Ben, "You got to the *women?*"

"Or maybe you already knew, you got the books. It's in the books, ain't it, Commander? *Mutiny on the Bounty? Pitcairn Island?* Them native girls, man, they love it! They're minks! Rabbits! Well, I got me one."

"Simmer *down,* damn it!" Ben's head began to throb. His first thought was yaws: all the *Shenandoah* needed was a case of VD a thousand miles from the nearest land mass to become the laughingstock of the fleet. Well, he could probably hush that up with the medics. "She look healthy?"

"She could run," said Watkins softly. Their eyes met.

"Run?" Ben whispered. "Oh, *no* . . ."

"She could run," Watkins nodded. "See, Commander, there's something them books don't say."

"What?" asked Ben, dully.

"She might be a goddamn jungle bunny with her tits hanging out on a island a million miles from nowhere, ain't never ate anything but a fish, but——"

"What?"

"She ain't near as black as me."

"I see," said Ben.

"And she might want a white baby, but she don't want a black one, not for all the Hershey bars on the fucking ship!"

"So she ran. But not fast enough?"

The ponderous, scarred head shook gently. "Not fast enough."

Ben moved back to his desk and sat down. He toyed with the dispatch he must answer. "Rape," he said finally. "We never had a rape. We burned down the EM Club in Bremerton, and Mize hit that *kanaka* cop, and they wrecked that shack in Tacloban and stole the pig. And we had that fairy for a while. The judge advocate general wrote us at Pearl, about AWOL's, but that was before Captain Langley made captain, Watkins, that doesn't really count. You like the captain, Watkins?"

"He's a great man, sir." The hazel eyes met his. " 'Course, from where I am, the commissary officer looks like God."

"Yes. Do you think Captain Langley would make a good admiral?"

"I think he'd make a right good president."

"That's nice," Ben said bitterly. "You think he'll *make* admiral?"

"Jesus, Commander, I was *drunk!*"

"Did the rest of the crummy bunch get laid?"

"If they did, nobody hollered. All *them* cats was white, of course. I'd a had to ride in the back if they wasn't scared shitless."

"O.K. Go to sick bay and get cleaned up." He tossed the book across the desk. "Get rid of this."

Watkins did not move. "Commander, they ain't putting me in jail."

"Oh, yes we are. Probably."

"No, sir. I mean it. They can hang me, they can shoot me, whatever they do. But I ain't going to jail again."

"We'll see," said Ben. Watkins started for the door. "Watkins?" asked Ben.

"Yes, sir?"

"They speak English on that island?"

"They don't *holler* in English, sir. Why?" A glint of hope came into the hazel eyes, and tears. He leaned forward across the desk. "Commander? The boss-man's just a Navy chaplain! You reckon———"

"I reckon," Ben said sharply, "you'll be lucky to get twenty years."

He was angry at Watkins, who had so much potential, for throwing it all away at nineteen. When the door closed he stripped to his skivvies, lay down, and turned out the light.

He was restless. He had thrown it all away himself at seventeen on a summer afternoon dripping with San Francisco fog, and in boot camp too at eighteen and on the *Nevada* and again on the old *Lex*, but each time someone had helped. No one could help Watkins, though; no one could even communicate with the woman.

He had a sudden idea. After thirty years under Jap control, he would bet that the natives spoke Japanese. He flicked on the reading lamp and picked up the phone by his bed and dialed Epstein's stateroom. "How'd you like to take a ride to Fassarai tomorrow?"

"I'll *walk* to Fassarai to get away from the flag."

When he hung up he was still jumpy, from worry over Watkins or the raid or the ship. He went to his safe, drew out his emergency fifth, and poured a long blast into his glass. He gave it a squirt of water, apologizing silently to the engineer. But when he turned out the light again he found that he still could not sleep: ghosts glided through his mind, wreathed in San Francisco mists, ghosts from his last summer in high school in 1929, when San Francisco had dripped under twenty-two consecutive days of fog.

FOUR

Driven past Washington Square that summer on North Beach affairs of state, the liquor overlords staring through bulletproof windows had probably longed for the sun of Palermo. In a city which during Prohibition was convicting three murderers for every hundred murders, it was almost too miserable to kill.

Above the dynastic battlefield the cheap corniced houses clawing for safety up Russian Hill squeezed together in the mist. In his back bedroom Ben, chaste at seventeen through conviction, fear, and, up to now, lack of opportunity, spent a damp vacation fighting for his virtue.

Twenty feet away, framed in her bathroom window, Terry Bellini tortured him twice daily with what he innocently thought innocent carelessness. On vacations she bathed morning and evening and then spent an hour combing her hair in her underwear.

He was six feet tall, a good linebacker and fair basketball center. With the gym closed for the summer, with solid fog curtailing swimming at China Beach, he was a hot boiler of sexual pressures. Sometimes Terry would forget to pull the shade, and he would writhe for hours. Even if she lowered the blind her silhouette as she drew her slip over her head and stepped from her underthings was excruciating: rounded hips, that should be solidly on his squeaky bed, tiny, virginal belly, firm breasts for his hands and lips.

He was currently convinced that masturbation slowed one

up on the basketball court, so he marshaled Jack London, Rafael Sabatini, Herman Melville, anyone else who could take him to sea, away from the rent in his own window shade. Their magic would work for a few pages; then an erotic moan from the horn on Alcatraz Island or the aphrodisiac chime of fog trickling from the rainspout would draw him to the window, pulse pounding, body throbbing.

Terry waited in ancient wisdom. Her mother owned a laundry in North Beach and worked in its steamiest corner fourteen hours a day. Her father was a fisherman, reputedly Black Hand. He was narrow-eyed and wiry and seldom smiled. All that summer he had chugged alone into the gauze emptiness outside the Gate to toss a token net, it was said, and wait for the Vancouver whiskey boat. He left the house early one Monday, the mother followed, and Ben found himself next door. Terry's pull was planetary in a vacuum of boredom or he would never have pressed the button. Mafia or not, the old man was Sicilian. In the lore of the neighborhood he would literally kill him if he found them alone in the house. But she had the fullest, cleanest blue-black hair he would ever see, and the reddest lips, and moistest. She was one of the few girls he knew who could pout and smile at the same time; at sixteen she had already perfected her throaty voice. Hand shaking, he pressed the forbidden button under the sign "Private Family. No Admittance." There were enough whorehouses on Russian Hill to warrant the sign, all right, and his own mother considered them O.K. for Italians but bourgeois, and anyway they never had any trouble except one night when he and **his** sister Porky screwed a red light into the outside lamp to see what would happen.

Terry opened the door immediately. Even then she had loved opera, and they put on a record but she sensed that it bored him, and they ended up playing checkers in a gloomy little dining room under a print of Mount Etna and the lewd smile of a cherub with a clock for a belly button. Someone— later they would argue who—dropped a checker. They bobbed together under the table and bumped heads. She moaned in pain, some of it real, and emerged, rubbing her temple. Checkerless, he took her to the imitation stained-glass window. There were tears in her eyes but no visible mark. Suddenly she was very close. Her leg, firm and warm, touched his knee, her soft round hip pressed his thigh. He looked into her wide amber eyes, and they were afraid but knowing.

There was a sound from the front door down the hallway. An electric shock doused his passion.

"Newspaper," she whispered.

"I got to go," he croaked, "anyway!"

"No," she murmured fiercely. And then: "What about the checker?"

So they crawled back under the ornate table and in five minutes he was no longer chaste. The cherub chimed his belly button. Terry made a sound and he thought she was sobbing for lost maidenhood, but then he noticed that she was not crying at all but chuckling.

"What?" he asked nervously, wishing he were gone.

"That silly statue, from Rome," she grinned. "It's my daddy's idea of class. You suppose he'll *talk?*"

Ben scrambled out, helped her up, and left. The foghorn on Alcatraz moaned and the terror began. Stumbling down the wooden steps, he spotted Frank Glioto tinkering with his motorcycle on the steep sidewalk. Frank crossed the street, wiping his hands.

"Hey, Ben, oh, Ben! Look, you ain't getting any of that?"

"I like her, is all."

He didn't, particularly, not then. Sometimes in class her breath smelled of garlic. His longing for Terry had never got far past his loins, while there was a girl named Sharon with a delicately tilted little nose whom he worshiped cerebrally. She was a doctor's daughter from Pacific Heights who had refused to go to Burke's or Sarah Dix Hamlin's because she wanted to see, presumably, the shoddier side at Galileo High, and she clung to him and no one else at the dances in the gym. She would go well with a fireside in a rustic beach house when he retired from the Navy as an admiral or became first to fly the Pacific. If not, under some future dock light stood a Golden Girl in a trench coat out of Hemingway by Erich Remarque. No, he didn't like Terry particularly, but already he felt stirrings again: if he didn't see her tomorrow he'd bust.

Frank Glioto glanced at her door. "You better watch it," he grinned. He tugged at his teeth with his thumbnail, jerking it away in the purported Black Hand sign of death.

"Fuck you," Ben said pleasantly, to hide his fear. "And keep your goddamn mouth shut, you understand?"

It did no good. Next week school began. To sense the mood of the neighborhood, Ben sneaked out the red Model A his stepfather had bought with last month's Radio Common "profits" and took Frank Glioto and Bugsy Calahan cruising through North Beach while his mom and stepfather were at a union banquet. Frank measured the front seat and the clearance under the wheel and searched for Terry's footprints on the dashboard upside down. For once he was funny but Ben wished he'd shut up.

"Look, you bastard," Ben said finally, "that's all over, you understand?"

"All over Fisherman's Wharf."

"If it is, you spilled it. I didn't *do* anything, anyway."

"What if you knocked her up? I wouldn't touch her with a ten-foot pole."

"You couldn't touch her with what you got," offered Bugsy. "She's in love. She's in love with Benny!"

"They're gonna get him out on that boat," Frank predicted happily, "haulin' nets full of booze. 'Captain, sir, Captain Bellini? Look, I'm your son-in-law, sir. Can I take a piss now? I been haulin' on this fucking net since breakfast!' "

He was parked safely on the hill at home, checking the car for cigarette butts, when he heard someone climbing the sidewalk steps. Terry's mother was heaving homeward, a mammoth with a market basket and a moustache. There was no escape.

"Good evening, Mrs. Bellini," he said. His face felt like cardboard.

She paused under the streetlamp, regarding him through Terry's enormous, beautiful eyes. She breathed in gargantuan earthquakes from the climb. Her mouth twisted downward and she grunted as if reaffirmed in some ancient judgment. Then she moved swiftly to her door and unlocked it. He climbed from the car and she stopped him with the lift of a Roman finger. "Giovanni," she yelled inside. She added something in Italian. Startled, he slammed the car door and made a break for his steps. He was too late.

Giovanni Bellini stood on his wooden stoop in an old-fashioned underwear shirt, buttoning his pants. Ben caught a whiff of sweat and wine and fish. The face was dark and the black eyes slitted and a cigarette dangled from his lips; he removed it in a cupped hand like a prisoner and motioned him inside with his head.

"Mr. Bellini, I got to——"

"Come in, eh?" demanded the wife. Ben was no match for the scorn in her eyes or the threat in her husband's. He followed him to the dining room where it had all happened, Mama cutting off escape to the rear. Terry, clearing dishes from the fine lace tablecloth, looked up and almost dropped a plate. Ben knew suddenly that she had not talked; it was Frank Glioto's big mouth, nothing more. It gave him strength, but only temporarily. Terry asked her mother something sharply in Italian; she got no answer, but the woman, moving with astonishing speed like a battle cruiser, took her arm and steered her to the kitchen. He heard a solid slap, and Terry yelled something angrily; another slap, and then angry sobbing. Terry did not reappear, but the mother did, and planted herself across the escape route again while the father sat at the head of the table. He scratched his armpit meditatively, never taking his eyes from Ben's.

"Look, Mr. Bellini——"

"What you gonna do?"

"About what?" His knees began to tremble. He had dived headlong once into a charging set of guards and the Mission High backfield without a qualm; now he felt that he might drop from fright. "What do you mean?"

"Teresa," said the man.

"You going to marry her, Benny?" asked the woman. She mouthed his mother's name for him deliciously. "You think your mama like you to marry her? All one happy family, eh? One Sunday, we go next door for dinner, next Sunday over here? Your mama invite the PTA ladies to tea." She crooked a finger and lifted an imaginary teacup. " 'Please to meet my sister-in-law, Lucia Bellini. She don't speak English so good, but she's very good at the laundry, and the spaghetti she cook—mmm—' " She kissed her fingers. Suddenly she was in garlic range, glaring into his eyes. "You think she gonna like that, eh?"

He took a breath. "Look, Mrs. Bellini, I'm not going to

marry anybody! You think I'm nutty? I'm not even out of high school!"

She ignored him. "Your mama's a schoolteacher. Every week, how much? Fifty dollars? Maybe she thinks she got us to feed, the fishing goes bad, the laundry don't do so good?" She moved closer. "You don't have to worry about that, Benny." She murmured something in Italian. Bellini, without taking his eyes from Ben's face, dug into his hip pocket. He pulled out a mass of greasy bills, tossed them on the table. Ben stared at the first fifty he had ever seen; he hadn't known they printed anything larger than a twenty.

"That's today, Benny!" she leered. "Today! You think we got enough for a *dote di sposa*? Good fisherman, eh? You marry Teresa, you think you got to take care of him?"

"I'm not marrying anybody!" he squeaked.

"That's right, Benny," she said suddenly. Her eyes were full of scorn. "You're *not* going to marry her. She going to marry somebody *we* are not shamed of. She's going to marry in Saint Peter and Paul's, and after, there's going be a hundred people, a thousand, at Fugazi Hall, and a cake from Gallo's going to weigh a hundred pounds! And who she marries going to find out he's a rich man! But I don't think you going to be there, Benny. I think you going to be a long way gone."

Anger began to throb dully. Who the hell was she to threaten him? It wasn't his fault alone, and anyway, she didn't know, she didn't have proof.

"What do you mean by *that?*" he asked hoarsely.

Bellini broke his silence. "She mean what she say! Or we maybe cut off your balls! Now, *vattene!*"

"Get out," spat the woman.

He stumbled into the chill night, knowing that now there was no escape, he would have to tell Steve.

Steve Casco had drifted into their lives a few years after their father, who had crinkly gray eyes impossible to lie into, returned from duty as navigator of an old four-stacker convoying doughboys across the Atlantic—returned to die of flu. Ben's mother, an alumna of Mills College, had grieved and then gone to work as an English teacher; in a few years she had tenure and nothing short of joining the Wobblies could lose her her job, and she did not quit even when she married Steve.

Steve was a benign man with a blond shock of hair that always shot forward like a kid's, leaving a clump sprouting in back. He'd been their father's closest shipmate before the war; they were officers on the Oregon line. During Steve's courtship he was mostly at sea, but when he was ashore there were noodles from the soup carts in Japtown, *panettoni* laden with fruit from Russo's bakery down the street, litchi nuts from Chinatown, where he knew everybody. He was heavier than their father, but not as tall. He had dark-brown eyes, easy to look into at all times; he was a boisterous tosser of children into the air, a playmate who wore a plaid cap and bright ties.

Steve went to sea after the honeymoon for a few trips as master, and it was a good thing that his bride had not resigned, for one day he came home for keeps, carrying his sacred Plath sextant. The ship had struck a scrap barge in Puget Sound. He lost his ticket. Afterward he seemed to shrink in size and he never used the plaid cap again and for years he wore ordinary neckties like other men.

For eight years now he had been an underpaid official in the Masters, Mates, and Pilots' Hiring Hall. This fall, he had been shouldering every lunch hour with Italian pastrycooks and butchers and one-room salami factory owners into a Washington Square brokerage, watching the Big Board. He had built up his wife's tiny estate to nine thousand dollars;

it was in hock now as collateral against a hundred shares of
Radio Common, worth fifty thousand dollars and climbing
each night.

The evening of Bellini's threat, Ben found that the market
had slipped badly and that he could not pile another problem on the big sloping shoulders, and next week came
Wall Street's Black Tuesday and thank God he had not said
anything, because if he had he would have blamed himself
for what happened. On Wednesday morning, strangely,
Steve squeezed his arm, leaving for work, and kissed his
sister Porky and held her very close, but they thought nothing of it. That afternoon their jaunty Model A was found
empty on the ferry in the Oakland slip, holding up a honking
line of cars. No one had seen Steve go; perhaps the Goat
Island horn had shouted and no doubt the bell buoys clanged,
but no one would ever know, for there was no note, no matter how hard the police and insurance people looked, and the
body was swept through the Gate as they always were, and
out to sea and never found.

By the time the services were over and his mother had settled into her second widowhood there was a Packard following
Ben with three men in it. Two were marble-eyed Italians
who might have been brothers of Giovanni Bellini, with
high, rare-steak cheekbones; the third was a fat, affable slob
who rode next to the driver and grinned at Ben whenever
their eyes met. Then Terry disappeared from school. Pregnant? Banished to a convent? Chained to her bed? Ben had
nowhere to go for advice but to Antonelli, the barber, who
was Milanese and hated Sicilians, but who knew everything
because the Sicilians seemed to forget he was Italian and
talked in his shop. Antonelli regarded him from beneath his
white Caruso mane and snipped a few stray hairs.

"Not pregnant, no. Or I would hear. She's with her aunt,
in Fresno."

"Why, for Christ's sake? She won't graduate!"

"You got to understand this Bellini, Benny. See, he's just a little shot. Fisherman, bootlegger. Millionaire? Maybe. Maybe he's got it all in a sock someplace, but in the mafia he's just a little shot. But a beautiful daughter, and so smart she is, too. So they laugh at him. Now he's *ludibrio:* a fool, a clown, you know? They laugh so he think he gotta do something. The *siciliani*, they knife you in the back for a dollar, but they think they got honor. Like Japs, you know? Losing face. So he sends *her* away, to make sure it don't happen again. Then maybe when he runs *you* away he brings her back."

"Well," Ben said, "he's got a long wait. Nobody's running me out of town!" His voice sounded squeaky. "Nobody!"

That night he crossed the street to see Frank Glioto. Frank was scared. He sat pretending to yawn, in his parents' parlor in the yellow-satin boxing robe they had given him when he fought South of Market. He moved casually to the window and shifted the blind a little, peering out. From down the hallway his father yelled a question at him in Italian; Frank yelled back, "Benny Casco!" and the voice down the hall exploded. Ben knew no Italian, but the sense was clear: "Get him the hell out!"

"Gray Packard?" repeated Frank. "Yeah, I seen it."

"If these guys get me—if they lay a hand on me—you're the one who did it! You understand that, Frank?"

"I'm sorry. I thought it was funny, is all. I mean, her old man's a bootlegger, and your old lady's being a teacher, and you—"

"Me, what?" Ben turned. Frank looked smaller. He was practically a pro, but for the first time in his life Ben felt he could take him.

"You being such a brain and all—"

"Brain my ass," he exploded. "She drove me out of my

fucking brain, and you guys stirred them up, and now they want to kill me for it!"

He went into the fog, taking giant steps up the sidewalk stairs, teeth clenched. In three steps he regretted leaving, but then it was too late.

Behind him he heard a car grinding up the hill. He was scared to turn. He climbed more slowly now, hoping that it would pass before he crossed the street. It did not pass. He stopped and turned. The Packard waited, door open.

"Hello, Romeo," said the fat man in front. "Get in back."

The man in the rear had on his lap an oddly truncated shotgun that could pick him off before he'd gone a step. He got in.

It was a short ride, far too short, but long enough to teach him some Machiavellian truths. Football, he learned suddenly, taught you to play football, street-fighting was handy on the streets, but absolute power was absolute. He had been a student of the Tarzan-d'Artagnan-Douglas Fairbanks school of self-preservation, victor over dozens of bandits in his room and white slavers invading the study hall, but he was being kidnapped by three illiterate mobsters without moving a muscle. He was a good guy, they were bad; the laws of fiction demanded their downfall; in any movie they were doomed and he would fight his way free, but he remained paralyzed, too scared even to yell.

The gray Packard glided downstream like a battleship through the hairpin curves of the Lombard Street Hill. No one said anything. He counted the turns, familiar from childhood skate scooters; he'd passed the point of terror; he was drifting in a nightmare and only the rich smell of the Girhardelli Chocolate Plant behind Galileo High seemed real. A school visit to the factory was more vivid than the Packard's stately rumble through darkened waterfront streets.

They rolled past Fisherman's Wharf into the shadow of a

warehouse. They parked and for a moment they sat silent. Ben found that he could speak, hoarsely, "What are you going to do? Why?"

The fat man glanced back but didn't answer. He got out of his door, motioned Ben to follow him. Ben shook his head. The man with the shotgun poked him and he stumbled out, Shotgun behind him. He followed the fat man toward the warehouse, but at the warehouse wall, without warning, Shotgun somehow yanked his leather jacket down over his arms; simultaneously Fatty turned and his huge fist flashed in the yellow light of a streetlamp. Ben was all at once on his face in the dirt, his right cheek numb. He rolled over, licked his lip, and tasted blood.

The fat man looked down at him with the trace of a smile; the other cradled the shotgun and picked his teeth with no expression at all. He lay for a moment with shame and fear and a nameless, all-powerful rage rising in his throat. He had never been struck by an adult; he'd had no idea that so fat a man could hit so hard. But he hadn't killed him, and before he did, he was going to have a crack at the son of a bitch....

He scrambled to his feet, fought free of his jacket, and charged insanely, forgetting science, head down, fists flailing at the big belly.

But it was not fat, it was muscle. It was like punching a bag of potatoes. The man never moved. When the nightmare ended and Ben ran out of steam, Shotgun nailed him from behind; his neck was vised in a wiry arm, a hard hip dug into his butt. He was bent backward, stomach wide open....

Slowly the fat man cocked a fist. Then he hit him in the gut, and Ben was down, vomiting, strangling, fighting for air. He would suffocate unless somebody helped him; he could hear his own heart pounding; if he didn't breathe he would die. He croaked for help; he needed air, air, air. . . .

The spasm passed. He was lying on his back, flat, belly throbbing, but at last, at least, the blessed, foggy fish air was shuddering into his lungs. He was somehow aware that while he had been thrashing in the dirt the two men had moved away. Now he played possum, feigning unconsciousness. He moved his head and could see the fat man and Shotgun back at the car; the other had never even bothered to get out. He could hear the rise and fall of their soft Sicilian voices. The big man laughed at something. Then Ben caught the flash of a switchblade knife as he flicked it open and showed it to the others.

They were going to do it! They were waiting until he could feel it, and they were going to castrate him! He rolled deeper into the shadow of the warehouse, groaning as if still struggling for breath. A chill racked him; a vomit taste seared his throat; but no one near the car seemed to notice his movement. It was now, or not at all. Suddenly, without conscious effort, he was up and sidling along the building, keeping to the shadow, tense for the roar of the shotgun or the sound of running feet—let it be that, let them chase him on foot, because he could outrun any of them, he could outrun Paavo Nurmi himself. If they just didn't start the engine . . .

He rounded the warehouse, sprinted sobbing along the street until he got to North Point, cut up toward Columbus Avenue. If he could get to the bright lights of the Columbus restaurants, or to a cop, or anywhere the damn Packard couldn't follow, he would never ask God for anything more.

He got as far as Antonelli's Barber Shop before he started to vomit. He stepped into the shadow of the locked entrance, puked, and stumbled three more houses to the flat where

Antonelli lived. He pressed the bell, put his forearm on the wall, and prayed that he was home.

FIVE

Mr. Antonelli sat at the kitchen table in an incredible nightgown and tasseled nightcap, like a character from *Pinocchio*. Ben swirled the raw Dago-red around his mouth, moved to the sink, spat it out. He took another mouthful and spat again. Antonelli moved over and tousled his hair. "They *let* you go."

"Let me go? Jesus Christ, they were going to *castrate* me! One of them," he said, choking, "held me still. And that fat bastard slugged me in the gut! What *happens* to him?"

"Someday," Antonelli said simply, "somebody gets *him*. And his soul goes to hell."

In the past few weeks heaven and hell had lost ground with Ben; he wanted to see the fat man sweat here and now, just in case God lost track. "I want to get him *now!*"

"No. What you got to do, you got to let them know you're scared. You got to let *Bellini* know you're scared."

"I'll write him a note. 'Dear Mr. Bellini: O.K. I'm scared. Please stop getting me beat up. Love. Ben Casco.'"

The old man's eyes were distant. For a long moment there was silence, except for the murmur of simmering coffee. A horn honked somewhere and Ben thought of the gray Packard and lifted his cup too soon and burned his tongue.

"Benny?"

"Yeah?"

"You *got* to get out of town."

"I graduate in six months. Damn it, I've been working my ass off! I want my diploma!" He was talking more to himself than Antonelli.

Antonelli ignored him. He asked Ben his number and moved to a telephone on his kitchen wall. In two minutes he had arranged for Ben's mother to meet them at the Ferry Building. Then he drew his chair across the room, climbed to the sink counter, felt behind a steam pipe. When he got down, grunting, he extracted ten tens from a thick stack of bills. Ben tried to refuse, but he pressed them on him. "You can pay it back."

"How's Bellini going to know I've gone? I don't want them fooling around home."

"I'll tell your friend Frank," Antonelli said. "In five minutes, everybody knows."

SIX

Ben told his mother about Terry, in a booth at the Ferry Building coffee stand; she was angry—not at Ben but at her. She said all the things he'd expected: that the police wouldn't let anybody hurt him, that this was a civilized town, that he'd miss his graduation, that they'd move out of the neighborhood if necessary.

In the end it was his bruised cheek and Mr. Antonelli's patient, stubborn wisdom that convinced her that a Packard full of impregnable murderers was going to outweigh her arguments no matter what she said. Ben told her his plan: he'd enlist in the Navy at Vallejo; they'd send him to San Diego for boot training; he'd be not too far from home but far enough from the local hoods. Maybe from the ranks you could get an appointment to Annapolis, which is what he wanted after all. Someday he might even go to Pensacola and join the select eagles who every Navy Day led the Fleet through the Golden Gate. By the time he had finished talking he had almost convinced himself that it was all for the good. He gave her his gold football for Sharon and basketball for Porky and told her Bugsy could have his dinghy if he'd paint it; he kissed her good-bye and stepped aboard the ferry.

His eyeballs felt full of sand, his cheek hurt, his mouth was cut, he was more exhausted than he had ever been, but on the upper deck the damp dawn wind cleared his head. He did not even look back at the city; the fog was gone and the rising sun was warm on his cheeks and the blood warm in his veins and three hours before he had thought he was going to die or worse. Not even the bell buoy tolling for Steve off Goat Island wrecked the fragile golden moment.

He was unharmed, and he was free.

PART TWO

The Rape

CHAPTER ONE

ONE

Fifteen miles astern the carriers loomed like distant seacliffs across the vast lagoon of Ulithi. Ben leaned next to the bearded boat-pool coxswain at the landing craft's helm. A horrible diesel groaned below. Supported by heat waves ahead, floating mystically above the surface of the lagoon, slept a narrow alligator of an island with white-coral flanks and palm trees thick on its backbone.

Barney Epstein, Atabrine yellow from his Philippine duty, squatted forward like a Jewish Buddha cast in brass, holding his shirt open to catch the wind of their passage. In the cargo well two Seabees in marine fatigues slept among jerry cans and crates and cardboard boxes, the weekly ration for the island's natives.

The coxswain blasted an airhorn. Off the wavering shoreline slid an outrigger paddled by two bronze, sleek-muscled little men with frizzled hair. They turned as escort through the coral reefs, keeping ahead effortlessly. They were sullen and refused to look at the LCVP, pretending to search for a channel. The coxswain spun the wheel, reversed his engine, and then moved forward slowly. "Usually," he said, "they're jumping with joy. The chaplain must have corn-holed the chief." The ramp clattered down and Ben and Epstein strolled ashore. They climbed the ridge up a coral-bordered path and found a sign pointing to a tent with a wooden floor and half-wooden walls: "Ulithi Military Government Unit." The canvas flaps were raised for coolness. They walked up two creaking steps and peered into the shadow. On a desk made of a packing crate sat a monkeypod plaque: "Lieutenant Peter García (Chaplain Corps) USNR." They entered and a skinny man with a scraggly beard swung his feet over the side of an iron bunk.

"I'm just the yaw expert, gentlemen. Al Singer, pharmacist's-mate third. Island's out of bounds, but you're lucky, the chaplain's with the king. No," he said, glancing down the walk, "this is him. He."

A solid, shirtless young man tanned almost black, wearing a baseball cap with a small golden crucifix where the officer's insignia should have been, came up the path. He was handsome, vibrant, with expressive dark eyes; he gave the impression of being vulnerable, which was good, and fearless, which was bad. He shook hands without particular enthusiasm, and said, "I'm Father García. Frankly, gentlemen, we're not encouraging sight-seeing anymore. King Pul was concerned because his people were being treated like monkeys in a zoo." He smiled to take the sting off it. He had a luminous smile. "The stores boat usually off-loads in about an hour, so if you'd care to return to her, now, I'll try to take care of my weekly crisis." He nodded at the paperwork on his desk and sat down.

"Your weekly crisis," Ben said softly, "may be the reason we're here."

The chaplain's eyes flicked to Ben's. "That, gentlemen, is a different matter. Was he your man, Commander?"

Ben became aware of a rumble of surf from the seaward

reef, of children's voices far distant through the palm groves, of someone hammering on the beach. Feeling oddly unlike the exec of a capital ship in the presence of one lieutenant who was really a lawyer and another who was really a priest, he told what he knew of the gig's visit.

"Your steward's mate admitted it?" the chaplain remarked. "Why?"

"I guess he figured I'd find out."

"Or he likes you."

"He does. And he was scared."

The chaplain looked at Epstein. "And Mr. Epstein? Are you the legal officer?"

"No," Epstein said wryly, "I'm Admiral Howland's intelligence."

"He speaks Japanese," Ben explained. "I thought we'd better be able to communicate."

The chaplain's eyes flashed darkly. "You can communicate with _me_, Commander. If there's one thing we don't need around here today it's somebody speaking Japanese." He moved to the side of the tent and looked down at a crystal cove. "That's where they landed," he said bitterly.

"Our gig?"

"I wish it had, I'd have seen it. No, the Japs. They'd run the place since nineteen-fourteen, but you know what they did after Midway?"

"No." Ben studied the chaplain. Color was rising on his cheeks; he was getting angrier by the moment.

"They sent troops ashore right down there. As usual, they raped. Ulithi's in the Yap diocese; they beheaded the Catholic fathers. Then they moved most of the population off Ulithi to Koror and Babelthaup, three hundred miles away, without regard to family, so a wife might end up on one atoll and her husband on another. Some of them aren't back yet."

"Why?"

"We're too busy." The chaplain shoved back his chair. "And we don't care much. Hell, before we landed we bombarded the Japs on the atoll, who'd already left. We killed five natives, but that was all right with the survivors: at least we weren't Japs. We didn't rape. Right?"

"O.K., Chaplain. I get the idea."

"Not all of it. Now *we* had all these little islands with the few little people the Japs hadn't moved already, so what did we do? Why, gentlemen, we moved them again, here to Fassarai. Safer, anyway: they had yaws, a minor form of syphilis inflicted on them by the white man some three hundred years ago. We moved forty-seven off Asor, and a hundred and sixty off Falalop so we could build an airstrip, and thirty-nine off Lossau, why I don't know, and ninety-five off Mogmog so we could throw up two officers' clubs and string a mile of barbed wire around a baseball diamond and build the biggest reefer in the western Carolines to cool beer."

"Beer for white-hats who spent three years trying to take the Japs off their goddamn backs," flared Ben.

"Sure, we liberated them," agreed the chaplain. "And they can still see home on a clear day. And what if we did make the place a zoo for the brass afterward, as the king says? We couldn't be blamed for that: it's not like the Micronesias or the Marshalls, or Guam, with junk spread all over. Not yet. Because for some reason these natives alone, out of all the islanders, lived just like the pictures in the story books. Grass skirts, breechcloths, outrigger canoes! Not a corrugated roof on the atoll. A zoo! 'Glad to have you, Admiral. Would you like to see a live king? Just don't feed the natives, sir!' Well, not anymore!"

"That's some indictment, Father," Epstein said, "but your alleged rapist is a Negro who's been similarly shoved around

all his life. And he had nothing to do with the Japs raping
the natives."

"He did his own raping! Commander, you could have saved
yourself a long hot boat ride if you'd simply dispatched his
name to the port captain, as I asked. What would you do if
this were a white woman in Pearl? Would you go to this
trouble to smooth it over?"

Ben controlled his anger. "It depends. A prostitute or a
bar girl, maybe. My God, Chaplain, he could get ten, twenty
years at Terminal Island! This girl will have laid half the
western Carolines by then."

The chaplain studied him for a long while. Finally he
said, with a tremor, "Gentlemen, would *you* like to do some
sight-seeing?"

"I'd rather get this squared away," said Ben. "If we could
talk to the king—"

"Good idea. He'd like to talk to *you.*"

"Maybe invite him aboard the ship—"

"Today? He'd turn you down cold."

"Well, maybe send over a couple of cases of cigarettes—"

"Ulithians don't smoke, yet. Shall we go?"

TWO

There was no one to be seen, but the homes were
superb: tall, stately, with woven-palm roofs on ridgepoles.
The high-peaked buildings dwarfed the grove in which the
village lay. Ben had expected the shacks and rubble of New
Guinea; he saw a thatched Swiss village transported to a
tropic isle. The arrow-straight paths between the houses
were swept clean by the trades or by hand.

"German mandate, until nineteen-fourteen," the chaplain

explained. "They pick the best of what the white man shows them."

"Including religion?" asked Epstein.

"Oh, they had a choice. In seventeen thirty-one."

"Between what?" asked Epstein.

"Well, paganism or Catholicism," smiled the father. He took them to the only wooden building in the grove. "Here's the new church. *Ecclesia,* they call it."

It was a typical Seabee structure of unpainted pine. They stepped past a holy-water font made from a half-coconut husk jammed into a five-inch shell case. The altar was a plank laid across two ammo boxes; on it flickered a candle and a smoky ship's lantern; Jesus suffered sootily on a cross above. Epstein remarked that the church was empty.

"They disappear after a funeral, too," the chaplain said.

"You could use a new altar," Epstein suggested. His eyes met the chaplain's, and the priest flushed.

"No," he said softly. "You don't understand at all, do you?"

"Could we see the girl?"

The chaplain shrugged. "If she'll see *us,* sure."

At the end of the path they stood outside a thatched home while the chaplain ducked like a Limbo dancer under palm-frond eaves two feet from the ground. He returned in a moment and nodded. Ben and Epstein crawled in.

It was very cool inside. The darkness was almost total. When Ben could see, he noted that the house was immaculate. There were palm mats spread neatly on the floor; others, apparently for sleeping, were rolled to the side under the eaves, which slapped them softly in the rising breeze. The girl sat close to the overhang, plaiting a coconut mat. Her father, a hugely tattooed little man with white hair, hovered nearby, never taking his eyes from Ben's face; the girl had not looked up once. She was a miniature Polynesian except for a Micronesian explosion of black, frizzled hair. She knelt on her heels, her legs thoroughly hidden under a full grass skirt; her bare breasts were lush and full. Her skin shone coppery in the dusky light, and in contrast to every native he had seen in the Solomons, the Marshalls, and even on Guam, she was immaculate. Her face was flat and round, her lips were beautiful, and her black eyes were red from weeping. The chaplain squatted beside her and for a while they talked softly in the native dialect. He got up, finally. "She asks if I think she should leave the island. She thinks she has shamed me and the church and her family."

"What did you tell her?" Epstein asked quickly.

"That the man will be punished."

"What did she do to prevent the rape?" Epstein wanted to know.

"You *are* a lawyer, Mr. Epstein? Legal officer or not?"

"Yes."

"I thought so," the chaplain said, smiling savagely. "Well, she was bathing down at the southern end of the island when he found her. They're very modest. The women bathe with their skirts on, for instance. He approached her there, and she ran toward the village, so scared she hid in a *yeeper,* and he caught her again—"

"What's a *yeeper?*"

"A menstrual hut, no men allowed, and it was empty at the time, and he raped her in there."

"A menstrual hut," Epstein said thoughtfully. "I'll be damned. . . ."

"Yes, Mr. Epstein. By our own standards, tantamount to violating a nun on the holy altar. I'd like to be charitable but I hope he gets thirty years."

"Chaplain," Epstein asked suddenly, "do they have *mesphil* here?"

Ben had never heard of *mesphil,* but whatever it was the chaplain's face flamed. *"Mesphil?* No, they don't. There have been Catholic priests on this atoll for two hundred years, Mr. Epstein. It's as Catholic as, say, South Boston. Perhaps it's too bad, perhaps not, but nobody even remembers the old chants anymore, let alone *mesphil."* Tenderly he touched the girl's wiry hair. "We've been wasting our time. Let's see the king, Commander, and then I'll take you to your boat."

As they crawled out into the heat, a chubby little boy squatting at the side of the house looked up at Ben's wings with wide eyes. Ben unclipped them and handed them down. The chaplain smiled. "Her brother. If he was a year older, you'd never get him to take them."

The interview with the king was useless. He was a fine-looking, steely little man with bushy white hair, clad in a loincloth like everyone else. He sat cross-legged at the end of a tall thatched house almost exactly like the girl's. He had gentle, wise eyes, and he listened to Ben's apologies, but apparently nothing would satisfy him but blood.

"He says," said Father García, "he told the village that Americans weren't like Japanese. Now the village thinks he was stupid. He's lost face."

"Tell him I'll send Watkins ashore to apologize."

"No. They don't like force, but I think they'd kill him."

Ben glanced around for Epstein. He had slipped out. Damn . . . "Well, ask him what we *can* send ashore. For the village, or for him."

The chaplain shook his head. "No."

"Why not?"

"We're dealing with a mortal sin, Commander! He knows it. What *can* you send ashore?"

"All right," Ben said abruptly, "tell him the man will be punished."

"I've told him."

"Thanks," he said bitterly. They found Barney Epstein at the landing craft, talking to Singer, the yaw expert. Epstein seemed strangely thoughtful.

"Thanks for stranding me at the royal audience," Ben said sourly.

"My hands are clean," said Epstein. "I went out backward."

Ben told the priest that he would have charges written up before they left. Watkins would probably be tried at Pearl, but the sentence would appear in the court-martial orders. "Along with the name of the ship, unfortunately. And you can spread the pound of flesh around the parish."

"Commander," flared the priest, "it isn't only spiritual! It's medical. If they lose confidence in me, Singer's dead, too. Right, Doc?"

Singer glanced at Epstein, and Ben caught the merest tremor of a shrug. "That's right, Padre." Singer smiled at the priest, Ben thought, almost paternally. Then he turned and ambled toward the headquarters, kicking coral hunks along the beach. The chubby little boy Ben had lifted came splashing down the beach and handed the chaplain a package wrapped crudely in a taro leaf. He glanced at Ben, eyes full of tears, and scampered off. It was the pair of wings. Ben boarded the boat with Epstein and the ramp squealed up behind them. Ben watched the island recede in the ripple of the afternoon trades. "What's *mesphil?*" he asked Epstein suddenly.

"Gang-bang. Old native custom. A virgin reaches puberty, all the bachelors in the village get to break her in."

"Damn," muttered Ben. "All the snatch in the western Pacific, and he had to get turned loose on *them!*"

"Ulithians?" smiled Epstein. "Rabbits."

"What?"

"You don't need a Hershey bar. They put out for fun."

"What are you talking about?"

Epstein shrugged. "Means nothing to them."

"Are you serious?"

Epstein nodded. "Ask Singer."

"Well, why the hell did she holler rape?"

"Glad you mentioned that," Epstein said. "Give me twenty-four hours, Commander. I'll find out."

CHAPTER TWO

ONE

Catlett was hard on Watkins' scent. He came to Ben's office with a list of minor offenders for exec's mast, but his mind was on the Negro. He glanced at the torn copy of Melville. "I don't know what, yet, but he did something besides just rip that book in half."

"I told you I'd take care of it," Ben said tersely. "It's my book."

"Yes, sir," Catlett grinned. "And of course he's your mess-boy, too."

"What do you mean by *that?*"

"Well, you don't want to brig *him*. It's almost like in the family, isn't it?"

"Catlett," Ben said suddenly, "you know what I'm going to do when we get back from this strike?"

Catlett's face froze. For a moment the massive scar on his chin seemed even whiter. "Get me transferred, sir?" he murmured.

"Yes."

The chief smiled faintly, as he had fifteen years before, when he had shattered Ben's dreams with a word. "When I leave," he murmured, "this half-assed crew will come apart at the seams."

"That's right," agreed Ben. "Like a seaman recruit that just got laid. But when we get it all glued back together it'll be a crew and not a bunch of zombies."

"I'm surprised you waited so long," Catlett shrugged, "considering."

"Considering what?"

"San Diego."

"Do you really think," Ben asked curiously, "that's why I'm going to do it?"

Catlett said affably, "Of course not, sir. No naval officer would hold a little brig time against his old drill instructor. Not even a mustang officer. Sir."

Ben studied him. "You know," he suggested, "there might just be enough there to bust your ass?"

Catlett appeared to ponder the question. "I don't think so, sir."

"Get out," Ben said softly.

"Aye, aye, sir," grinned Catlett. He closed the door behind him very carefully, and with great respect. Ben scanned the service records Catlett intended to soil with "late to quarters," "dirty dungarees," "malingering on a working party." He tossed them aside and turned to commissary lists and ammunition tallies but, as if Catlett had never left the compartment, the broad smile and cold green eyes lingered, reminding him that his own enlisted record was a skeleton locked safely in the ship's vault.

Catlett had marred it the afternoon before Thanksgiving in 1929, on the day of the Great Crab Race in Ben's boot barracks. No, that wasn't fair—Ben had marred it himself, but Catlett had goaded him into it and made it stick, where any other DI in camp would have punished him unofficially.

The economic gale Ben had escaped after the crash had been howling in San Diego beyond the boot-camp wall.

Some of the recruits in his company were ex-citizens of San Diego's Hooverville at the mouth of the Santa Fe tracks, which was swelling like a snow-fed lake as bindlestiffs who preferred not to freeze in the north dropped from each new freight. None of the boots were emaciated, ordinary bums, though; the laws of natural selection were at work and Navy doctors who in prosperous civilian times might have enlisted consumptive cretins were already rejecting out-of-work college graduates for unsightly warts. It was hard to pass the Navy physical: even the Hooverville body lice, survivors of delousing, head-shaving, baths, and a ten-day quarantine, were well above average athletically.

Ben earned twenty-one dollars a month. On the cement floor of the great bare barracks lay ten dollars of his first Navy pay in a white sailor cap, while Ape Gorman, a hairy, barrel-shaped boot, scratched his pubic hair and urged on the squad's entry, a crab louse named Lindberg. A half-dozen visitors from the third squad were cheering their champion, a magnificent *Phthirus pubis* named Admiral, crawling mightily after Lindberg from the center of a ring sketched on a mattress cover.

Ben, acting squad leader by virtue of high-school ROTC, spotted Catlett first, swept the arena from the floor, stuffed it into a seabag, and kicked the sailor hat with the stakes into a corner. Chief Oscar Catlett loomed in the doorway, outlined in bronze by the afternoon sun. He was a silent terror to the company; omniscient, in the air it breathed. He wore a duty CPO armband and white gloves and carried a short DI sword.

" 'Tention!" Ben barked belatedly, but there was no need. Every man in the room was as stiff as if the Cat were the drill officer; stiffer, perhaps.

"Thanks, Casco," said the chief, smiling. "I was wonder-

ing." He began to stalk the room, his eyes crinkling with
good fellowship, perfect teeth sparkling. A dozen pair of
eyes studied the plaster walls dead ahead. "Look at all the
extra company we got!" Catlett said thoughtfully. "Crap
game?" He saw the hat and money and prodded it with a
toe. "Who's got the dice?" He squatted and slapped the
seabag nearest the hat, raising an explosion of golden dust;
he arose quickly and clapped his hand to his face as he
sneezed. A sharp flash of pain glinted in his eyes; false teeth,
thought Ben, and he had almost lost them. For an instant the
chief turned away, fumbling with his mouth. When he turned
back, his eyes scanned the recruits; Ben realized suddenly
that he was the only one not staring dutifully ahead. "Casco?"

"Yes, sir?"

"What's so goddamn funny?"

Ben found nothing funny; he was chilled with fear, but
he was damned if he'd show it and he held the cold green
eyes. "Nothing funny, sir."

"Who's got the dice?"

"No dice, sir."

The green eyes glinted. "They won't like that at Annapolis, if you get there. Honor system, you know, and that
shit?" Catlett grinned suddenly at the rigid recruits. "You're
all restricted to the barracks until chow. Not that you got
anywhere to go. You, Casco, I want to see in the drill office.
And this is for you."

He handed Ben a message and left. Ben glanced at the
note: "Call San Francisco, Operator 21." He tensed, anger
and fear of Catlett forgotten: something had happened at
home; nothing less than catastrophe would have enticed his
mother or sister Porky these days into a long-distance call,
Thanksgiving eve or not. He picked his bet out of the hat and
pulled on a blouse.

"Hey," Ape Gorman demanded, "where's Lindberg?"

"Casco killed him," said Deacon, a sallow farmer from Tennessee, handing out the rest of the bills. "He murdered him trying to stay off the report. He thinks they're going to ship him off to Indianapolis, you hear Catlett?"

"*Ann*apolis," Ben muttered, squaring his hat in the communal mirror. He had passed his exams for the Academy prep school; he was well on his way to an appointment.

"Hey," said Ape, "five or six years from now, me and you, Deacon, we're swabbing the shitter on some battleship, he's going to come along and goose us with his big long sword."

"I'll wear white gloves," promised Ben, "because you'll probably still have crabs."

The Ape scratched his genitals with sudden hope. "You know something? I think he's back."

TWO

The nearest pay phone was outside the Administration Building; Ben ran all the way. The line crackled and when finally he got through it was his big brother Joe who answered, not his mother. "Ben, Porky's been in an accident—"

Oh, God, no. Joe, yes; even Mom, but not Porky . . .

"What happened?" he croaked.

"That goddamn Glioto hit her."

"*Hit* her?" Bellini? The mafia? "On purpose?"

"Hell, no. He was screwing around outside on his motorcycle, no hands, and she was watching, and he damn near took off her foot, and busted his collarbone—"

"I wish he'd busted his neck!"

"She's pretty bad, Ben. They're operating in the morning."

"I'll be home tonight."

Emergency liberty, or leave, or whatever the hell they called it! He stumbled into the Administration Building, almost deserted for Thanksgiving already. In the duty officer's cubicle he found Chief Catlett, feet on the desk, waiting for a cup of coffee from the Owl, a bespectacled boot in Ben's company who had drawn Thanksgiving messenger duty. Catlett sipped the coffee and let him finish his story. "Where's your neckerchief?" he asked suddenly. "You're in the Administration Building."

"Sorry, sir," he said tightly. "What do I fill out?"

"Nothing. You aren't going anywhere."

Ben leaned on the desk. "Chief," he said hoarsely, "it's an emergency!"

"Before you could get emergency leave," Catlett said, "I'd have to check with the Red Cross. They'd telegraph the San Francisco Red Cross, and then they'd check the hospital and telegraph back. You *want* me to check?" He put his hand on the telephone and waited.

"You're damn right! Yes, sir!"

"What hospital's she in?"

Ben had forgotten to ask. The chief sat back. "You got poontang outside called you, or you set it up with home for Thanksgiving, is all."

"Jesus!" Ben borrowed a nickel from the Owl and trotted back to the pay phone again. He made the operator ring interminably, but Joe and Mom must have left for the hospital. He burst back into the Administration Building.

"Chief," he pled, "I can't get anybody. I got to catch a train! Give me leave! I'll prove it when I come back."

"Oh, hell yes," Catlett grinned. He rolled a cigarette. "There's a saying, Casco: 'Sing your troubles to Jesus, the chaplain's gone ashore.'" He looked up. "You're breathing hard, boot. I don't like it when you do that. It scares me, you know? What you thinking of?"

The moment froze. "I'm thinking," Ben blurted, "of knocking those false teeth down your fucking throat."

The chief sat back. His chair creaked. The Owl rattled a cup on the rack. Ben clenched his fists to grab the words and bring them back, to grasp their fleeting menace. The clock on the wall jerked forward: one minute, one click. Oh, God, let the new minute wash out the old. . . .

"Say again?" Catlett coaxed. He beckoned delicately, as if drawing words from a bashful child. "What was that?"

"Chief," Ben begged, "I got to get home!"

"Yeah. But what was that you said?"

"Nothing. Nothing, sir."

"Messenger!" the chief purred. "What'd he say?"

"I was washing out the coffee——" the Owl squeaked.

"What'd he *say?*" This time the words lashed out and the Owl folded.

"He'd knock your teeth down your throat?" Behind round glasses the Owl's eyes pleaded with Ben.

"What kind of teeth?" wheedled the chief, grinning again.

"False?" the Owl quavered.

"And what kind of throat?"

"I didn't hear——"

"What kind of *throat*, goddamn it?"

"I think he said 'fucking' throat, sir."

"You think?" Catlett slapped his desk. It sounded like a shot. "Or you know?"

The Owl looked as if he were about to cry. "He said it, sir."

Catlett sat back. "Write it down, then. Just like you heard it. Casco?"

"Yes?"

"Yes what?"

Ben wouldn't answer. His throat was tight, his world had crashed, it was his own fault but he was goddamned if he was going to grovel further. For three more ticks of the clock he stood, rock-still and silent, while the green eyes studied him. Finally the chief said, "Go back to your barracks. Be damn sure you don't leave it: I'll be checking every half-hour. Captain's mast Monday."

The next day Porky's foot was saved, and Monday Ben stood before Lieutenant Mitch Langley, the drill officer, god with gold wings and braid Ben now could never wear. Langley was genuinely distressed, but he had no choice, and the following day Ben was sentenced by a deck court officer to ten days' bread and water. He left the courtroom and reported to the marine court orderly, a hard-mouthed Pfc with a mirror-gloss .45 swinging from slim hips. The marine smelled like a shoe store and creaked when he moved as if his neck were really leather.

"Go to your barracks, Swabbie. We'll pick you up."

"You won't forget?" Ben asked anxiously, to prove that he didn't give a damn about the twenty-thousand-dollar education and the braid and the dream of golden wings.

"Full seabag, Asshole," grated the marine. "You got ten minutes."

THREE

The San Diego brig had smelled of Borax and marine gun oil. The cell was three paces long and one pace wide. If you avoided banging your shin on the seatless toilet at one end or your hip on the cold-water basin at the other, you could walk thirty paces per minute, or almost a mile an hour. But it made you dizzy, and after a while hungry. You weren't allowed to lie on your bunk but you did, until you heard the squeak of gyrene shoes and then you got silently to your feet. He was hungry all the time, but the hunger was not the worst. The lack of privacy was. He was a bug pinned in a collector's case. At any instant the fat young marine who had their cellblock would appear quietly at the lattice steel bars, leering in, daring him to be sleeping or even sitting against the wall.

He continually told himself that he wasn't really starving; that he had a full ration coming every third day; that plenty of people lived on less than his portion of bread, which was often buttered or soaked in gravy; and that at least he had all the water he wanted. But by the third day his dungaree pants were hanging from his hips, and when finally he faced Lieutenant Langley again, he was bitter and hard.

The lieutenant stuffed a pipe and lit it. "How's your sister?"

"She's home, sir."

"Good. You lost weight," Langley observed. "Learn anything?"

"To keep my mouth shut, sir," Ben admitted stiffly.

"That," the lieutenant said, "in your case, can be good. Or bad."

"It's what they built the brig for, isn't it, sir?" Ben asked. "And boot camp?"

Langley studied him, puffing at the pipe, which murmured softly and smelled faintly of rum. "Do you bear *me* any resentment?"

"Of course not, sir," Ben answered.

"Catlett?"

"That's different."

Langley studied him. "You know how Catlett got that scar?"

"He was a doughboy in France, I heard, sir." And, he added silently, I wish to hell they'd hit him six inches higher.

"No, Casco, that's scuttlebutt. He's younger than he looks. He was a gunner's mate third on my first tin can out of Annapolis. Quiet, nice-looking, popular: I heard half the young ladies in Panama were after him. Well, a sailor passed out and fell off the bow of the liberty boat one evening, and the coxswain panicked and swung the stern into him. Catlett dove over the side and grabbed him, and the screw chewed him up. Lost half his jaw, but——"

"Why's he have to ride us so hard?" Ben demanded. *"We* didn't do it!"

"Lost half his jaw," Langley said sharply, "and never let go of the drunk."

Ben wouldn't quit. "I don't question his guts, sir. But he baited me into that, and he lost the Navy an officer it could have had for life. Because believe me, sir, I'd have made it, if I had to study twenty-four hours a day!"

"You can *still* make it," Langley blurted suddenly.

"Make what? Chief, like Catlett?"

"Warrant officer! One deck court isn't going to stop you!"

"Warrant?" Ben asked bitterly. "In how long? Thirty years? Forty?"

"Things change," the lieutenant said.

"In thirty years," Ben said, "I'd be almost fifty. And I'd still be saluting twenty-year-old ensigns out of Annapolis. Wouldn't I, sir?"

Langley sat back. "You? I don't know." He was still impersonal, though his eyes were kindly again. "O.K., Casco. Report back to your company. Catch up with the drills. I'm finishing you on schedule. Your company's slated for a draft— the USS *Nevada*."

"Thank you, sir."

Ben slung his gear to his shoulder and trudged to his barracks. Ape and the Deacon and the Owl were glad to see him, and if he hadn't hated the sight of white-duck leggings and the sound of a floor called a deck and a water fountain called a scuttlebutt, he would have been glad to be back. But at dinner after ten days of semistarvation, his stomach had shrunk or something and he could hardly eat at all, and he saw that he was risking the wrath of the chow-line master-at-arms for filling his tray too full, and if there was one thing he was steering clear of for the next four years, it was trouble, so he slid his portion to Ape, who wolfed it, of course, as he did in the wardroom today, when they could get him to eat there at all.

In the passageway outside Ben's office a steward chimed first call to dinner. Ben regarded Catlett's haul of service records on his desk. The hell with Catlett; you didn't punish a seaman for dirty pants when you were going to take him a half-hour off Tokyo Bay and very likely get them blown off his butt. He sent the records back to the personnel office and went to chow.

FOUR

Thunder rolled northeast of Ulithi, scoring the movie on the hangar deck with a threat of torrents to come. They were halfway through the picture when Ben heard of the great theft. He was sitting next to Mitch Langley in the center of the row of honor; from the forward bay, beyond the screen, came the sound of a night-check crew changing an engine, but everyone not working or on watch was here.

The film was *West of the Pecos*. It was a tradition, a part of *Shenandoah* culture like the stewards' choir at Happy Hour singing "When the Saints Go Marching In" or Foghorn Bailey's battered slide trombone. The picture had been sucked long ago from the veins of the Fleet movie exchange, and God help the first projectionist who inadvertently returned it by highline to a tin can or a tanker. The print was scratched and spliced and the sound track unintelligible, but that was all right, because it was always played silent.

Everyone knew the dialogue, but there were specialists, too. There was a signalman contralto who spoke Robert Mitchum's lines, and a basso-profundo yeoman named Cassidy who dubbed Barbara Hale. The second division were warbling Indians and Kwong and three other radiomen clacked coconut shells for hoofbeats and a storekeeper from Brooklyn could neigh like a horse. The number-one five-inch mount had a stock of inflated balloons ready for the final gunfight, and Foghorn and a drummer from the band swung into the *William Tell* overture at the drop of a chase.

Barbara Hale, eyes dewy, towered above them in the hangar bay. She rested her tidy curls on a rough-hewn corral rail and looked up at Robert Mitchum. Her lip trembled. "Matt," she boomed in a deep bass voice, "be careful. He means trouble." Mitchum looked deeply into her eyes. "I'm new to Pecos," he lisped, "but trouble is my middle name." He leaped to his horse, the storekeeper neighed, Kwong and company clattered their shells on the steel deck, and Foghorn Bailey's trumpet blared.

"Commander," said Catlett, looming above him in the dark. "Somebody's stole the fucking altar."

CHAPTER THREE

ONE

The *Shenandoah*'s chaplain's office was off the ship's library in the gallery above the hangar deck. Ben was tense with impatience. The gig, fastest boat aboard, was being readied, but he had to calm the troubled waters first.

Chaplain Schram was a full commander, USN, bitter at the Japanese for cutting off his retirement with Pearl Harbor; with the war almost over, anything that got in the way of a smooth final lap was a personal attack. "It takes three men to move it to the hangar deck. Damn it, Ben, who'd *want* it?"

"Well, the first lieutenant?" Ben proposed, wondering how Epstein and Watkins had got it through the hangar deck in the dark.

"Why, in the name of God?"

"I told him to get rid of all extra wood before the strike," Ben said weakly.

"*Extra wood?*" bleated the chaplain. "My God, they cost a hundred and thirty-six dollars! The father got it blessed by the archbishop of Seattle! It's Title C! Who signs the survey?"

"I'll sign the survey," Ben said hurriedly. He had to cut them off before Watkins was murdered by angry natives. "Go on back to the movie."

In five minutes he had evaded Catlett and was making the captain's gig, unobtrusively, down a rope ladder from the forward boom. He gauged the swell and dropped into the stern sheets, looking up in the moonlight at Rainey, the fat-faced coxswain who had caused it all. Rainey leaned back on the stern rail, chewing gum, tiller in hand. I'll get you, you bastard, Ben promised him silently.

"Hospital ship, Commander?" Rainey leered, nurses in mind.

Ben smiled evilly. "Fassarai."

Rainey's jaws stopped. "Sir, that's out of bounds."

"Yes. You think you can find it? At *night?*" he added.

"That black son of a bitch!" Rainey blurted. "Look, sir, I never even went ashore! I just——"

"I asked you if you could find it," snapped Ben. "Now shove off!"

TWO

They almost caught up with the landing craft by the time it hit the beach, but not quite. Great anvil thunderheads carved in silver were riding in from the northeast across the pulsing moon. From a thousand yards off Fassarai he could see torches; first a few firefly winks and suddenly a whole line of them moving down from the village as if they had never heard of a blackout. The gig drew three feet of water and must not touch coral. Ben told Rainey to stand fifty feet off and splashed ashore in his shoes.

He sloshed into the circle of flickering torches as the landing ramp slammed down. No one even noticed him; all eyes were on the cargo well. Forward loomed the altar in its

Navy cover. Barney Epstein, shirt drenched with sweat, tugged at the canvas. He worked it off, and a little moan of ecstacy broke from the crowd.

It was a standard Navy altar, made of turned oak, with no more sheen than a desk or a Navy chair. But in the torch-light it seemed to come alive; it occurred to Ben that the populace had never seen any wood more carefully finished than, probably, an orange crate. The king, carrying a torch, stepped up the ramp and touched it reverently; all at once it was surrounded by excited natives.

Ben slogged aboard. The cargo hold was suffocating; the torch smoke stung his eyes; the brutal humidity sucked sweat from his itching armpits and sent it pouring down his flanks. Epstein's eyes widened. "What the hell——"

"Where's Watkins?"

There was dead silence. A thunderclap sounded distantly. Everyone was staring aft. Ben turned. Watkins moved from the deckhouse shadows, bare-chested, skin gleaming like oiled leather in the flickering orange light. From behind Ben a low grumble began, and it was not thunder now but the growl of a murderous crowd.

"Jesus," he heard Epstein mutter.

"Say *something*, for Christ's sake," Ben said. "Now!"

Epstein looked at the chief, pointed to the altar, and then to the church. *"Ecclesia!"*

The chief whirled suddenly and yelled. Slowly, the wave of hate receded. The girl's tattooed father shouldered through and peered up at the Negro. His head came to Watkins' bicep, tense as carbon steel in the lamplight. He spoke to the chief, who nodded.

Suddenly Watkins squatted. With a swift motion he en-compassed the whole width of the altar. The crowd gasped. His corded back muscles sprung him erect and he stood swaying, the altar clasped to his great ebony chest.

"Where's their goddamn church?" he grunted.

Another clap of thunder sounded to the east. It began to rain.

THREE

The odd, deep rumble started as they neared the church. The rain had begun in globular, infrequent splats, as if celestial barkeeps were flipping over individual shots of warm water. It rained hard enough, while the procession was winding up the beach, to put out half the torches. It rained in sheets, in torrents, in rivers; it turned the neat path up the island's backbone into a miniature Missouri, so slick that Ben could hardly keep his own footing and Watkins, lurching under the altar, slipped and slid and staggered until the natives closest to him were moaning with anxiety. They would dart in to steady his load; when he would turn his straining eyeballs on them, they would fall back.

It stopped raining once and gusts began. Now Watkins caught the full blast on the face of the altar and Ben reached toward his gleaming back to steady him. He shrugged off the hand. Ben's legs ached, unburdened. There was no relief in the wind, it was too moist and hot; suddenly it was raining again, harder than before. Ben noticed a sound he thought was the boom of the surf of the seaward side, but it was not; it was the natives chanting. The rhythm was Micronesian, exultant and proud. They moved along the crest. In a flash of lightning, Ben saw the altar tilt. Watkins righted it.

The line slithered through the village to the black shape of the church. Inside, torches began to glow as the natives entered. On the threshold Watkins stumbled to his knees; had it not been for the king and the girl's father, the altar would have crashed to the wooden floor. Somehow, he struggled back to his feet and staggered up the aisle. He turned, knocking over the old altar and tilting Jesus on his cross. He set the new altar on the floor and straightened up, stretching his back, his face contorted.

"That make them jungle bunnies happy?" he demanded.

The chant died away. There was a long silence as the king moved up the aisle. In front of Watkins, he bowed suddenly, like a Japanese, and put out his hand. Watkins regarded it for a moment, took it in his huge paw, and bowed too. The king bowed again. Watkins bowed. All at once the church was full of natives giggling and laughing. The chant grew louder. Suddenly the side door opened and the singing stopped.

The young chaplain appeared in the doorway. He shook the water from his hair. Behind him was Singer, the pharmacist's mate. The chaplain noticed Ben and frowned.

"What are you doing here, Commander? My God!" He stared at the altar. "Where'd that come from?"

"USS *Shenandoah*, sir," rumbled Watkins.

García faced Ben. "No, *sir*. I'm sorry, Commander, but no. It doesn't change a thing."

"It's changed something," Ben said. "They don't want to kill him."

García's jaw tensed. He swung toward Epstein. "It's still a mortal sin," he said, very low and very fast. "They're children, and you're trying to bribe them, but the girl has to live with it. There's guilt, and the man has to atone for it. It just isn't this easy, and you know it! Your own faith tells you that!"

" 'An eye for an eye'?" asked Epstein. "That's *old*, García. You can do better than that. 'It is more blessed to give than to receive'? 'Love thy neighbor'? 'Turn the other cheek'? 'Cast not the first stone'?"

"No!" yelled García. His eyes were filling with tears. "They've been had long enough! They've been cheated and fooled. They've been despoiled!"

"Father, shall I ask the girl?"

García shook his head. "She's innocent. She doesn't have to decide!"

The girl and her father were standing at the altar. She put out a slim hand and touched the wood. Epstein said something in Japanese. The girl glanced at her father and he nodded. She talked for a moment with Epstein and then she giggled.

Epstein said, "She doesn't want him punished. She's grateful for the altar. I doubt if she'd testify against him." His eyes narrowed. "Would you like to know why she ran?"

"She ran because—she ran . . ." The young priest's lips worked spasmodically. He turned from the room and from the door Singer called, "Mr. Epstein!" The corpsman's head shook imperceptibly. Epstein smiled and touched the priest's shoulder. "We won't ask her that, Padre. You know better than she does. But will you use it?"

The father's voice sounded strangled. "Use what?"

"The altar?"

The rain drummed and the surf roared below. In the rear of the church a baby cried.

"Will you use it, Father?" Epstein asked again.

The priest turned suddenly. "I don't know." His head came up. "Now get off this island! All of you! Understand? Off! Now!"

Ben turned at the door. The natives were clustered three deep around the altar. The chaplain spoke from the corner, in pidgin, and then more loudly, in dialect, but no one looked around. So he moved behind the altar and straightened Jesus. He looked at his flock and smiled and the natives giggled. Some of them started up the chant, tentatively; the priest nodded, and the chant gathered force; when he left through the side door, Singer stepped aside, regarding him curiously.

The father was laughing. Singer shrugged at Ben and followed him out.

FOUR

Epstein slipped the coxswain of the landing craft ten dollars and they transferred to the captain's gig beyond the shoal and by that time it had stopped raining and the great clouds were scudding southward on the trades. Perry Watkins loomed hugely outside the gig's canvas top. He leaned down once. "Lieutenant," he asked Epstein, "what do you reckon that little chick would have said if you asked her why she run?"

"I did ask her."

"I *thought* so. What she say?"

"She was afraid."

"I *know* that. I been black most all my life."

"Oh, no." Epstein smiled. "That wasn't it."

"What you mean, 'that wasn't it'?"

"She thought you were too big for her."

They made the gangway. Ben saluted the quarterdeck and the OOD. It was Ape Gorman, who had been commissioned after Midway and was a j.g. in the Air department. Ben said mechanically "Permission to come aboard, sir?"

"Jesus, Ben," murmured Ape, "I didn't even know you was gone!"

"We weren't," said Ben. "Remember that."

CHAPTER FOUR

A rust-scarred tender held the submarine net politely open while Hammering Howie Howland's task group,
first of the three in the task force, glided seaward in column
through Ulithi channel. Nine of Howland's eighteen destroyers led the way. Behind them churned two fast battleships and then his flagship *Shenoandoah;* then three other
carriers and three more battleships. Nipping at their sterns
were four cruisers and the other nine destroyers, tightly
spaced to minimize the net-open time. The group was full
war strength. Before Midway it would have been a fleet itself, twice the power the United States could have put to
sea, but now it was only one of three units which would
leave that day: two identical flotillas would slide from the
anchorage in the afternoon to take position out of sight on its
eastern flank. Together the three sunburst patterns would
form a task force with a skirmish line a hundred miles deep
and three hundred miles from end to end.

Twelve hundred miles northeast, the Imperial Navy's surface fleet lay shattered in Yokosuka and Sasebo and along the
Inland Sea. The battleship *Yamato*, one light cruiser, and
eight destroyers had perished on a one-way suicide attempt
to beach themselves and expend their last shells on the in-

vasion forces at Okinawa. Japan was bone-dry of oil. B–29's from Saipan and Iwo could pound the islands at will; the Japanese Army was out of planes and gasoline. But the Imperial Naval Air Force had gas and planes and pilots and bombs and everyone from lower magazine to flag bridge knew it was saving its punch for a few last cracks at the U.S. fleet.

Clear of the channel, the cans began to race for their exposed positions on the outer ring. Ben, standing by Mitch Langley's leather chair on the bridge, looked down on a destroyer cutting close to port: stretching from fantail to after turret was a Japanese sign and a huge arrow pointing abeam. He leaned over the rail and saw Barney Epstein on the flag bridge, his bald head, encircled by curls like a monk's, bare in the morning breeze. "Father Epstein?"

Epstein looked up. Last night's forced march had not tired him a bit; he was fresh and starched, as became a staff officer; even his moustache seemed trimmer. Salvation agreed with him.

"Yes, Commander?" he asked impassively.

"What's the sign say?"

" 'Carriers that way,' " said Epstein.

Ben looked down at the bearded destroyer skipper. Very funny, he thought bitterly. The ships turned north and slowed to wait for the other groups. It was good to be underway, making your own breeze after three weeks in the molten lagoon, but he was uneasy and troubled. A gun captain in a five-inch turret below, head through the hatch, was reading a comic book, battle helmet beside him. Ben had a sudden picture of the Empire crouched over the horizon like a wounded sea dragon while eighty thousand U.S. sailors approached it, noses buried in Dick Tracy. He glared at Golden Boy Lee, riding the director above the bridge, and jerked a thumb at the mount. Golden Boy nodded and said something into his sound-powered phone. The gun captain dropped the comics and jammed on his helmet.

Ben should have felt better, but didn't. Catlett came topside, drew him aside, and read him the list of men for captain's mast. It seemed like a travesty to put Watkins before Mitch for a mere slap on the wrist, but he had to be punished somehow and Rainey did too, and the gunnery strikers who had gone ashore; the story of the five-dollar jaunt was all over the ship. He had already told Mitch the facts, unofficially, and Mitch had agreed.

"Commander?" Catlett asked suddenly.

"Yeah?"

"You hear anything about that jig and a native girl over there?"

"Yes," Ben said. "It was nothing."

The captain's yeoman placed the service records and the charge sheet on a writing stand which had been moved aft of the pilothouse on the bridge level, so that Mitch would not have to leave the bridge for mast. A following breeze was goosing their own stack gas along with them; it stung your eyes and squeezed your lungs and yellowed the morning sun. Catlett, coughing, stepped from the watertight door herding his culprits; he looked tired. The men began to line up behind a white-painted chain suspended from two white stanchions to separate judge and judged. Six bells dinged, the boatswain stepped to the mike on the wing of the bridge, piped, and announced, "Captain's mast, captain's mast." Mitch, in his scrambled-egg hat, stepped from his sea cabin and nodded pleasantly.

Catlett called the names. The men stepped forward, tugged off their hats, and told their stories. For each man a division officer would move forth to sing his praise. Mitch would consider each case for a long, unhurried time, as if it really mattered; finally he would decide.

He fined three gamblers and brigged two enemies for fighting in a bomb magazine; he broke Rainey and brigged him and gave the gunnery strikers fourteen days, extra police duties, despite Golden Boy Lee's eulogies, and then it was time for Watkins.

"Perry Watkins, steward," Chief Catlett said, his voice so full of malice that even Mitch looked up. "No middle name."

Watkins, hat in hand, took a giant step forward and stood looking down at the captain. Mitch nodded at him and read the specs, AWOL and out-of-bounds, and Watkins admitted the charges.

"Well," said Mitch, "I think two weeks' extra police duties for you."

Ben heard Catlett draw in his breath. *"I'm* god damned!" And aloud, "Captain?"

Mitch glanced at him, surprised. "Yes, Catlett?"

"Before you make up your mind, sir? I'm responsible for that report sheet. It might not be complete."

Mitch Langley hid his surprise. "Commander Casco mentioned further charges against him. He investigated them. Charges will not be pressed ashore, so—"

"Charges of rape?" interjected the chief.

For an instant the yellow stack haze cleared and everything seemed more colorful; the fox flag squealed to the yardarm as the ship prepared to turn into the wind to launch the evening patrol; a forty-millimeter gun below slewed and chattered to a stop; from the pilothouse door a quartermaster sang out the radar distance to the nearest ship in the screen.

The action, when it broke, was so incredible that no one

moved for an eternity but Watkins and his victim. But Watkins moved. He moved with a bellow and it was impossible afterward for any of them to remember if the yell came first or the act; Ben saw him grab the white chain and yank it loose from the stanchions and swing it in a flashing arc in the sunlight and saw Catlett lurch back against the light armor shield of the rail, his hand moving in slow motion toward a rakish slash on his cheek that looked for a moment like a scarlet rope placed tightly against the skin; the slash turned instantly to a streaming torrent down his neck and over his shirt.

Catlett recovered. He flung his arms over the rail, lifted his feet, and arched, catching Watkins in the lower stomach, so that on the second swipe he got only a slice on his lower leg.

It was like trying to fend a battleship off a pierhead with his feet. Ben lunged for the steward, caught a backhand swipe in the ear, and found himself on the deck. He scrambled up as Mitch yelled "Orderly!" and glimpsed an assistant MAA spinning gracefully past the flag-deck ladder, bouncing off the island structure, and slamming against a splinter shield. His bright silver badge wobbled down the deck and stopped. Christy Lee charged low and hard and caught the Negro's knee in the face and sat down hard, incredulously.

"Watkins!" screamed Ben. Watkins shook his head and wove toward the chief like a boxer, feinting, chain rattling. Catlett watched him, smiling twistedly, ready for the next swing. Ben saw Christy Lee scramble to his feet and tense for another charge. Mitch Langley, pushing fifty, seemed himself to be gauging a chance to jump the Negro.

"Stay put!" Ben yelled at Mitch. He stooped and lifted the sacred writing stand high, spilling reports, service records, and log sheets, and brought it crashing down on Watkins' skull. The huge Negro dropped to his knees. Catlett leaped from the splinter shield. His foot swung and he caught Watkins on the temple as Christy Lee slammed into him too, rolled clear, and got to his feet.

Watkins lay flat on his back, the chain dead in a scupper. Catlett, streaming blood, had his foot back for a coup de grâce. "Chief!" Ben croaked. "Hold it!"

Reluctantly, the chief lowered his foot and grabbed for his hip pocket. He produced a pair of handcuffs and knelt on Watkins' wrist. Quickly, he shackled it to a stanchion in the waterway at the base of the splinter shield.

Watkins opened his eyes. "I'm going to kill you, Cat. You know that, don't you?"

"I'll be dead a long time before you get out," the chief said, grinning gorily. Blood splattered on Watkins' face, but he did not move.

Ben rubbed his back. He had strained it, lifting the podium. God, how had he ever done it? "Brig Watkins," he told the assistant MAA, "and get Catlett to sick bay." He followed Mitch into the tiny sea cabin behind the chart house and the captain poured him a cup of coffee and sat back on his bunk, his eyes full of pain. "The fleet ought to love this."

"It wasn't the ship's fault, Captain. He went crazy, like an act of God. That goddamned Catlett!"

Mitch shrugged. "He thought I wasn't getting the full story."

"Bullshit, sir! I'm going to can him, after this strike."

Mitch studied him, and Ben wondered if he was remembering the days when Catlett was his shipmate on Mitch's first destroyer, or Ben's brig time in San Diego, or both. Finally the captain nodded. "O.K. And transfer Watkins, first fueling, with charges."

"Aye, aye, sir. In irons, by highline, and I hope to hell it breaks."

Ben assigned Christy Lee as investigating officer because much as he hated the son of a bitch, he had to admit that everything Lee was assigned got done in hours.

But speed made no difference this time, for the kamikaze attacks began the next day, earlier than anticipated, and there was no fueling at all until it was far too late.

PART THREE

Golden Boy

CHAPTER ONE

ONE

They sped from Ulithi along the Marianas trench over the deepest water in the world. Overhead circled an endless combat air patrol. A few hours out of the anchorage, Task Force 38 had become a galaxy of three solar systems hurtling north. In each group the central sun was a diamond of carriers. The planets nearest the suns were battlewagons and heavy cruisers; farther out sped light cruisers; remote from all, like a steel ring of lonely Plutos, steamed the destroyers of the screen.

The rings were not inflexible, but organic, contracting to protect the vulnerable inner suns when radar sensed danger, expanding again when hazard was past. The groups could shift direction, too, like checkers on a giant blue board, to zigzag or launch into the wind.

The western system would be closest to Japan, and in its center rode the *Shenandoah*. Two other task groups, under Davison and Sherman, lay over the eastern horizon on Admiral Howland's right flank, so far that even the outer satellites could not glimpse each other except on radar.

Hundreds of miles behind the task force, the vessels of the train trailed like cosmic dust: ships and tankers which would sustain the fighting craft for weeks, if the force was not mauled so badly off Honshu that it had to retire.

Between the westernmost destroyer of Howland's task group and the easternmost corvette of Sherman's rode a hundred and fifty combat ships with a thousand aircraft. Between the vessels lay the vacuum of outer space.

Each ship was a world. Across the void between them voices might reach on short-range TBS or signal-flags flutter or semaphores whip in the wind; lines might arc across and hawsers and the great looping fuel hoses transfuse oil over ten yards of racing chop, and movies and mail and the sick sometimes might pass between. But to a seaman on a tanker or a lieutenant on a tin can, life extended from keel to top and starboard to port. To the grimy oil king at his fuel valves in the guts of the flagship *Shenandoah*, the oil king on the cruiser *Biloxi* was a Martian. He felt more empathy for his own captain, whom he might not have seen for months, or Hammering Howie Howland on the flag bridge, whose name he might not even know.

In the world of each ship were many countries: admiral's country, wardroom country, warrant country, snipe country, marine country, airedale and first-division country. There were lines across the strata, too, in each community at every rate and every rank, for reserves had come and the Navy would never be the same. There were tanned airedale gunners whose best friends were the ensigns with whom they flew, and pasty storekeepers who had been on the ship for years and in all her actions never seen an enemy aircraft or a catapult launch and who could not have told their position now within a thousand miles. There were quartermasters on the bridge who could have taken the ship through the Great Barrier Reef, and ninety-day wonders in the crypto room who could not have pointed out the North Star. There were en-

listed fire-control men from Georgia Tech spinning cranks
in five-inch plot, and chief warrants with third-grade edu-
cations sipping coffee in the machine shops. For all, the
world was the ship: they drew their thoughts into it when
danger threatened as the admiral drew in his steel-ringed
screen; the other ships were light-years away; there was
plenty to worry about when you rode a floating powder
magazine with a quarter of a million gallons of high-test
aviation gasoline without fretting over others similarly
perched.

The destroyer screen was first to be hit, the second morning out of Ulithi. Outside of CIC or the bridge, few on the
Shenandoah knew it at once. Ben saw it from his general
quarters station at dawn GQ. An invisible paintbrush had
slapped strokes of red and purple on the southern horizon
but that to the east was brassy; there was the hint of a swell
and a moist gusty wind. At 1900 a destroyer on the western
flank, two hundred miles from Kyushu, took a Kate loaded
with TNT abaft her bridge. Ben could not even hear the
guns firing or the explosion when it hit, although he could
see faint flashes along the horizon and then a mighty flare.

It was hard to associate so remote a glimpse with danger to
the *Shenandoah*, but when finally they secured GQ and he
sat at the head of his wardroom table for breakfast, he noticed that everyone was preoccupied and laughter—even
among the junior officers at the other tables—was subdued.
He lingered as usual, holding minor court for busy officers to
speed up their day: he promised Josh Lowery water hours
and the gunnery officer midmorning sandwiches for the
mounts. The wardroom mess treasurer, Ensign Harvey
Baccus, all zeal and Adam's apple fresh from the Academy,
slipped into the chair next to him.

"What's up, Stud?" Ben asked wearily, knowing what it was.

"That frigging Ape! I know he's a friend of yours, sir, from when you flew Spads——"

"Watch it, mister," warned Ben.

"Well, whatever they were. But he won't pay up again, sir. He's an officer, he's got to join the wardroom mess!"

Ape Gorman had started it a year ago, as a new ensign. He had simply pocketed his gold bars and stayed in the chief's mess and he never paid his wardroom bill.

"You really want him back?" remarked Ben.

Once, when they had forced Ape into the fold, he had sat next to Harvey. He had spilled soup on Harvey's clean khakis, picked his teeth with a fork, and belched so loudly in Harvey's ear at the height of Harvey's first typhoon that the mess treasurer had left the table.

"I don't want him back," Harvey said. "He's a goddamn *slob,* sir. You can't change a leopard's spots. What I want is his money!"

"A leopard's spots," murmured Ben. "That's very interesting. Did you know I'm ex-enlisted?"

"No, sir."

"Tell me true, Harvey?"

"Well," Harvey reddened, "I thought it was scuttlebutt."

"You couldn't believe it?" prodded Ben. "A gentlemanly sort like me? Well-read? Urbane?"

"Come on, Commander," Harvey said suddenly, "I'm just trying to do my job."

Ben relented. "O.K., Harvey, I'll take care of it." From his office he sent for Ape. "Ape," he said, "pay your mess bill in the next fifteen minutes or I'll get you a utility squadron in Kodiak, Alaska."

"Look, Ben——"

"Commander, you boot!"

"Look, Commander, I don't like wardroom chow; everything I say in there goes over like a fart in church, and every time I pick up my fork that goddamn Harvey puckers like I was going to jam it up his ass! I wish to hell I'd stayed chief!"

"I wish you had too."

"How about if I join the *warrant* officers' mess?"

"You're a j.g.," Ben said patiently. "Wardroom mess."

"You sound like Catlett!" exploded Ape. "We was better off boots with Catlett than officers on this frigging barge!"

Ben found himself on his feet. "Knock it off! I'm canning Catlett, for your information, and it could happen to you!"

"Yes, sir," Ape said stiffly. He was really hurt now, and Ben felt his own anger leave.

"Ape?" he said softly.

"Yes sir?" Ape turned. His jaw was jutting and his eyes were stricken.

"No kidding, pay it. Or I'll make *you* mess treasurer."

Ape relaxed. His eyes twinkled. "Aye, aye, sir. Don't forget, Catlett knows about your brig time, but *I* know about that broad in Pedro and——"

"Shove off," said Ben. "And don't forget your mess bill."

"And that jarhead lieutenant with a busted jaw," mused Ape. "Kodiak, huh? Alaska?"

"Get your ass out," said Ben. He went into his bedroom to shave. He felt better. Standing over the stainless sink, which would have been such luxury a dozen years back, he thought, while he shaved, of the old *Nevada* and Pappy Shea and the nameless marine lieutenant. Bad days, bare of hope and, after the lieutenant, heavy with dread; always cold with the chill of saltwater swabs and wet teak decks on bare feet, for a seaman could never afford rubber boots. Bad days, and the worst of them the miserable dawn, steaming into Pedro after the '31 war games, when he had fallen from Chief Pappy Shea's grace.

TWO

Under a slice of tangerine moon the U.S. battle force, nine gray dreadnaughts which annually saved the Panama Canal, had been churning darkly north. The ships plowed toward L.A. on a track used twice yearly—once south for the winter to Panama and then homeward in the spring— a great circle as unwavering as one of Saturn's rings.

The Pacific fleet's two aircraft carriers were gone. Yesterday they had eased to starboard at the tip of Baja California; their own home port was with the cruisers and destroyers in San Diego. The battlewagons continued north. They seemed to ride more easily with the flattops out of sight. The surface Navy in the '30's pretended to cherish its planes and rather liked the carriers it had, although everyone knew them to be too vulnerable for the next battle of Jutland. Paternally, the Navy called its air arm the "eyes of the fleet" and often launched flybys when it visited ports on the yearly "society cruise" up the coast. "Battleship admiral" had already become an insult, even to admirals whose only carrier visit had been to lunch with a classmate. The modern skipper of a capital ship seldom forgot, if the weather was good, to catapult a floatplane to spot for main-battery practice and sometimes actually used its calls if the haze was too thick to mark shot from the foretop.

Hitler had become Chancellor in January. In March Japan, angry at Geneva over Manchuria, had quit the League of

Nations and everyone knew that she would withdraw from the Naval Conference to build all the carriers she wanted. It was said that Roosevelt was a Navy man, but breadlines still wound through the Bowery and soup kitchens dotted the Loop and unemployed longshoremen gathered ominously on San Francisco's waterfront. Planes were not cheap and wore out more quickly than ships. The Bureau of Navigation admitted that the carrier would someday be queen of the seas, but the Great War had after all been won without them; so, meanwhile, half the Navy's aviators were serving as deck officers and there were less than thirty students at Pensacola.

The battle force steamed in column, as ships of the line had cruised since Dewey's Great White Fleet. Each battlewagon was an island, part of a steel archipelago against which the dark Pacific swell had no more effect than had the ships been fast aground. The flagship *Maryland,* a monolith with towering cage masts, drew a green phosphorescent highway astern, up which glided the *California,* the *Texas,* the *Idaho,* the *New York,* the *Oklahoma,* the *West Virginia,* the *Montana,* and the *Nevada,* whose engines had earned her the nickname *No-Go Maru.* The ships kept pace with sleds towed by the vessel ahead to mark the proper distance, and God help the officer of the deck who straggled or crept up.

Beneath the force's armored decks, ten thousand bodies swayed under dim blue battle lamps. They swung in hammocks; bunks were for officers' country; sleeping space was for ocean liners. Men-of-war were built not for comfort but for battle, as in the days of Drake and Nelson. Men slung hammocks where they could: in messing compartments, handling rooms, around turret bases that reached halfway to keels forty feet below. They slept butt to butt, belly to belly, canvas rasping with the roll against hammocks on either side. When a man stirred, the ripple passed down the whole row swinging in the blue darkness, and if the man next to you snored, or stank, it was simply too bad, for hammock space, once claimed, was inviolate and no one could change. A seaman might spend six years aboard without seeing the transfer or promotion, the retirement or death, that would move him away from a man he disliked or a whining ventilator or the constant blue stare of a battle lamp.

It was seven bells on the midwatch: 3:30 A.M. An hour and a half earlier, the wheel and lookouts had been relieved: in twenty minutes the last of the oncoming watch would be called; in thirty minutes, at 0400, the column of steel giants would really stir: the watch would be relieved, the lifeboat crew mustered, the ship's cooks and messmen called. At 0500 each ship would come fully alive; reveille would sound and the boatswain's call would begin its shrill keening and hardly quit until taps.

The tunes of the pipe wailed down through the centuries and the steps of the dance had not changed. John Paul Jones would have recognized the songs; Sampson or Sims would have known the daily routine. A *Texas* sailor transported miraculously in his hammock to the old *Bon Homme Richard* would have awakened to piping he knew; whisked one ship astern today to the *California*, the identical schedule might have fooled him for hours.

At 0350 Ben Casco, seaman second class, riding twenty feet below the waterline at the base of the *Nevada*'s number-four turret, felt a hand shaking his shoulder.

"Pea-coat weather, quartermaster said."

The messenger dipped his head and scurried under the bulbous hammocks to awaken the next watch stander. Ben lay for a long moment listening to a shipmate's snore and the whirr of a ventilator too far from him in tropic waters and too close in the north.

A rhythmic thumping intruded: the pulse of the great propellers. This far aft the beat was always there, making shivering bull's-eyes appear in your coffee and rattling your locker door. You never really felt it until the rhythm changed; now Ben drowsily estimated six turns over standard speed; the old *No-Go Maru* must have fallen a few yards behind. As always when the turns were changed, ghostly blue faces arose from their shrouds and listened and lay back to sleep. It was then that you knew that the ship had a soul, that you were cradled in a living womb. Once you learned her heartbeat you winced for her when she was hurt. At night firing, when her main turrets vomited flame and jarred her to her kneel just to send a few two-ton red-hot projectiles arching toward the horizon, racing each other like children at play, you resented the shells, knowing the jolt they had given the ship at birth.

The rhythm eased again, the heads raised up and dropped. Ben envisioned the massive screws, twice as tall as his mother's house, slowing aft. Last winter he had gaped up at them from the bottom of a San Francisco dry dock and felt like an ant.

But he was not an ant: ants were individuals. In his hammock he was meat hanging high with a thousand identical carcasses; in a few hours, waiting for chow, he would become a milk bottle in a dairy, jerking forward with his hat tucked into his waist and stopping and jerking forward again until he was filled and recapped; at morning exercises he would be a puppet flailing his arms in concert with a division full of similarly reluctant puppets; at movies that night he would sit like a book jammed with identical volumes into a bookcase and at tattoo he would begin dutifully to string himself up again in his canvas shroud. "No one is allowed out of hammocks after taps except for urgent calls of nature."

He was dozing again when the smell of baking bread awakened him, joining the nighttime smell of paint, fuel oil, disinfectant, and a thousand jam-packed bodies. He was ravenous, and he had a four-hour watch on black Navy coffee before he would be relieved for chow. He swung his feet over the side of the hammock and let himself down its shrouds, winced at the cold steel deck which had been so hot in the tropics a few days before. He triced his hammock, tossed it by a bulkhead for the hammock stowers, and stumbled into the head. Back at his locker, when he had dressed for his watch, he did not forget to cross off the day on a calendar full of Harlow-blonde nudes. It left him one year, nine months, and six days to go. He climbed to the bridge and slid open the door to the red-lighted chart room behind the pilothouse.

Commander Hammering Howie Howland, squat and sandy, sipped coffee at the chart table and leafed idly through the *Nautical Almanac,* looking for the time of sunrise. His wings, tarnished green, caught a dull gleam from the glow of the hot plate under the coffeepot. Ben had liked him at first; he had twinkling eyes and an easygoing smile if you made a mistake. But then he had noticed that the eyes grew cold and the smile strained when the mistake could endanger him before the captain. He would hate to be in a pinch with no one to back him but Howland.

An open mahogany sextant case lay beside the commander. Chief Pappy Shea, father to Ben, mentor and spur and cross to bear, started a hack chronometer for the morning round of sights, although anyone could see that Howland was looking for an excuse to drop the whole dreary task.

"No horizon, sir," Ben reported hopefully, lips stiff with cold.

Pappy Shea was as dedicated to the dawn round of stars as a Carmelite monk to morning prayers. His eyes snapped. "Dammit, son, get out there and start looking."

Ben returned to the wing of the bridge. He moved his eyes a trifle higher than where the first faint line of horizon would appear. Pappy had taught him that night vision was more acute if you looked away from what you were trying to spot. But he was wasting his time, and he knew it; even if they got a horizon, clouds were obscuring nine tenths of the stars. When his hands were decently numb he bobbed back in.

"Still no horizon, sir," he told the navigator. "No stars. Sky obscured, sir."

Hammering Howie closed the sextant case with care. He faced down the chief, who had begun to eye him reproachfully.

"Note 'sky obscured' in the workbook," Howland yawned, showing a tooth broken in Academy football twenty years before. He left for another hour's sleep in his sea cabin. Ben began to sweep the dust from the dead-reckoning tracer. The light on the traveling bug, which moved on a chart in step with the ship itself, showed them halfway up the Baja coast; they would make Pedro before dark.

"He's saving his strength for tonight," Ben remarked.

"He was a good navigator," the chief said sharply. "When he was aboard as an ensign, I was third class——"

"You told me," Ben said quickly. He wrote down a chronometer error. "You told me, Chief."

"He'd shoot fixes you could cover with the eraser on your pencil! Then he'd do 'em over because they weren't tight enough!"

"Well, he makes a good passenger," remarked Ben. "He never gets seasick, and he sure sleeps good."

"Flight training done it!" rumbled Pappy. "An airedale, all they want to do is sleep and eat!"

"Sleep and eat," Ben murmured. "Tonight I'm going to get me a milkshake and a hotel room in Pedro and a pint of hooch and a girl——"

"And come back with a dose of clap," growled Pappy. "What you ought to do, you ought to stay aboard and study for seaman first, before somebody sends you mess cooking." He tried to glare at Ben, failed, and stepped to the pilot-house to check the log.

Ben began to dust the navigator's gleaming sextant case. On it was a plaque: "To Ens. Howard H. Howland, USN. Robert M. Thompson Prize for Excellence in Practical Navigation, Class of 1915, U.S. Naval Academy." He was about to put it in its place of honor on the shelf, when on impulse he opened it.

The instrument lay in its chocks, German silver arc glittering in the gray light, ivory vernier hardly yellowed yet with age. He glanced from the port. The sky had cleared with daylight; the horizon was razor-sharp. Venus dangled alone like an emerald in the eastern sky. Swiftly he picked up the sextant and stepped to the door.

Once when his stepfather Steve had worn plaid caps and screaming neckties, before his battered sextant was laid away to gather dust, he had taken Ben and his brother Joe up to their roof and they had eased the orange, filtered sun to the top of Glioto's house across the street and Steve had taught them to read the altitude. Now, braced in the chart-house, Ben lifted the navigator's instrument. The handle felt good in his palm. Quickly he found Venus and brought it down, rocking the sextant in a sweeping arc as Steve had taught them, lower and lower until the planet barely kissed the clean horizon line.

The chief's voice, unsteady with shock, froze him. "What in the name of *Christ* do you think you're doing?"

Ben turned, rigid with embarrassment. Pappy's face was twisted as if he were holding back tears. "Put it back," he whispered. "Suppose *he'd* come in, instead of me?"

"He'd have had my ass, I guess," Ben admitted.

"And mine. Why in *hell* did you do it?"

"Oh, come on, Chief. I didn't screw his sister!"

"I asked you *why?*"

Ben shrugged. "I don't know. I saw Venus, and I got a horizon, and——"

"You know what else you got, Ben?" Shea's voice rose. The monkey eyes blinked uncontrollably. "Mess cooking! *Chiefs'* mess! You're off the bridge! For three goddamned months! You hear?"

The words were ludicrous, the bathos laughable, but there was nothing to laugh about in the content. He heard the clatter of greasy trays thrown hurriedly for him to wash in the great steamy sculleries, saw the gaping coffee kettles caked with grounds, smelled souring milk and boiling soapy water, and felt the slimy tables he must wipe and the slippery messdecks he must swab. Now he would wear, finally, the stumpy white cap that was supposed to keep hair and dandruff out of the food he must serve to chiefs who would not even know his name. For the next three months he would know the indignity of short arm inspection every Saturday. And here, on the bridge, the breeze would be flowing fresh.

Pappy would ease the sentence perhaps if he seemed contrite and apologized again. But the words wouldn't come: he was damned if he'd beg.

Viciously, he dressed that evening for liberty and went ashore with Ape. He awakened the next morning in a strange, rootless vacuum of time and place. Propellers were drumming and yet he was not in his hammock. He opened his eyes in a bed, and the bed rocked with the queasy land motion you felt when you had been a month or so at sea. Bronze pellets of early sunlight peppered a worn blind and struck fire from a brass knob over his head, paining his eyes. But there was the damn drumming, and it was not the pounding of the screws but someone knocking on the door and finally it stopped and he could hear footsteps receding down a wooden corridor, squeaking with marinelike precision, a hundred and twenty steps to the minute. A brig? No.

He remembered suddenly. He was in the Algonquin Apartment Hotel, over Gunner Crowley's Locker Club near the liberty-boat landing.

Across Wilmington Channel a ship bleated her intention to back into the stream. Somewhere on the floor above, bedsprings squealed lasciviously; the place was halfway a whorehouse. The room smelled of stale smoke and sweat; he wondered how the golden girl beside him could stand to live here. He turned over and chilled.

Last night in Gunner's tiny speakeasy bar she had been a young goddess, a prize to be pried safely away from a dozen shipmates and from Ape. Well, he had her now, but in daylight the golden skin had turned to brass and the shimmering hair grown tangled and dry and somehow during the night she had aged twenty years and crow's-feet had attacked her eyes and her neck had sagged, and damned if she hadn't snored.

He couldn't remember where they had ditched Ape; then he decided that the pounding on the door and the squeaky shoes had been Ape trying to get him up to catch the liberty boat.

Well, the hell with the liberty boat; if he missed it he'd just stay AWOL. Not much additional misfortune could fall to a messcook this side of the brig. He had enough money for another liberty: he'd saved four dollars last night from the eighteen he'd come ashore with. He had an awful thought. He got up and staggered to his wallet, lying in the ring of his pants next to a scratched and battered bureau. It still had two two-dollar bills. The girl was O.K.

"All right, you son of a bitch," she murmured. "All there?"

"Look," he explained shamefacedly. "My last port was Panama!"

"Give me a cigarette." He found a pack on the bureau. He noticed that they were sea stores. He lit one for her; the taste was dry and sour in his mouth. She lay back, drew a puff, and watched him through lowered lids as he began to dress. She blew a cloud of smoke at him and said, "What's my name?"

"To me," he said, looking for his shoes, "you'll always be . . . Golden Girl."

"Thanks, Ben," she said dryly. She grimaced and rubbed her temple. "Oh, God . . . lemon-flavored gin! Why the hell do you drink lemon-flavored gin?"

"I don't like cherry."

"Very funny. How old are you?"

"I can vote," he lied. "Or I could if I weren't in the Navy."

"How old am *I*?"

He shook his head. He wanted no games, he wanted out. The sun-drenched streets beckoned; in here the smell of smoke was awful. If he hurried he might still make the liberty launch. His nerves were suddenly jumping with impending doom. Something was wrong, somewhere. He started dizzily to pull on his pants and almost fell over, so that he had to brace the small of his back against the bureau. He got the legs on and buttoned the thirteen stupid buttons on the front flap—unlucky buttons, no wonder everybody caught clap. He stumbled to the bed to put on his shoes and socks.

"How *old* am I?" she insisted.

He dredged up a smile. "Old enough to vote?" he suggested.

"I voted," she said, "for Harding." 1920, 1924? He couldn't recall. He was trapped. If he deserted he'd starve and if he stayed in the battle force he'd finish his enlistment sleeping with widows of the Spanish-American War. "Harding," she reflected. "Warren G. Harding!"

"I can't believe that," he murmured politely. "Where the fuck's my other sock?"

"Where you flang it, Admiral." She pointed to a tattered, overstuffed chair. Beside it was an ashtray lamp with a half-chewed cigar. He held it up. "You smoke these too?"

"My husband."

Well, half the battle force was sleeping with somebody else's wife. "Where," he inquired, "is he?"

"The *Montana*. First sergeant, marine detachment."

He tensed. "She's in, you know."

"He never gets the first liberty boat. Mostly he never gets the last one."

The pounding on the door, the squeaky shoes, the *marine* shoes . . . "He got a key?" he demanded tensely.

"I don't know," she shrugged. "Why?"

"Somebody was beating on the door. . . ." He listened. Oh, God, he heard it again, the purposeful cadence down the creaky hall, the protest of new leather mirror-shined. She heard it too, and snuffed out her cigarette swiftly. "Get, sailor!"

He lunged for the window, pulled aside the blind. No fire escape, and four stories to the white concrete. He saw liberty launches loading at the pier: *Colorado, West Virginia,* his own *Nevada.* If he once found safety in her steel embrace, he would never go ashore again.

"Get *where,* for Christ's sake?" he whispered hoarsely.

She pointed to the bathroom. "Maybe he'll take me to breakfast. But *get!*"

In one step he was inside, easing shut the door. A shower curtain hid the tub. He drew it aside and almost yelled.

Inside, head under the tap, lay the body of Ape Gorman. His neckerchief was still tied neatly. On his stomach lay his white hat, perfectly centered. Silently Ben bent and pulled him to a sitting position, banging his head on the faucet. Ape came awake. Ben stepped into the tub and stealthily drew the curtain. Ape started to speak and Ben held up a hand. "Pipe down," he breathed. "Her husband!"

A clump of sprouted hair at the rear of Ape's skull began to wilt in the dripping shower head. He looked sick. "Husband?"

Shut up, Ben mouthed silently. He could hear a murmur in the other room, and then an argument. The bathroom door opened a foot away. He had a momentary impression of Ape's teeth bared in terror. Someone urinated loud and long into the toilet; it flushed, then water ran in the sink.

"Linda?" a male voice spluttered, "where do you keep the towels?"

They hung from a rack in the tub behind Ben; he had a crazy impulse to hand one out. "Never mind," said the voice. The shower curtain jerked suddenly open. Two feet from him, eyes squeezed shut, a lean, tanned face dripped soapy water; six inches from Ape's belly, heavily veined hands groped for the towels. Ape sucked in his gut and tried to blend into the wall.

Ben swung. He swung with all he had, and he swung at the point of the jaw. The man spun, crashed against the bathroom door, and collapsed across the entrance like a uniformed rag doll, head under the sink. He was wearing marine greens. Ben stiffened.

Over one rangy shoulder glittered a Sam Browne belt; on the cloth strap rode a silver bar.

"Jesus, Mary, and Joseph," breathed Ape. "It's an officer!"

The woman stood in the doorway, looking down at the body; she was knotting a dressing gown and her face was flushed, so that she looked younger again and prettier. "My God," she murmured. "What did you hit him with?"

Ben rubbed his knuckle, which was strangely numb. "I thought you said 'sergeant!' "

"He's the lieutenant," she said primly. "He came to tell me Mike had to stay aboard."

"I'll bet he did," Ben said. He opened the door, glanced down the hallway, and faced the girl. "What's *my* name?" he asked softly.

"You're a short, fat civilian," she mused. "And you must be a peeping tom, because I never saw you before in my life. The question is, will I see you again?"

She looked better by the minute, not at all as if she had voted for Harding. But he was damned if he was standing in this particular line again.

"Sure," he said, "I'll be the one in a sailor hat."

The desk clerk eyed them oddly but they made the last liberty launch after all, and Ape huddled next to him on the thwart, mumbling about the years they would draw at Terminal Island when the lieutenant tracked down his assailant. Ben's knuckle throbbed miserably and he knew he had broken something and he was as scared of prison as Ape, but he heard hardly a word Ape said. His eyes were on a great red-faced chief with an Indian hawk nose and a hat like a halo askew riding a white shock of hair. The chief perched with grim displeasure in the stern sheets on a cruise box. It had been hauled aboard at the crook of a kingly finger by two drunken white hats who would probably have hesitated to move for a commander. The chief's other gear, seabags and suitcases, lay about him like imperial tribute: strangely, atop it all, lay a parachute.

He was apparently just reporting aboard *Nevada*, but somehow you already felt that he owned the ship's number-two motor launch and did not want title at all. Miraculously, he was smoking. No sane man would dare to smoke openly in the launch, even if he cared to risk the wrath of the coxswain, for there was a j.g. aboard who had missed the officers' boat. But the chief, a cigarette held delicately between thumb and forefinger, was puffing away as if he were already in the mess; the coxswain was pretending to gauge his approach to the landing stage and the j.g. was studying the profile of his own ship as if he had never seen it before.

The old chief bore himself like an admiral, but it was not that, or rows of ribbons on his chest, or thirty years of hashmarks on his sleeve, or even the mysterious rating device in the crow on his arm that fascinated Ben. He was no officer. Imperious or not, he was just an enlisted man.

But he was wearing golden Navy wings.

THREE

Ben was afraid to turn in to sick bay with his shattered knuckle and that first mess-cooking night he watched the chiefs' mess try in its own fashion to digest Crazy Charlie Horseman, chief aviation pilot, USN. Pappy Shea, mess president, introduced the new chief from the head of the table, formally, and the cadaverous cook second for whom Ben found himself slaving muttered, "Wardroom horseshit! Next thing they're gonna want chimes before supper."

Pappy clinked his glass for attention. "You guys! Pipe down, you hear?" Conversation slackened, but not the slurping of soup. "You all know Charlie Horseman?"

The white-haired chief snorted ungratefully at Pappy, the mess, and life in general. He continued to spoon his soup. A blue-jowled chief water tender cackled from the foot of the table, "Jesus Christ! Crazy Charlie, the flying Indian! What you doing on a wagon, huh?"

Crazy Charlie laid his soupspoon in his bowl. He took a pair of glasses out of his pocket slowly, blew on them, wiped them on his shirt, set them on his eagle nose. "Well, Kosloff! I'd a thought you'd a been busted by now."

"Nope," grinned Kosloff. "I'm water king."

Horseman held his water glass to the light, inspected it, and set it far out of reach.

"You ain't had a drop anyway in twenty years," pointed out the water tender. "How come you ain't on a carrier? Can't you climb into them cockpits no more?"

"I can get into any cock pit you can," Horseman said. "Including your old lady." He took off his glasses and began to dredge his soup for meat.

The water tender addressed the mess, "Goddamn throttle jockey! I just hope he don't get seasick."

"Kosloff," warned Pappy Shea, "he's wrung more salt water out of his socks than you sailed over."

Kosloff ignored him. "This bucket's going to hell! The main batteries already can't hit San Clemente at two miles on a calm day, and now they send us Oro-ville Wright's granddaddy to spot for 'em. Hell, he can't hardly see across the table."

Crazy Charlie Horseman's spoon stopped. He put it down delicately, rolled his napkin, and slid it into a lacquered ring brazed with his name in Chinese and a pair of Navy wings. "It ain't bad enough," he said to Pappy, "I got to mess with a bunch of black-shoe chiefs on a goddamn battleship should have been scrapped fifteen years ago. It ain't bad enough they're slapping the hat on boots that got less time in their racks than I got in a fighter upside down . . ."

Forty aging chiefs, none with less than twenty years at sea, digested the canard stolidly and held the middle ground.

Crazy Charlie stood up, dabbed his lips with the rolled napkin, and tossed it onto the table. "It ain't bad enough I got to fly a barn door with a float at ninety knots for a bunch of half-assed gunner's mates that'll probably put one through the wing before they ever see the target——"

"Come on, Charlie," Pappy pleaded. "Sit down and eat your soup."

"No, that ain't bad enough," Crazy Charlie continued. "I got to take crap from a Russian water tender that could never have got past seaman apprentice in any aviation squadron I ever saw this side of Tsingtao."

He slammed from the mess. Pappy Shea looked pained. The symphony of slurping recalled its key and continued.

"That's the trouble with them brown-shoe chiefs," complained Kosloff. "They're sensitive. Like officers."

Pappy Shea sighed. "Save him his chow," he told Ben.

FOUR

Ben dreamed of golden wings like Crazy Charlie Horseman's. He pleaded for orders, he cajoled, he demanded, he sulked, he brownnosed Pappy Shea, he haunted the captain's office in the bowels of the ship, checking on enlisted flight-school quotas. To prove his worth he spent a few nights studying and the next week made seaman first with the highest score the *No-Go Maru* remembered since the college boots of '17.

His knuckle grew so bad that he had to brave sick bay after all, and a finger was splinted. He was temporarily excused from mess cooking and sent back to the bridge; so, having failed to get Pappy Shea to sign a request for flight training, he began to stalk the navigator. His chance came when Pappy sent him one afternoon to Hammering Howie's stateroom with a sheaf of daily logs.

Officers' country was ten degrees cooler than the compartment, steamy with bakery odors, in which Ben slung his hammock. Respectfully uncovered, he passed a half-dozen green-felt curtains: the chaplain's, the gunnery officer's, the chief engineer's. It was a turquoise world of carillon chimes and gleaming stainless steel and doors instead of half-ton hatches: even the toilet stalls in the heads were private. In Ben's circles you squatted on toilet seats suspended over a saltwater trough and were lucky if you ended up wiping your own ass; the height of camaraderie was to light a fire ship of crumpled toilet paper and float it downstream to watch a shipmate leap from his perch.

Howland's curtain was open and the navigator lay in shorts, not in a hammock, but on a bunk. Ben knocked.

"Come in, Casco." Hammering Howie swung his legs to the deck. Ben handed him the logs, which he took to a built-in desk, painted Navy gray and decorated with his wife's picture and one of himself in a football uniform and long hair: "Howland 6, Army 0, 1912."

Ben scanned the room: curtains over the brass port, uniforms hanging in a clothes locker glittering with braid and doubtless brushed daily by his Filipino steward, shoes automatically polished and standing at attention below the uniforms, a sword dripping gold tassels hanging on a hook. There was even a stainless-steel washbasin: it explained why they were immaculate at quarters, they did not even have to stand in line to shave. There was a Victrola and a radio all his own, and a private ventilator poking its snout at a tiny reading lamp built into the head of the bunk; you could turn off the lamp when you felt like sleeping so it would not stare at you all night. Even the ubiquitous pipes on the overhead were a delicate green, and when the main batteries fired and showered the room with lagging from above, there was probably someone to sweep out the crumbs before the navigator even came below. Passengers? Ben thought. *First-class* passengers: no wonder you never saw them anywhere but on the bridge.

Hammering Howie scrawled the last signature and Ben made his pitch, fast, succinct, and well rehearsed. Hammering Howie seemed genuinely surprised.

"Pensacola? Son, you're dreaming."

"There's an enlisted quota, sir. I saw the ALNAV."

"I haven't seen an enlisted pilot for years. Except old Crazy Charlie, and that squadron on the *Lex*."

"I'd like to put in for it, sir."

"Well, see the chief sometime."

"I have, sir. He won't sign my chit."

"He needs you on the bridge, then." Hammering Howie's jaw set. "The chief first. Then me. Just like in the book."

"Aye, aye, sir," Ben said, and that was that.

He was sick with envy of Ape; instead of striking for quartermaster he should have asked, like Ape, for the aviation division, for that, although Ape hadn't known it, was the logical path to Pensacola. Ben was sure that the senior aviator, a tousled lieutenant with a cheerful grin, would have bucked a chit to the captain if one of his own men wanted to fly. He decided to transfer. There was plenty of time for his scheme: he and Ape were afraid to go ashore anyway, for there was a rumor that the shore patrol was watching the landing. Ben began to haunt the catapults, helping Ape and the other airedale strikers hose the floats and scrub the wings of the gawky 03U3 biplanes. He greased-up Crazy Charlie, who spent Sundays fishing off the fantail with a handline wound on a lead-line spindle. The old man accepted his idolatry but shook his head. "I ain't going to steal a striker from Pappy. You got a home there. He knows more navigation than all them navigators put together. You just listen to him."

"I don't want to learn navigation! I want to learn to fly!"

The chief felt a nibble and jerked his line. He missed and Ben caught a swift and searching glance. "Oh, hell, kid, what's the use talking about it? Nobody gets through Pensacola anymore. Nobody but officers."

"There's still an enlisted quota, I told you."

"Sure, it's a act of Congress, they got to let some white-hats in. But they don't have to *graduate* you. We can fly the ass off half the officers in the fleet, but we don't hardly know what end of a teacup to grab. Admiral Moffett hated our guts, and they still do. Well, you can't piss up a rope."

"You got through."

"When I went through, they didn't have to wash you out; when a wing fell off, they buried you."

"I want to try."

"Why?"

"I'm as tired of this battleship crap as you are."

"I'm a chief," Crazy Charlie reminded him. "I got a right to be tired."

"I like airplanes," Ben said.

Crazy Charlie jabbed his fishhook into the spindle and jerked his head toward the floatplane on the port catapult. "You probably never *seen* an airplane, because that sure as hell ain't one. But if you *like* 'em, you're crazy!"

Ben stood numbly as the chief's voice rose. Something he had said had triggered him, and the whole new plan of attack crumbled. Crazy Charlie's words came in a torrent: "The engines are dirty and the gauges lie to your face. They build the cockpits too small and you freeze your balls off before you get to ten thousand feet. On a carrier the landing signal officer's mostly some blind j.g. couldn't get a box kite down in a cow pasture. If he cuts you so you miss a wire, you nose up in the barrier with a mouthful of stick. The goddamn airplane smells of gas all the time and it goes off like a bomb if you light a cigarette."

He took out a pack of cigarettes, put one in his mouth, felt for matches and found none. He threw the cigarette over the side. His hands were trembling. "Take a *good* look, Casco. You can stick a thumb through the wing, the ass sticks out, hell, they ain't as pretty as a battleship, even. How can you *like* airplanes?"

Pappy Shea joined them. To finish Ben off, Crazy Charlie

Horseman said maliciously, "Your fair-haired boy wants to be an airedale."

"Over my dead body, I told him already. Charlie, I read a blinker from the flag. Your flight physical's tomorrow."

Crazy Charlie seemed to shrink. "Where?"

"On the *Lex.*"

"Who runs their sick bay? Who *is* that lard-ass chief? Davis! Wrinkle-Meat Davis! Ain't it?"

"Yeah," Pappy Shea said nervously. "I guess."

Crazy Charlie took out the pack of cigarettes again. Savagely he demanded, "Ain't anybody got a match?"

Pappy handed him a matchbook and he lit up and hurled the match into a butt kit. He puffed for a moment, looked at the floatplane in a sort of silent agony, and finally said hoarsely, "Pappy?"

"Look, Charlie! Suppose somebody wants to know what all the blinker's about?"

Crazy Charlie gazed into the gnarled face. Whatever it was he wanted, he barely got it out. "Pappy," he murmured, "please?"

Pappy folded. "*O.K.*, goddamn it! I just hope he answers, is all."

"He'll answer," Charlie Horseman said, "or they'll throw him out of the mess." He seemed suddenly relaxed. He studied Ben. "Look," he said, "we got the fleet weather hop today. You ever been up?"

Ben's heart began to pump. "No—no, sir."

"That's it!" Pappy spluttered savagely. "Steam him up some more!"

Crazy Charlie put a hand on his arm. "Kid wants to be a AP. He ought to know what it's like up there; what it's *really* like?"

Pappy got the message. He smiled. "Yeah . . ." He turned

to Ben. "Benny, you go. You go with Crazy Charlie, and then we'll talk about your chit."

Ben had got the message too. His knees were weak with fear and Ape had to help him with the safety belt because his hands were shaking, but nothing short of a gun at his head could have torn him from the cockpit, and when the engine splintered the universe and the catapult fired and slapped his skull against the headrest and his guts slid solidly against his backbone and the plane rocked faster and faster down the track, he found himself yelling in wild animal joy.

They banked and he looked back at the *No-Go*. A tiny white-capped figure stared up from the fantail. On the forecastle he could see microscopic sunbathers. A mass of white hats sitting on the face of the number-four turret watched two ants sparring on the after deck.

They climbed. The *Lex* and *Sara* were up from Dago, and they became barge-size. The battlewagons shrunk to cruisers and the cruisers to destroyers and finally to bathtub toys, and he could see the open ocean beyond the breakwater, and Catalina crystal-clear in the sunlight. Suddenly, without warning, the universe began slowly to revolve about Charlie Horseman's helmeted head. Ben gripped the sides of the cockpit. When the earth lay squarely at the tip of Charlie's skull it stopped. They hung suspended for an age. The seat belt clutched his legs together, jamming his testicles tight, and he was afraid to shift; his eyeballs popped from his head, his pulse began to pound unbearably in his ears. If the seat belt broke he was doomed, for he was too disoriented to find the rip cord and he was not at all sure the handle was still where Ape had pointed. He was freezing in the open cockpit. A low howl began as the horizon rose slowly to Charlie Horseman's shoulders and the howl climbed to a wail of distress and then a shriek of terror.

They were heading down, straight down. He caught a glimpse of the Terminal Island ferry, loaded with white-hats fore and aft, drawing an arrow wake toward Wilmington's waterfront. Then it disappeared under the lower wing and all the organs that had jammed his head reversed and gathered at the soles of his feet and he was gripped in the seat in a giant vise, so that he could not have lifted a hand if he tried.

Suddenly, with a crack and a lurch, they were rolling again and the spinning horizon, centered on Crazy Charlie's head, wound clockwise and back and clockwise again like the hand of a stopwatch gone mad. Ben smelled gasoline and oil and ancient sweat and tasted the greasy pork he had had for Sunday dinner. He closed his eyes and quickly opened them: it was far worse when you lost your frame of reference.

The torture lasted forty minutes. Ben hung on to his lunch, damned if he was going to give the crazy chief or Pappy Shea or Ape or the other mechs cause to laugh at him; damned too if he was going to spend the rest of Sunday cleaning the cockpit. Crazy Charlie said not one word: isolation was part of the treatment. Ben crouched deserted in his frigid cage, gripping the tubular cockpit braces as the blood drained from his head to his feet and to his head again.

It might have lasted longer, but Crazy Charlie lost his glasses when he shoved his goggles back to wipe the lenses. Something went out of his flying, then; he turned back to land and the plane became leaden and more cautious. They were not more than fifty feet above the water when Ben saw an excursion launch standing bravely out from behind the granite-solid hulk of the *Maryland.* It's orange-and-white-striped awning fluttered in the breeze. It was churning directly into their landing path, crammed to the gunwales with tourists. His voice failed him for a moment, and then he screamed into the gosport mouth, "Chief! Motorboat! Starboard bow!"

The snore of the cut-back engine turned to startled clamor. The launch drew closer and still the plane slipped lower, clawing for a hold on the sky like an astonished duck. Then the engine caught, a wing rose awkwardly, and they were clear and skimming down on the lazy chop of the bay in a rush of water. They stopped almost instantly. For a moment they wallowed; at last the chief headed for the *No-Go* in an angry shower of spray. He said nothing. Ben, still fighting nausea, watched a red tide climb the weathered neck. Deposited by crane back on the *Nevada*'s catapult, Crazy Charlie seemed shaken. He climbed out and drew Ben to the fantail.

"Was that motor launch from the flag?"

"The flag?" Ben gaped at him. "That was a rubberneck launch! Tourists!"

The chief's eyes snapped angrily, as if he didn't believe it, but then he leaned on the lifeline and gazed away. "Yeah," he said finally. "I guess it was." His eyes scanned the other battleships, the carriers and the cruisers and the destroyers, the great floating islands *Lex* and *Sara*. "You know something?"

"What?"

He jerked his thumb toward the plane. "I got ten thousand hours sitting on my can in them things. Fighters, torpeckers, hogs, flying boats—everything but balloons. Hell, I used to hook onto *dirigibles*. I flew into the crater at Mauna Loa once, for pictures. I smashed up a few airplanes, everybody did. But I never hurt nobody, not a scratch."

Pappy Shea walked up. He handed Crazy Charlie a piece of paper. "From Wrinkle-Meat Davis," he said. "The horse's mouth."

Crazy Charlie took it wordlessly but did not even look at it. Pappy Shea glanced at Ben. "You O.K.?"

"Just fine," Ben said acidly. "Why do you ask?"

"You look pale. You still want to aviate?"

"Not right this minute," Ben said. "Give me half an hour."

Crazy Charlie studied him. "You still hot for Pensacola?"

"Yes, *sir!*" Ben said.

Crazy Charlie turned to Pappy. "Why don't you sign his chit?"

Pappy's face worked into creases of disbelief, Caesar surprised by Brutus on the forum steps. "Charlie, you said yourself! Why set him up so they can kick him in the ass?"

Crazy Charlie smiled grimly. "He's goin' brown shoe some way, or he won't ship over. You been feedin' me all this about his 'career.' Well, you're slowin' it up. Sign it, you old bastard!"

Pappy glared at Charlie. "All I've done for you today!" he squeaked. He turned on Ben. "No! You stay on the bridge! I told you!"

Ben braced. He had one last chance, and he used it. He held up his splinted hand. "Pappy?" he said softly.

"Yeah?"

"You heard about the marine lieutenant? At the Algonquin?"

Pappy turned white. "*You* hit him?" he breathed. "Is that why you been staying aboard?"

"That's why."

"Then *stay* aboard, goddamn it!"

"Forever? Jesus, Pappy, this is our home port!"

Pappy began to pace the fantail, his features wrinkling

and unwrinkling like an agitated monkey's. Finally he stopped short. He poked his nose into Ben's face, jaw outthrust and eyes hot. "O.K.," he quavered, "I'll sign it! But I hope you bust your ass!"

"Thanks, Pappy," murmured Ben, fervently. He squeezed his arm. Pappy shrugged off his hand, stumbled over a padeye, and strode blindly forward.

"Thank *you*, Chief," Ben said to Crazy Charlie.

"Hell, you ain't *there*. You ain't even started. You got to get two more black-shoe signatures before you get past the captain, and you got to pass a flight physical."

"I'll pass."

"Then they count your brains and then you wait for orders from BUNAV. If you get past the gates, even, the first thing they'll tell you is you got two strikes against you and they're achin' to fan you out."

"Well, they won't, dammit."

"Keep half a dozen uniforms you never wear in a new bag for bag inspection, and no matter how hot it gets stay awake in class. You forget to salute some reserve ensign don't know a rudder bar from a aileron, they'll bust you out on your butt—smell for 'em, don't wait until you see 'em. Keep your airspeed up. When they cut your gun on takeoff, land straight ahead. If you do all them things . . ." His voice trailed off.

"Yes?" Ben urged.

"Well, you do all them things and if you're *goddamn* lucky, someday they'll strap an F4B fighter on your back and you can reach out and pat its tail and it's got five hundred horses haulin' you straight up at a hundred knots and a goddamn fireman striker on the Asiatic station couldn't make it spin unless he wanted it to. It flies upside down just as good as right side up, and you couldn't tear a wing off in a typhoon. You sit there with *that* stubby little bastard glued on your ass and you might not be nothing but an AP, but— Aw, screw it!"

He crumpled the paper Pappy had given him and hurled it off the fantail. It began to float away from the hull on the ebbing tide. Ben glanced at him, wondering what it was. The old man's eyes were glistening. He turned on Ben. "Curious bastard, ain't you?"

"I didn't say anything, Chief."

"Well," the chief said, "that was the eye chart off the *Lex.*"

He shambled forward in his sweat-soaked flight suit, looking very old and tired and not at all like the imperial monarch Ben had seen first in the motor launch last month. In a week Charlie's rate had changed from chief aviation pilot to chief mech and when he flew it was in the rear cockpit, although he refused to take off the golden wings. He had quit fishing from the fantail and begun to spend his Sundays in speakeasies and Crowley's Locker Club and Legion halls ashore.

Ben felt sorry for him, but was too busy sweating out the quota to worry. Within three months he was pulling away from the *No-Go's* bulk for the last time, sitting on his bag and hammock with his orders to Pensacola in hand, praying that no shore patrol were on the dock. He spotted a monkey shape leaning on the bridge, watching. He waved. Pappy Shea raised a hand, turned quickly, and disappeared into the chart house.

He liked Pensacola from the first. He crossed the neck of a bayou over a trim bridge in a Navy bus with a dozen other enlisted candidates. Gulls floated under drooping trees on mirror-blue water. The station was all lush lawns and scrubbed seaplane hangars leading to the tepid water of

Pensacola Bay. Everything was white, green, fresh, and sparkling, so that you did not mind the fetid smell of swamps or acrid paper mills to the north. He did not even mind the wringing heat or great whale-bellied clouds which massed all morning over the Gulf and dumped rain every afternoon on the steaming runways so that, if you were an enlisted candidate instead of a cadet or student officer, you had to help the ground crews pull tarps over the cockpits.

He found that all that Crazy Charlie Horseman had said was true. The cards were stacked. Within three months only Ben and one other enlisted man were left from the busload. The others had fallen to down checks or the heat in the drowsy engine classes or had bilged their radio code.

But Roosevelt was a big Navy man and flight training was stepped up; there were suddenly planes everywhere, on the ramps, in the chocks, circling mainside and the outlying fields. Ben realized that his only chance was to get through in the rush. He hung on desperately. He learned tricks in shining his shoes and developed a hungry look in class, as if he were starved for the words from the front of the room. He learned to anticipate an engine emergency from the instructor's head in the front cockpit, having noticed that when he was about to cut your gun he invariably looked for a smooth field first in case the engine quit for good.

He soloed in nine hours. Alone, he learned other tricks for the flight checks that stretched endlessly ahead. He found in the open cockpit that the caress of wind on a cheek would hint that you were sideslipping and the smell of hot metal warned you that your engine was laboring long before the temperature gauge showed it.

He learned to fly by sound. He found an ear for the doleful whispers you heard when you throttled back for a no-power spin, holding the nose higher and higher above the smoky

horizon while the rudder pedals grew sloppy and silence
deepened and the plane seemed to hold its breath in fear,
and you teetered on the edge of the void, trying to stop her
dead-still in midair, reining tighter and tighter until the
bottom fell out and her starboard wing dropped and you
were spinning, slowly at first, down an invisible vortex,
counting the turns by the white steeple on the Baptist
church of an unknown town in the swamp below. There
had to be precisely two and a half turns and your instructor
lay by his yellow convertible on a mattress on the shoulder
of U.S. 90, counting them, hoping you'd miss, or preferably
that you'd never recover and have to hit the silk, or better
yet, perhaps, that you'd freeze and go in with the plane, thus
proving again that a white-hat's place was swabbing decks on
a battlewagon, not in the cockpit of a five-thousand-dollar
Navy airplane.

He drew a lieutenant named "Downcheck" Laski for his
final aerobatics check. Laski was the Grim Reaper, the devil's
advocate, Attila the Hun. He was a tubby, morose officer
who, it was said, had never recovered from watching his first
primary cadet stall, spin, and burn. Ben got a "down," of
course, and on his recheck with another instructor droned
through Immelmanns, snap rolls, and loops until he was
soaking in the chilly cockpit and so nauseous he could
hardly land the plane. But he knew he had flown a perfect
hop. By the blackboard outside operations he found Laski
arguing with the check pilot, a young ensign. Something
snapped. In a searing, careless rage Ben challenged Laski,
who had probably two thousand hours to his own two hundred, to an illegal dogfight over Foley, Alabama, the tradi-
tional trysting ground. Laski looked into his blazing eyes,
decided quite correctly that Ben might try to ram him,
shrugged, and walked away. The check pilot struggled for

a moment with his prejudices. Thoughtfully he drew a vertical line on the board. Then, while Ben stared like a downed gladiator watching the emperor's box, the ensign added an arrowhead. The arrow pointed up.

Twenty-one months off the *No-Go*, Ben pinned on the golden wings. He was strangely disappointed; he felt the same man with them on as before. But with the wings came the crow of a first-class petty officer and orders to the enlisted fighter squadron on the *Lex*. By then Roosevelt was using WPA funds to buy airplanes. Rates in the tail-hook Navy loosened up; by 1936, when Ape Gorman reported aboard with his own set of new wings, Ben was up for chief himself.

At mail call one morning on the *Lex* he got a letter in Pappy Shea's neat, quartermaster printing. A new ensign on the *No-Go* had crashed with Crazy Charlie on a catapult shot off Pearl and he had been buried at sea. Planes from Ford Island had flown over the ceremonies and they had even dropped a wreath, which was not bad for a rummy enlisted man who hadn't had a stick in his hand for almost four years and had half the black-shoe officers on his own ship gunning for him for his acid, bitter mouth.

Next week the squadron exec called Ben into his cabin and shook his hand and called him "Chief" and that night he stood blindfolded at attention in the CPO mess, drinking from a sick-bay bedpan what turned out to be warm soup and oysters and paying fines for imagined crimes two years old. He bought his uniforms at the receiving station at Dago, driving past the brig in a new secondhand Ford and wondering what misguided recruit stared from the cell he had once owned. He bought blues and whites and the sacred visored cap, and for all the years he wore it, he cocked it as Charlie Horseman had, ten degrees to port.

CHAPTER TWO

ONE

All day, as Hammering Howie Howland's task group plowed north toward Kyushu, Japanese snoopers hung high on its western flank. But when the combat air patrol was vectored toward them, the Japs found it easy to dive home to Sasebo or Kagoshima or Nagasaki. At dusk another picket destroyer was hit by a kamikaze and again Ben could see from his GQ station a ruddy glare. Now he could hear the guns from the other destroyers in the screen pounding vainly at the kamikaze's escorts, who escaped. That night he left his seaboots at the side of the bunk and his pants and socks on; when the general alarm clanged, far too early, he was into the boots and groping for the ringing phone in his office almost before he had awakened. He noticed that the stateroom was heaving under his feet, as if they were mounting great swells. He punched a stopwatch on his desk and picked up the phone.

"CIC watch officer, sir," a cheerful voice announced. "A large group of bogies sixty miles northwest . . . Belay that, sir. Two groups now, sixty miles northwest and seventy miles west."

"Thank you," Ben said. Damn . . . It should have been a

free ride all morning. Action this early would foul up the refueling schedule.

His battle station was under the overhang of the flight deck, within feet of the extreme bow, so that if the bridge was knocked out and the skipper killed he could take over from the eyes of the ship. It was wide open dead-ahead, very cold from the speed of their passage, and at this hour pitch-black except for a rosy glow from the auxiliary binnacle between the anchor chains, where his emergency helmsman was checking the wheel now. Next to his helmsman the auxiliary engine room telegraph man jingled test messages to main-engine control. Against the starlit sky he could see gunners in the forward quads, helmets on, breaking out ammunition. The whole area was hushed in deference to Ben. A quad motor started, whining as the trainer spun the mount; a loader lost his balance and cursed, but softly.

Ben felt along the bulkhead and found his life jacket and battle helmet; he yanked them from the rack and put them on. His stubby talker Markowitz, trailing a phone line, appeared at the binnacle and handed him a cup of coffee.

"Good morning, sir. Five-inch batteries manned and ready, steering-aft manned and ready, sky control manned and ready, forty-millimeter batteries manned and ready, and . . ." He listened and repeated, "Damage control central manned and ready, all emergency aid stations manned and ready, engineering spaces manned and ready, damage-control parties one through sixteen manned and ready, brig prisoners released——"

"Wait a minute," Ben said, thinking of Watkins, "under guard?"

"Yes, sir."

"O.K.," Ben said. "Go on."

The litany continued; the ship was shadowboxing, nerve ends flicking into life as the last few talkers manned their phones and the five-inch batteries jerked and slewed and came to rest again. And she was buttoning up, too: thirty feet below the rushing waterline, lonely men were sealing themselves into cubicles from which, should the worse happen, they could never snake their way. Damage-control parties, white cells ready for the infections of fire or flood, dogged hatches and settled down to wait.

"All stations, manned and ready," Markowitz concluded. "Condition Zebra set."

Ben punched the stopwatch again. He held it to the binnacle light. Four minutes, eighteen seconds, he noted. Not bad. He moved forward over the anchors and looked uneasily down at the dark swells. He smelled weather, and it was typhoon season, too.

He flicked to CIC on his bulkhead intercom. A fighter pilot's voice crackled with distant static: "Believe it is a Betty, angels twenty." Ben felt a twinge of envy for the fighter. Ten or twenty miles ahead, snug in his stocky F6F, hunched behind the green eye of his intercept radar, all of his being must be squeezing together, focusing on the tiny screen until, at the ultimate moment, his hopes would pour down the barrels of four jarring fifties and he would make his kill and never even have to see the plane.

"Commencing pass," he heard him report to his wingman, and then after an interminable wait, "Break left, Charlie. Left, goddamn it!"

Markowitz grasped his arm excitedly. "Dead ahead, Commander!"

Ben saw a far-off orange glare and suddenly a blinding red flash, and then solid darkness. From the intercom the fighter pilot's voice screeched to his director, "He just blew! Splash one, splash one! I got one! Holy Christ, he just blew up!"

It had been no ordinary explosion. Ben's stomach constricted. Gasoline? Or . . . This far out, Betty with a *baka?* There was nothing more from CIC. The night fighters returned at dawn. Five minutes afterward the catapult overhead was slamming and gull-winged Corsairs, heavily fueled, were bursting from the flight deck and sinking with ponderous grace to Ben's level ahead. Their engines roared for a moment into his steel cavern and then, tucking their wheels neatly, they clawed skyward like long-nosed hawks.

Each carrier launched nine fighters and a dozen SBD's to hit Kagoshima, holding all else in reserve. Then Hammering Howie swung the group contemptuously from an upwind course back to a zigzag along its original track, not even deigning to change it. A high overcast gave not enough cover. The remaining Bettys, if there were any, waited somewhere between the force and Kyushu, so the *Shenandoah* ate no breakfast. She stayed at GQ, and the stubbled gunners in the quads grew nervous and red-eyed as always, without even coffee, but stayed alert enough from fear.

It was a forward quad gunner who saw the first Betty arrive at ten. She was a decoy who had hidden from the radar screens under returning fighters and she passed majestically over the group to draw fire. The forties began to pound, then the staccato twenties, and then it was no trouble at all to find Bettys, because they were everywhere. A *baka* from nowhere undershot the new *Lex* by yards and for a moment there was nothing but spray and then a bright yellow flash and Ben could see men on her flight deck, tiny figures against the pallid horizon, racing to starboard to see the debris. Gray sky, gray tracers, gray weapons, gray water, frozen in steel harmony. Suddenly it was all over except for the rising howl from a mother plane, one wing afire and tail chewed off jaggedly, spiraling into an invisible whirlpool as if someone had pulled a plug in a sink, spinning faster and faster, trailing a black rope of smoke and roaring defiance from runaway props. She hit, exploded, and there was utter silence. All at once everyone was hammering again at a tiny doll swinging beneath a strange, gossamer parachute. *Poom . . . poom . . . poom . . . poom . . .* from the forties, staccato *pah, pah, pah, pah* from the twenties. For a wild moment the figure looked like a target in a shooting gallery and then they got the word out to cease firing, and Ben found the Jap in his binoculars. There was no way to tell if he had been hit or not. Ignoring Markowitz, who was begging at his elbow for a look, he followed the dot all the way down, certain time and again that in the next second it would strike the water, but still surprised when it did, in a shower of spray.

The canopy sifted into the sea. Ben thought that the pilot had been caught in its folds, but a tiny black head bobbed up just outside the heaving pool of silk. A tin can slicing across the formation began to blink furiously, answering a message from the *Shenandoah* flag. Ben read: "ROGER. WILL DELIVER DEAD OR ALIVE."

On the TBS radio Ben heard that the Jap pulled a water-soaked revolver and tried to fire on his rescuers. Within ten minutes Ensign Susumo Yokawa, Imperial naval reserve, was lashed in a litter and on his way to Barney Epstein over a highline from the destroyer racing alongside.

TWO

The morning strike report came in, and it was good, but it was bad: sixteen enemy aircraft destroyed on Kyushu airfields, four shot down taking off, a locomotive damaged, two yard-patrol craft in Kagoshima Harbor sunk. But antiaircraft had been heavy, and Skip LeMasters, a lanky dive-bomber pilot from Arizona, was down in Ariake Bay. His wingman was circling a life raft under fighter cover but running low on gas.

As always, the dive-bomber squadron drew together when one of its planes was down. Alex Scliris, the solid, dark young air-group doctor, wore the wrong kind of wings but was closer to the fliers than Ben. He was jumpy and scared for the pilot: Skip was his liberty buddy, his favorite acey-deucy opponent, his partner when the wardroom turned to bridge. Ben loitered next to him on the edge of the crowd hugging a ready-room intercom.

The battleship *Washington* launched a Kingfisher float-plane and they heard in driblets that it had landed by Skip's raft in sight of the shore batteries and picked up one of the two men aboard, but it was not until the man had been passed from the *Washington* to a destroyer and was on his way back by breeches buoy that they found that the survivor had been the gunner and not Skip, who had died on the raft. Ben went with the doctor to sick bay. They found the gunner, a jockey-sized, hot-eyed seaman named Barnaby, sitting on the examining table. There were tear streaks down the grime on his face. He was already well oiled with medicinal whisky from the *Washington*. He regarded Scliris with loathing. The doctor, surprised, told him to lie down. Barnaby shook his head. "I don't need no physical. Go check your first-aid kits, you want to stay busy!"

"Listen, son," warned Ben, "you're not the first guy to ever have to ditch! You're talking to an officer, so watch it!"

Scliris raised his hand. "Barnaby, what's on your mind?"

The gunner got up and moved close to Scliris, nose to nose. "The aid kits, Doc. In the rear cockpits? They ain't complete! It ain't all there, Doc, you understand?"

The catapults began to wham above and a sterilizer gurgled and in the next compartment a sick-bay patient coughed. Scliris put down the blood-pressure apparatus.

"Morphine?" he whispered.

"Whatever it is," said Barnaby. "They ain't none!"

"Oh, Christ," murmured Scliris.

Barnaby nodded. "He was hit in the nuts, or maybe his pecker. He still got her down in one piece. And he held on, he never even hardly groaned, until we had the raft in the water. And I got him in, and I opened up the goddamn kit . . ." The little man's voice rose. "And I took out the fucking syringe, and guess what, Doctor? *Guess what!*"

Ben picked up the phone and dialed the master-at-arms office. "Get Catlett," he told the duty MAA. "Sick bay! On the double."

"It took half an hour," the little gunner said. "It took a whole half-hour, Doctor. He went out screaming. Can you imagine that? Old Skip-boy screaming? He was *hurting!*"

"Yes," Scliris said, "he was."

He studied the seaman for a moment, unlocked a safe, and poured him another shot of whiskey.

THREE

Ben stood with Catlett and the flight surgeon in the senior medical officer's office and looked at the pile of first-aid kits on the desk. Scliris lifted an empty syringe and wheezed air through it.

"Not one c.c.," he said savagely. He tossed the syringe into the pile. "Check every man aboard for hype marks," he demanded. "And then every officer. Lockers, safes, voids, I want every goddamn one of them searched!"

Ben regarded him sadly. "I'm sorry, Al. You know we can't. Not here, anyway."

Scliris seemed not to have heard. "I'll take the air group myself. You know what to look for, Chief? Knots on the veins, and not just the forearm, either. Thigh, hip, and——"

"I know, sir," said Catlett.

Ben shook his head. "We can't call off the whole operation to check for one narco!"

"One? Or a half-dozen! This goddamn bucket!"

Ben faced him angrily. "Why does it have to be the *ship?* How do you know it wasn't the air group? Who has access, anyway? What's wrong with the plane captains? I wouldn't *have* a plane captain who'd let anybody in my airplane, dammit." He sat down, mulling the problem. "Chief," he decided, "the corpsmen will check every cockpit before dawn GQ. From then until flight quarters I want one of your men guarding every five planes."

"I don't have that many men," Catlett said.

"Deputize some, like in the Westerns," Ben said. "Tell the major I said to lend you some marines. I don't care how you do it, but do it. You understand?"

"Aye, aye, sir. One for five."

"It's protecting the planes," Scliris said, "but it's not finding the guy that did it."

"We'll find him," Ben said.

"I want to find him *now*. He might get killed on this goddamn strike, I want to find him all in one piece."

He capped the whiskey, changed his mind, and offered it to Ben. Ben shook his head. Scliris poured himself a shot, but half of it spilled down his shirt.

FOUR

Ben told Mitch Langley in his sea cabin. Mitch's jaw tensed and his face grew taut. He almost never swore, but now he said, "Jesus Christ, Ben! In the water, screaming!"

"We'll get him, sir, whoever it was." There was a knock and Christy Lee brought in the charges against Watkins, typed in the rough. Wordlessly he passed them to Ben, who read them and nodded coldly and gave them to the skipper. Mitch O.K.'d them for a final draft.

"By tomorrow morning, Mr. Lee," Ben said.

"Aye, aye, sir," Lee said stonily. He left and the skipper looked up at Ben.

"What have you got against him?"

Ben had no intention of confiding even in Mitch. "Does it show?"

Mitch nodded. "Did you meet him at Annapolis?"

"Yes."

"Did Terry?"

Ben stiffened. "I'd rather not go into it, Mitch."

Mitch nodded. "Terry was too pretty. You were both too young. When I saw her I should have canceled your orders."

"My God, sir, it's not your fault! I was lucky they weren't to Siberia!"

Mitch Langley grinned. "You know, you're right? The *Golden Gate Bridge!* Heavens above . . ."

Ben stepped from the sea cabin, glancing down at the afternoon fighter launch. The action below never ceased to thrill him, no matter how professionally or detachedly he watched it, or how critically. He slipped into Mitch's swivel chair to gaze down, chin on hands, remembering when a launch was an event and cooks and bakers would climb topside to the catwalks to watch. The hose-nosed, dull-blue Corsairs with their brawny gull wings became squat F4B biplanes, bright with paint, and their destination was not Kagoshima Bay but the new Golden Gate Bridge and the city that, while it disdained the sailor, loved the fleet.

FIVE

Ben had launched from the old *Lexington* one scrubbed morning in May of '37, thirty miles off the Gate, leading the fleet's enlisted stunt team "Four Goshawks." When his wingmen, Ape Gorman and Jockstrap Latham, and his tail-end-Charlie, Ug Pflueger, slid into position at the points of a tight little diamond, he climbed the tiny biplanes toward a single turreted spire of cumulus capping the northern tower of the glittering bridge. Scornfully the overpowered little fighters outdistanced the floatplanes and scouts from the *Sara*, already drumming toward old Fort Point. Ben looked down for the first time on the bright-orange span, empty of traffic, which tomorrow and forever after would become the symbol of his city.

Newsreels on the hangar deck had for weeks shown Hitler's planes and Mussolini's pounding Barcelona unopposed and the scuttlebutt from the China Station was of Japanese bombers wingtip to wingtip on Manchurian airstrips, but in the ready rooms the briefings dealt with the giant Frisco flyby and in the chiefs' mess of tail at Sally Stanford's and the bars on the Oakland waterfront. It was a golden age of Navy E's and naval ease. The U.S. Navy saw its next enemy engagement, if at all, as a fleet review under a 1918 dogfight. Ben's squadron—enlisted men with officers or CPO's for section leaders—was short on fighter tactics but owned an E in gunnery and another in formation flying and Mitch Langley as skipper and its four-plane stunt team was the pride of the force.

Mitch had launched Ben early to practice tomorrow's exhibition. "Pick your own routines." Ben trimmed the aircraft at fifteen thousand feet, flew hands-off for a moment, and stretched in the tiny open cockpit to lower his wingmen's guard, extending his hands where they could see them, wiggling his fingers in the light summer flying gloves like a swimmer loosening up for the start of a race. When there was a good chance that they had relaxed too, he dropped a hand swiftly to the stick and dumped the nose. In his rearview mirror he could see Ug sticking like glue just above his slipstream; he snatched a quick glance port and starboard and found Ape and Jockstrap wedged perfectly in place, their lower wing a foot above his upper, chubby tires scrubbed ebony, propellers splintering shards of glassy sunlight fifteen feet from his head. He let airspeed build up, craned port and starboard to check past his cowl ring for air-corps strays from Crissy Field or civilian puddle jumpers, and eased back on the stick. At the top of the loop he snatched another glance: he found Ape and Jockstrap precisely where they should be, and Ug, inverted, as rock-steady on the tip of his vertical stabilizer as if he were driving a Cadillac down a state highway. Far out of the tiny cockpits poked the goggled faceless heads. They were automatons until, at the very zenith of the loop, Ape's left hand rose before his head, third finger straight in salute.

The plane was an extension of Ben's arms and his legs; the team was an extension of his mind. If he willed it to chandelle or to slow-roll or to snap or split-S, the four points of the diamond would follow as surely as if the planes were frozen in a chunk of ice. He yodeled in delight, then, too soon, he saw the first V of the *Sara*'s white-tailed fighters and the lemon-yellow empennage of the other *Lexington* aircraft and Mitch's F4B riding herd above his squadron. The tile roofs of the seven hills were brilliantly red behind them, the marina bright green, the whites dazzled him through tinted goggles. He looked aft under the bridge to see the *New York* battling chop behind a column of cans and cruisers. A Japanese freighter, doubtless full of scrap to drop on China and probably clicking pictures of the new bridge, was meeting them close aboard and dutifully dipping her flag for each. When he dropped a wing he could see the *Saratoga* launching the last squadrons and tossing spray halfway to her flight deck. Ben had a crazy impulse to dive on them and scatter them with his slipstream. Instead, he chopped his gun and led his own team gently down in a series of banking turns, frolicking over the rest of the procession so that by the time they joined up on Mitch every eye on Marina Green and Pacific Heights must have been on them.

He was home. He had returned an enlisted man and not

an officer, but he was flying the sweetest plane in the world, with the Navy's best on either wing, for the finest skipper in the fleet. He slipped the diamond into place above Mitch's F4B. The plane was rock-steady in the crystal air. He had not one care past Ape's port wingtip or Jockstrap's starboard, or the tip of Ugly's tail; he glanced down on the crimson bellyband of the squadron leader's plane and would not have changed cockpits with Mitch himself, not for three stripes on his sleeve or an eagle on his hat.

He had lost, the Cat had beaten him, but the Dago brig was far behind him, and maybe he had really won.

SIX

Dutifully after dinner he put his brother Joe's little boy to bed in what used to be his own room. He had bought him a sailor hat in the *Lex's* small stores, and it came down over his ears, but could not be removed until he was asleep. His sister Porky, burping her own baby, watched them. She had married a schoolteacher and was very happy.

"Have *you* met anybody, Ben?"

"Sometimes," Ben muttered, "I think I've met everybody." Morosely, he moved to the window. The light in Terry's bathroom was off; he wondered if she still lived there. Porky read his mind.

"She moved out, Ben. Or her Al Capone daddy *booted* her."

He had a quick memory of a lovely body against the bathroom blind and firm legs swinging up the hill. "She was lucky."

"She goes with Glioto."

"Then she must be out of her mind."

"She always was. He's a detective."

"Glioto? The *city's* out of its mind."

"On the vice squad!"

"He ought to know where they keep it. I'll bet her old man loves that."

"If he even cares. She sings. Kind of. And dances. I heard it's nothing but a high-class strip."

He felt his face grow hot. "Where does she live?"

"I don't know," she said. She dabbed at spit on her tiny girl's lips. There was a pregnant silence. Damned if he'd ask. He started for the light switch. She watched him inscrutably. With his hand on the switch, he paused. "Where's she sing?"

She looked away. "Oh, hell! Why don't I learn to——"

"Where, Porky? Cut the crap."

"La Cantina," she sighed. "Down on——"

"I know where it is."

SEVEN

Ben and Ape bulled their way through a reluctant headwaiter and retained their caps past an angry hatcheck girl. North Beach was peppered with dives, but none so low as willingly to let in two enlisted men. In San Francisco anywhere north of Market in 1937 it was strictly "Tommy, wait outside," and "Chuck him out, the brute," but the golden wings and Ben's magic hat sufficiently confused the management to get them in, and once they were planted at a ringside table, it was easier to serve them than to try to dig them out. They ordered depth charges, shots of bourbon dropped, glass and all, into a stein of Carta Blanca beer so that greenish tendrils of liquor formed above the sunken whiskey and uncoiled mysteriously, in time to the music, Ape claimed, like charmed snakes.

Ape had won twenty-seven dollars playing poker in the starboard shaft alley on the way up from Dago, so by the time the drums rolled and the fairy master of ceremonies skipped to the center of the dance floor in his toreador pants and announced Terry's act, the table was loaded with empties and wet with spilled beer and Ape's shuttered eyes had a wavering, crafty motion, as if he were waiting the proper moment to dash through a whirling propeller.

An orange spotlight jogged along the arched ceiling, bobbed, and found its place in a haze of smoke at the side of the three-man orchestra. Terry Bellini drifted to the dance floor.

Her hair was an ebony river touched with golden ripples. Her face was thinner, without the childish blandness, and utterly beautiful; her amber eyes shot flecks of scorn into the audience. She was pouting. She challenged the room and there was dead silence for a moment, and then, though she was wearing Italian peasant dress, though the combine beside her throbbed with an Italian beat, she stabbed her heel on the dance floor once with an explosive, Mexican crack, and began to sing.

Her voice wormed into the guts of every man in the room. She started low, almost in a whisper, and began to look full into the face of the men at the tables. The bare-shouldered blouse slipped, and you felt that in a moment she would be swaying full-blown and naked before the world.

"*Veni, veni, veni, veni, veni tusa bella bella*
Lonesome and true . . ."

"Jesus," Ben heard Ape breathe. He chopped him off with

a gesture. Her eyes flicked to their table and she looked away because a sailor, even a chief, was a drunk, and not to be tempted to lurch to the floor. Then, as if something had struck her, she looked back and her eyes widened. For a long moment they locked on Ben's.

> "Palm trees are gently swaying
> My heart is saying . . ."

Her voice trailed off.

"Forget *him*," Ape murmured audibly, "he's hung like a stud mosquito. Look at *me!*"

She caught the beat again and whirled, bare legs gleaming gold, and Ben hated every wet-lipped man in the room. When she was through she ignored the howl of applause and would not sing again but came directly to Ben's table. Ape gaped and Ben snaked a chair from the nearest tourist table and seated her. He ordered her a drink and gave her a ticket to the mayor's pavilion at the bridge opening. "The four-man team with the yellow tails," he told her.

"I'll be there," she promised, and then, softly, "Oh, oh. Here's our childhood playmate."

Frank Glioto was picking his way through the jammed tables. His face was heavier, and it made his eyes seem closer set; he had a self-conscious, virtuous look about the mouth that he had never had before. Badge heavy, Ben decided, like a seaman first on shore patrol. He flashed a grin and stuck out his hand; Ben ignored it and did not bother to get up.

"Well," said Glioto with a tight grin, "the fleet's in."

"That's right, Frank," Ben said. "Maybe more than you think."

"Don't count on it, sailor," Glioto growled.

"Chief," corrected Ape. He edged his chair back for action. "Benny, shall I toss him out on his ass?"

"He's a cop," warned Ben. "Leave him alone, you'll have more fuzz in here than a bushel of peaches."

"Fuzz," snorted Frank. "That's nice, a brain like you. Hey, how come you ain't made officer, 'Chief'? I'd a thought you'd a been admiral by now."

"No," Ben said. "Some wop bastard hit my sister on a motorcycle, and I got a court-martial for trying to get home. I'm glad *you're* getting ahead, though, Frank. What's a good, solid vice-squad man average on a good month?"

"More," said Glioto, "than you probably see in a year. Terry, you ready?"

Terry looked up at him radiantly. "I'm having a drink, Frank."

Glioto's eyes narrowed. "You a B-girl now? You finish that drink and there'll be a padlock as big as your head on that door tomorrow. And your daddy won't bail you out."

Slowly, deliberately, Terry lifted the glass to her lips, tilted back her head, and drained it. "Frank," she purred, "you're going to make some girl a lovely husband. You know that?"

"Move it," grated Glioto. "Now!"

Slowly she got up. She held out her hand to Ben and the amber eyes found his and for a moment they were alone in her father's musty dining room with the clock in the cherub's belly button chiming six.

They were cut off from liquor at La Cantina when Terry left but they wandered to Izzy Gomez's and then closed the 365 Club after hours on Market. The sun was high and the air group already taxiing to the runway as they stumbled from the *Lexington*'s station wagon at Alameda Naval Air Station Operations and sprinted through the awful clamor of a hundred Pratt and Whitney engines to their planes. Ben had no time for a preflight; he pretended to count the wings, signed the yellow sheet, and scrambled to his cockpit, sick with the smell of gasoline and exhaust and the jar on his eyes of bright ground-crew jersies.

The plane shone with care. Ben's name leaped from the fuselage in new red paint, his bright-blue section-leader belly-band gleamed with wax, the CPO crow that was the badge of the squadron had been newly retouched and polished. The plane captain, a freckled mech who loved the stubby fighter as much as Ben, strapped him in and wrinkled his nose.

"You going to fly it?"

"No," said Ben. He impaled the mech with a Von Richto-fen stare, "I'm going to taxi it around in ever-decreasing circles until I disappear up my own asshole."

The mech's face twisted in agony. He trailed his hand sadly along the cowling, ran his eyes from gleaming silver prop to shining yellow tail. "You'll never get her off the deck."

"Don't be sailor, silly— Don't be silly, sailor. Crank her up."

The glittering disk of his own prop hurt his eyes and he quickly dropped the tinted goggles and then it was not so bad. By the time he was lined up in the take-off spot with Ape and Jockstrap tight on his wings and Ugly spring taut on Ape's port beam, he felt better, and as he dropped his hand and eased on throttle and the four planes responded, he found himself hurtling down the runway singing Terry's song.

EIGHT

He would always remember the flight, but only in flashes like quick cuts in a flying movie. So he would never know exactly when they did it. Even the newspapers were vague and so was Terry; Ape didn't know and Ben could never admit to anyone else that he was too drunk to know himself.

He remembered dumping the nose at ten thousand feet, until the underside of the orange bridge span balanced precisely atop his sky-blue cowling. It looked good there, gratified his sense of composition, so he let the shriek of struts and braces build and the stick grow firm and the rudder pedals rigid and the slipstream turn from air to liquid paste and finally granite set in concrete, until he could barely budge the controls.

He saw in his dive a cable dangling sloppily dead-center from the girders below the bridge: a man could get killed, and sue. He banked to the left and the bridge leaned crazily; he straightened out as the great towers port and starboard widened to greet him. Suddenly he was in shadow and slammed in the ears with the echo of their engines, everywhere hurled back at him. He glimpsed giant orange girders thirty feet above and then they were back in sunlight, climbing, climbing, climbing, until they were suspended over the span upside down and he tipped his head back to see that the traffic which had begun when the mayor had cut the ribbon had stopped again and there were people opening car doors and people staring up so he looped it again, twice, and he might have tried it again but something told him that it would be wise to catch the squadron and land with them at Alameda, and so he poured on the coal and did.

He parked on the long flight line and, when Ape's prop stopped, sat in a vacuum, stunned by silence. His head throbbed and he longed for a gulp of the Old Taylor, but it was stowed a million miles away in his locker on the ship, past all the lines of aircraft, past the ugly gray dock cranes, celestially remote.

He looked across at his wingman. Ape was staring straight ahead. His eyes were open, but the mech was shaking him. Ben struggled achingly from his cockpit and climbed Ape's wing. The very fabric of the plane seemed to smell of Old Taylor and beer. On Ape's cheeks, making the steel-blue stubble shine, was a greasy film of sweat. His lips were pale; he looked like a dying gorilla glad to go. His furnace-red eyes rolled toward him. "I could have *swore*," Ape murmured, "we flew under that bridge."

Ben was suddenly sober, and deep in his gut a chill conviction grew that he was through, this time, for good. He backed away from the nightmare; he would not think of it. But Ape's pitiful eyes would not release him.

"We *didn't*, did we Ben? Fly under the bridge?"

"Yes," Ben said heavily. "I think we did."

NINE

Commander Mitch Langley sat at the desk in his stateroom, nibbling thoughtfully at a pen. Since Ben's boot camp days his hair had turned gray, but his eyes were clear and calm as ever, even now, when Ben knew he must just have been through hell in the admiral's quarters.

"Annapolis?" murmured Ben.

Mitch nodded. "Annapolis."

Annapolis to an enlisted pilot meant yellow floatplanes browsing on the Severn across from the Academy; it meant flying bored midshipmen in circles at ninety knots; it meant teaching survival and aircraft engines to young men who probably didn't care, men he would be saluting in a year. He thought of Ape and Jockstrap and the long echelon of nimble fighters stepped wingtip to cockpit to infinity, peeling one after another off to dive at a target-sleeve towed across a royal-blue sky; he felt the jolt of thirties and fifties in the cold calm air. It was better than another court-martial, though, or a Disposition Board that would cost him his wings. He must simply forget the tail-hook Navy and morning sunlight on his cheek when the fleet, ten thousand feet below, was still in darkness. He tried to look grateful. "Aye, aye, sir," he said. "Thank you."

At his locker he stuffed the Old Taylor under his blouse; the bottle was almost empty. He had thirty days' leave on the books and he decided to ask for it. He didn't want to fly with the squadron again, knowing that he was leaving.

His spirits were plummeting by the moment. He found Terry's number in the San Francisco book and called her from a dockside booth and told her that he had to see her; she hesitated.

"What happened?" she asked. "I saw you loop the bridge. You idiots!"

"That," he said, "is what happened."

He ordered a cab and when he stepped from the booth he had the shakes so badly he drained the rest of the pint. Leaving the dock, he hurled the empty bottle against the *Lex*. It shattered beneath the number-two elevator and showered to the greasy water.

TEN

At a table in La Cantina he told her what the squadron meant to him; instead of pointing out that he had thrown it away himself and was childish to moan over it, she took his hand and squeezed it as if she understood. She pleaded a headache for her one-o'clock act and they left, avoiding Frank Glioto. They went to her dank little apartment on the Hyde Street hill and let the phone ring and the downstairs doorbell buzz and she giggled at Frank, returning over and over to park double by the streetlight and peer up at her window.

"It serves him right," she said. "He was fine on a motorcycle, but when they put him in plain clothes, he got to be God!"

They left the light off to give Frank doubt and sat quietly in the glow from the streetlamp while the foghorns began in the bay. He asked her if she knew that her father had run him out of town.

"Yes. He didn't tell me until afterward."

He toyed with a lock of her hair. "Well, he used three hoods and he scared me shitless."

Her eyes misted. "Why wouldn't you be scared? You were just a kid. And it wasn't even your fault. I was so ashamed! I finally pried your ship out of Porky, the *Nevada*, or something, and then I was too embarrassed to write."

"The hell with it."

She had finished Galileo High and studied music at SFJC for two years, thinking of teaching, or really more of singing in the SF opera company, but her voice wasn't good enough. And one night she walked out on her dad.

"What happened?"

"He killed my kitten. Named Cleopatra. Just an orphan kitten I had; I found her coming home from an audition, at the car stop, and she looked as sad as me. She grew up and one night she was in heat and crying and Papa was drunk as usual and made some lousy Sicilian crack about

birds of a feather. Then he slammed her through my bathroom window and she hit the side of your house, and——"

Her voice was shaking and he tried to change the subject.
"I used to watch you there, taking your bath."

"I know, you bastard. Anyway—anyway—" Her voice was
tight with rage, and she was fighting tears. "She was dead,
and I left."

He took her to bed, and they listened to the foghorns,
that night and every night afterward. She loved the fog and
he did too, except at sea. They would watch the street-
lamps bloom yellow and the windows opposite her flat fade
and then they would be alone and wrapped in cotton above
the clamor of the Hyde Street cables. Ben taught her to
recognize a motorman by the rhythm of his clanging at an
intersection; each had his own signature and she had lived
in San Francisco all her life without hearing it. He made sense
of the ceaseless clack below: "Raggedy-Ann-and-Raggedy-
Andy, used-to-make-love-wherever-was-handy. . . ." and she
did too, "Rickety-rack-get-back-in-the-sack. . . .", so that the
clatter would arouse him, something like Pavlov's dog, and
he would want her again. He began to lose weight and to
wonder if some morning he would go up with the window
shade. He got to know the window shade very well, every
crease on it, because he couldn't afford to spend every night
at La Cantina and he wouldn't borrow money from Terry,
although she made more than he.

One night the eagle-beaked manager of La Cantina fired
her. Glioto had threatened him and the manager said,
"Look, Teresa, all I got to do is serve just one minor, or
maybe the public health don't like the kitchen. What can I
do?"

"Glioto," Ben grated. "That son of a bitch, I'll tear him
apart!"

She wouldn't let him. To stir up Frank would only mean trouble for her father, and then for her mother, who was trying to keep the old man away from the rackets now that it was all numbers and junk.

She needed work: she loved to sing. He took her to Izzy Gomez's Bar, last relic of the Barbary Coast. They passed under the old wrought-iron light with Izzy's name in script and climbed the creaky stairs. While Terry broiled their steak sandwiches in Izzy's kitchen with an out-of-work guitarist and a snowbird photographer, Ben asked Izzy if he would hire her.

Izzy, who had served him illegal beer when Ben was in high school, studied him with sad brown eyes, a sallow walrus in a derby hat. His yellow jowls hung in folds so that you could not really tell where face left off and neck began; it was impossible to know if he weighed two hundred pounds or three hundred, for he let the world come to him and was always in the narrow space behind the bar. Behind him blazed a mural by Rivera, with Izzy in his derby hat embracing all of the city's struggling great: Saroyan, Steinbeck, Henry Miller, Ansel Adams.

"You are unhappy, my friend," he announced, ignoring Ben's question. "Why?"

"I got myself kicked out of the hottest fighter squadron in the fleet. What about Terry?"

"You were one of the ones that looped the bridge?"

"I *led* the damn thing. Look, can you hire her?"

"No, Benny." He spoke with a beautiful British accent, although he came from Coahuila and claimed he couldn't read or write. He knew everything, like God, and when Ben asked him what Terry should do, he shrugged. "She's blackballed. You can't beat the SFPD, you know. Tell her to try L.A."

"Not until I leave. I want her here."

Izzy began to wipe the bar in long, sweeping arcs. He poured a shot of tequila for himself and one for Ben. They touched glasses, tasted salt, and tossed them down. Izzy asked, "You don't plan to marry her?"

"Maybe."

Izzy glanced through the open kitchen door. "She is very generous to the local indigent with my steaks."

"I'll pay for them," Ben said sourly. "Jesus, you've been supporting half the artists on Telegraph Hill for the last twenty years. I don't see why you can't hire her!"

Izzy shook his head. "Here she comes, I think. She has a certain *simpático*. But take care, Benny, she doesn't kick you in the balls."

"What do you mean by *that?*"

"In the balls," Izzy smiled, "right in the bloody balls." He polished the bar in front of a stool. "Sit down, my dear."

She flashed him a dazzling smile and began to nibble her sandwich, watching him lumber down the length of the bar to serve a tourist couple.

"It's practically against the law," she admitted, "but I hate that greasy bastard. You can't believe a word he says."

That night the fog turned the streetlight yellow and the cables clacked and there was a distant jangling of bells. "Powell and Jackson," she murmured sleepily. "Car number fifty-nine?"

"Hyde Street," he said. "Car sixty." He traced his finger down the perfect nose. When the cable car passed he would ask her; the minute it passed. The car clattered closer, and jangled below, and the clamor receded in the night, until he heard the conductor's faint warning when it rounded to Jackson Street: "Owfudacurve!"

He kissed her and asked her to marry him and her amber eyes widened. "Oh, yes," she sighed. "Yes, yes, yes . . ."

ELEVEN

He waited in the Bellini dining room, standing because the old man had not asked him to sit. He was in uniform, because Terry had begged him to wear it, for her mother: "She's been somebody to laugh at ever since I left. Now it can all be right again; in an hour it'll be in every boccie-ball alley in North Beach. She *got* the son of a bitch, after all. And in uniform!"

Bellini sat precisely where Ben had seen him last, at the head of the table. Spread before him was a pack of cards. Ben could hear a low Italian murmur in the kitchen: Terry telling her mother.

Bellini still smelled of fish and garlic, although Terry claimed that he never went out on the boat anymore but chartered it and lived off his share of the catch. He looked much smaller than Ben remembered him. Two ruddy spots on his iron-gray cheeks matched a tall bottle of red wine by the discard pile on the table.

"*Marry* her?" Bellini snorted. "You want to *marry Teresa?*"

"I'm going to," Ben said.

"You think I want her to marry a sailor? A *marinaio?*"

"You have no choice."

"Sailor?" Terry stalked in. She leaned on the table until her face was inches from her father's. "He's not a sailor," she said tersely. "He's a chief. A *capo*, like Uncle Nick, only the cops aren't looking for *him!*"

"If she wants to marry a sailor," Bellini growled to his wife, "she could marry any *pescatore* on the Wharf. Rossi, Baccigualippi, Rinaldi . . ."

"He's *not a sailor*," Terry yelled suddenly, grabbing Ben's visored cap and jamming it into her father's face. "He's an *ufficiale!*" She jabbed the golden wings. "An *aviatore!* Can't you get that through your stupid head?"

Her mother slapped the table. Ben saw that her fingers were slim and delicate, like Terry's, though folds of fat ran around her wrist. For the first time he noticed her rings: a thick wedding band and a diamond above it big as a dime.

"Teresa!" she warned. "You want only to fight your papa, is that it?" Suddenly she smiled at Ben, for the first time. To his amazement, she was radiant when she smiled, with all of Terry's beauty and fire shining through the same golden eyes. "Now," she murmured, "let's go into the parlor, is better. Giovanni, you will get some of the grappa, no, and we will talk about this like human beings, not like a bunch of stupid wops? Si?"

In an hour she had her husband hugging Ben's shoulders and they were toasting each other and testing each other, and half an hour later Father Pietro was there and the date was set at Saint Peter and Paul's. There was no talk of a dowry, but there would be a reception at Fugazi Hall afterward, the cake would be from Gallo, and the guests would bring bags to steal the antipasto, there would be so much. It would be a wedding North Beach would not forget, and certain loudmouths would see why a girl like Teresa could afford to wait a few years for the right man.

"The admiral!" Mrs. Bellini decided suddenly. "You can get the admiral!"

Ben shook his head. "No, Mrs.———"

"Mama!" Mrs. Bellini beamed. "Mama, Benny."

He got it out. "No, Mama. I am not in too good with the admiral this week. No admiral."

"*Il capitano?*" she suggested. "The captain of the ship?"

"*Il capitano,* maybe," Ben promised. "The captain of the squadron." At the door she remembered something else and clasped her hands. "For the pictures, you can cut the cake with your sword!"

He began to tell her that CPO's, *aviatore* or not, did not own swords, but Terry squeezed his hand and he shut up. They stopped next door and eased the news to his mother, who took it well because really she had expected it ever since Porky told her that he had moved in with Terry: she even got out something about not losing a son but gaining a daughter; you could have hoped for better from an English teacher. Porky and her baby arrived while they were there and Porky even managed to kiss Terry and wish Ben luck.

Walking down the Lombard Street hill, where once he had glided kidnapped in the Packard, he told Terry that "Mama" or not, the sword was out. "She ought to know CPO's don't wear swords!"

"She thinks officers do."

He stopped short. "Did you tell her I was an *officer?*"

She shrugged. "I guess so. CPO, officer, what's the difference?"

"That, my love," he said softly, "you may spend the rest of your life finding out."

TWELVE

The sword was not out, not at all; he used Mitch Langley's, because Mama Bellini had slipped a note into the skipper's invitation asking him to bring it. He stood before a huge table sagging with antipasto in Fugazi Hall, where the Sons of Italy met on Fridays, and stabbed a cake a yard high between a tiny cock-hatted naval officer and a tinier bride in a satin dress, feeling like an idiot with the sword before his squadron mates and half the squadron officers, even though they raised their grappa and smiled and seemed not to be laughing at all.

Bulbs flashed too, capturing the imposture forever. He kept the smile glued on and cut a piece for Mitch, who stood surrounded by a cell of wide-shouldered, wide-lapelled Bellini relatives whose combined incomes would have paid the squadron's gasoline bills and whose total jail terms probably exceeded Mitch's time in the Navy.

They escaped in a shower of rice to their flower-draped Ford. The honeymoon was a dusty montage of hot days and passionate nights in motels along Route 40, marred one morning in Cheyenne, when Terry rebelled at hitting the road at six A.M. Ben had to tell her that their leave was up in three days and it was a long way to Annapolis. She didn't understand that at all, and fought leaving to the end, and was cold all day. It was their first argument, but making it up was worth it, if somewhat exhausting.

CHAPTER THREE

ONE

Ben slid from the skipper's bridge chair and stuck his head into the chart house to check their noon position. They were two hundred miles off Kyushu, still heading north. He began to wonder if the admiral was going to run them out of fuel before he turned away to a rendezvous. Seas were still rising; if they didn't replenish pretty soon, they were liable to find themselves unfueled in a gale or worse.

Barney Epstein was waiting for him in his office, smiling wickedly with a plan to make the captured kamikaze talk. He told it to Ben, who thought it ridiculous.

"The admiral loves it," Epstein said complacently. "I think he'd like me to turn regular."

"I bet he loves it, you son of a bitch. My God, Barney, the lab's asshole-deep in strike pictures! They can't take home movies!"

"Not *home* movies. Newsreels! A captured kamikaze, interrogated by Hammering Howie? Does Halsey have his own kamikaze? Does MacArthur?"

"Intelligence!" snorted Ben. "I thought you guys could dig out anything."

Epstein smiled ruefully. "Not from this cooky. Always the bow, always the smile, always the *Tai-i*—lieutenant. But he won't even tell me his name. He thinks he's the family disgrace."

"Maybe he is. Why'd he bail out?"

"Fire got too hot, I guess."

"Start pulling fingernails."

"*You* want to?" Epstein asked coldly.

"No," admitted Ben. He made a last attempt. "*Still* pictures won't do?"

Epstein shook his head. "*Sound* movies. Hidden camera. And then *bang*, we show them to him. For after the war, we'll tell him, at his local movie house. That ought to shake something loose."

Ben dialed the photo lab, spent a few minutes talking to a raging chief photo mate, and finally concluded the argument: "Admiral's orders. So set it up." He got to his feet. "O.K., Goldwyn. Let's go." He led him aft to marine country and down the brig ladder past the little platform at which Sergeant Elmore, the warden, stood writing in the brig log. "We need your Jap for an hour or so."

The sergeant called a corporal named Rich as an escort. Ben swung down the remaining steps to the six-cell brig. In one of the far cells Watkins lay behind stainless-steel lattices, staring at the overhead. On the deck beside him lay a tray of untouched food.

Ben was more interested in the Jap opposite. He was a stocky little man swamped in a borrowed flight suit, sitting unhappily on the bunk. On his head he wore the sacred *hachimaki* band. He looked up as Corporal Rich, a baby-faced youngster with innocent eyes, unlocked the door. Rich snapped his fingers and jabbed a thumb at Ben. The Jap got quickly to his feet. His flat black eyes were tragic, but he had a certain poise. He pointed to the leaves on Ben's collar and looked at the corporal. "Commandel?" he murmured.

"That's right," the marine said hurriedly. "Now come on, Buster."

The Jap pointed to Epstein's bars. "Lieutenant?" he asked tentatively.

"*Hai*," agreed Epstein thoughtfully. "I wonder who's been drilling him?"

"Where to, sir?" asked Rich hurriedly.

"Flag bridge," said Epstein.

"*Flag* bridge, sir?"

"Come on," said Ben, glancing at his watch. "Let's go."

At flag-bridge level Ben stepped from the passageway. The wind was chill and the leaden sea was undulating with the same swell he had noticed before; over everything was an odd luminosity that made him jumpy and irritable. Hammering Howie sat in his padded leather swivel chair on the wing of the bridge, watching the returning strike. A Corsair took a wave-off over the heaving deck and tucked its wheels up, roaring angrily. Ben heard a faint whine from the movie camera hidden in flag plot and noticed a mike hung unobtrusively on the splinter shield. Then Epstein was speaking, loudly and distinctly, "Admiral Howland, this is the kamikaze we shot down this morning. He's been most cooperative."

Hammering Howie Howland, studiously dignified, swiveled the chair. Grimly he studied the little Japanese standing at attention before him. Finally, with just the right blend of scorn and pity, he permitted himself a tiny nod.

The Japanese bowed deeply. For a long reverent moment his head was down. A Dauntless thundered by. The Japanese waited. Slowly, as the sound faded, he raised his head. Ben felt Corporal Rich tense beside him. The little Japanese cleared his throat politely and with immense and heartfelt respect he said, "Fuck you, Admilal."

There was an instant of shock and an explosion of laughter from the hidden sound man in flag plot. The admiral sat for an icy moment. Suddenly he lashed out and backhanded the stolid face before him. The Jap staggered, his eyes widened, but he kept up his head and said nothing.

"Back in the brig," Hammering Howie snarled. He swept them all with a deadly glance, swung forward, and set his face to the damp wind.

Ben was starting down the ladder when a tubby reserve photo mate, rumored to have worked in Hollywood, grabbed his arm. He was smoking a fat cigar, which wobbled up and down as he wound a Navy-gray movie camera. "Commander?"

"What is it, for Christ's sake?"

"Can we do it again, for close-ups?"

TWO

After lunch he climbed again to the chart house and noticed that the glass was falling. The seas were rising, too; the swell was no longer greasy but a series of hills marching south and the sun had the coppery sheen he had noticed before typhoons. He told the first lieutenant to batten down. He found Mitch sitting on the port side of the bridge, quietly available to the OOD.

"I'm buttoning up below," Ben said. "I don't like it. Have you talked to the admiral, sir?"

Mitch Langley was incapable of criticizing a superior, even to Ben. He nodded. "One more launch."

The next sweep took off into an oddly glowing western

sky, and while they were gone, the seas built. You could stand on the after end of the flight deck by the LSO's net and feel your body go light as the stern dropped away, as if you were in the rear seat of a Dauntless going over the top on a dive-bombing run. What were surging hills became peaked mountains while the sweep was out. When the first aircraft returned, there were three waveoffs from the heaving deck before the first cut. Then came a barrier crash, and as the sun set, an SBD bounced over all the wires, skidded to port, and spun in slow-motion over a crouching gun crew in the catwalk, onto her back in the swirling wake, and though the destroyers hovered for a half-hour in the deepening twilight, the pilot and crewman were lost.

That night in the lurching wardroom, the mess attendants dropped a roast, which no one wanted anyway, and even half-filled water glasses spilled.

Ben climbed to the wing of the bridge after dinner; there was no GQ tonight because not even a suicidal Japanese could get airborne. He was bone-cold in moments; the wind tore at his eyes and hair and blew his lips back over his teeth as if he had stood up in the slipstream of an open cockpit. They were almost hove to, shouldering through at five knots, huge screws barely turning. The ship would creep over an abyss, shudder on the brink as her backbone strained, then fall off and dive into a dark canyon, bury the hawsepipes, and finally shake black water from her eyes to rise again.

He knew that a thousand yards off the starboard bow slogged the *Biloxi*, that in the void somewhere beyond the mountains breaking to port the USS *Washington* was smashing her bulbous bow into the marching ranges, but he knew it only on the radar screen and in his head; his guts told him that *Shenandoah* was alone in a maelstrom and that every other ship in the group had plunged to the bottom.

Shenandoah writhed with strains she had never felt before. Earlier, below, Ben had been shocked at the creaks and groans and screams of tortured metal as she bent and twisted and flexed. On the bridge he waited for a lurch to port, lunged uphill to the pilothouse door and was through it and hanging on for the next starboard roll. In the red glow from the curtained partition behind which the quartermaster wrote his rough log, Ben saw Mitch in his seat, planted behind the streaming windows. He handed himself forward from bulkhead to grab rail to Mitch's chair and offered to relieve him, but Mitch refused.

At 2243 the gunnery officer informed the bridge that a forty-millimeter-ammo handler was missing; he had been sent from the guntub along the catwalk for foul-weather gear and never returned; they radioed the cans astern, which ostensibly searched in the blackness, but, of course, it was hopeless and they all knew it. At midnight a snipe lost his hold on a ladder and dropped five feet to the fireroom grating; from sick bay they reported that he had a concussion and a possible fracture. Finally a Corsair broke loose on the hangar deck and Ben raced below to the gallery level.

He burst through a blackout curtain to a hangar deck lighted like a huge skating rink. He squinted down at chaos. There was an ugly smell of gasoline everywhere, and an idiotic damage-control party was laying down a film of foam as slippery as soapsuds, and by the time he shouted down and got that stopped the four-ton Corsair, rampaging through the afterbay, had slammed the tail from an SBD and with every roll was moving closer to a line of her sisters, cowering with wings folded over their heads.

He clung to the rail on the gallery deck while the plane captain and a half-dozen mechs stalked the aircraft, slipping and lurching on the foam-slicked steel; they cornered it and moved in. It squatted malevolently between an SBD and a Hellcat night fighter, dripping oil obscenely from its snout. The plane captain made a dash for the wing, slipped, and tried to slither out from under as the Corsair burst loose on the next roll. The starboard wheel passed over him. A mech pulled him from further danger and the hangar-deck chief miraculously swung to a wing and scrambled to the cockpit as the plane slammed into a row of TBM's. Ben clenched his fists; if a torpedo bomber broke loose too, the hangar deck would turn to a bowling alley. But the chief locked the Corsair's brakes long enough for his mechs to tie her down, and when Ben went to sick bay to see the injured man, Al Scliris told him bitterly that outside of a chest full of broken ribs and a crushed clavicle, he was hardly hurt at all.

By 0200 Ben was in his stateroom pulling off his boots. There was a knock on the office door. He opened it to Epstein. "Hello, Commander. I saw your light through the slats."

"What's a landlubber doing up on a night like this?"

"I've been in the brig. Vomitous."

"The *brig?* Why?"

"I thought the Jap might want to talk a little, a night like this."

"Did he?"

"Calm as Buddha. He ordered it. This is the Divine Wind."

"Yeah," said Ben. "The whole U.S. fleet will go down at sea."

"It feels that way to him. He mentioned the Spanish Armada, he's hoping."

"That's nice." Ben said. When Epstein left he found it hard to sleep. He had never been in a ship before, so far as he knew, with a man who wished her sunk.

CHAPTER FOUR

ONE

They battled the typhoon for two days. Two destroyers in the eastern group broke their backs and went down. The bow was torn from a CVL in the central unit. Nineteen floatplanes were swept from catapults on cruisers and battleships; hundred-and-twenty-knot winds tore fighters and dive bombers like leaves from the flight decks; a hundred and forty-six aircraft were lost, and with the destroyers over three hundred men. On the third morning, as the gales softened and the heaving mountains shifted from gray to green and finally to blue, the three task groups spun on their sterns and combed for survivors. They criss-crossed the storm area until dusk and picked up eighteen men in life rafts, life jackets, or even clinging to debris.

The typhoon had spiraled westward toward Japan and Hammering Howie "Hit 'Em Again, Harder" had an inspiration. The other two groups retired to refuel and lick their wounds; not Hammering Howie. He got permission from the task-force commander to fuel his ships last. If the typhoon had hit Tokyo, he wanted his planes over the downtown area to greet the city when it struggled to its knees.

So that night the *Shenandoah* group broke off and headed

into a gory moon. Radar told them twice that they were
being scouted and a night fighter shot down a Kawanashi
flying boat by moonlight, but for once the Japs dropped no
flares to keep them at GQ.

Perhaps the typhoon had grounded the flare planes. Or
perhaps the empire didn't want to scare them off.

TWO

They launched at dawn in seas still surging, a hundred and fifty miles off Tokyo, and the gun crews stood hungry at their GQ stations from 0400 until 0930, when the first
strike came back. Returning pilots reported the Ginza bright
with sunlight; photos showed that it had not even rained
during the night. So much, thought Ben, for Howland's
private storm.

The wind was off Japan. Standing in the eyes of the ship,
he could sniff moist night soil from the paddies and smoke
from the Tokyo-Yokohama industrial complex, and from
CIC he got word finally that they were less than seventy
miles from Tokyo. Circling above, the combat air patrol
could see the tip of Fuji.

He heard a squabble in one of the quad mounts between
a pointer and a trainer. The men, tired from the typhoon,
were irritable, facing a day of cold sandwiches in the guntubs. Maybe he could do something about it. He left secondary conn and moved aft along the catwalk and up the island
to flag plot. On the flag bridge he paused, looking down at
the departing strike. The air officer's voice grated over the
speaker, "Start engines." There was an instant of silence and

then the whine of starters began. A plane coughed, back-fired, and all at once the flight deck was a roaring jungle of slow-turning props, props balking and coming alive in spurts of flame, props tracing condensation rings in the morning sun. Everywhere were the yellow-, green-, red-shirted crews motioning and wheeling and pointing, dodging wings and tails and sidling past the deadly gyrating arcs until, watching them, your hands grew damp, but over the years since Bremerton the men had learned to dance with death and there was seldom an accident now.

In flag plot he found Epstein fruitlessly cranking a radio through the Japanese aircraft frequencies. The admiral was studying the huge plastic plotting board, behind which a seaman, writing backward with a grease pencil, would plot the outgoing strike. Ben could see the track of the morning Kawanashi ending in a triumphant burst of red. There were no live bogies on the screen.

"We moving out?" he asked Epstein quietly.

Hammering Howie heard him and answered from the plotting board, "No, Commander, why?"

"I'd like to feed the men, sir."

"Go ahead." Howland turned to his communicator. "Make the signal, 'Secure from air defense. Set condition three except in antiaircraft batteries.' "

It wasn't what Ben had had in mind, and he almost said so, but Howland seemed to want an argument, so he thought better of it. Instead he told Mitch on the bridge.

Mitch shook his head. "I don't like it. Set *modified* condition three."

Ben nodded. "Aye, aye, sir." It left more men at GQ, but Ben thought the group should have steamed an hour away before anyone budged from the gun crews, food or not. He passed the word and headed for breakfast himself.

THREE

Ben sat at the wardroom table, very aware of Golden Boy Lee standing at his shoulder, waiting as he scanned the smooth charges on Watkins. He was damned if he'd ask him to sit down. For over four years they had seen the same action, eaten at the same mess, gone to the same movies, shared liberty boats. Before Ben became exec, they had even stood watches on the bridge together. In all the years not one unnecessary word had passed between them. He knew that Golden Boy's cool blue eyes were on him, challenging him to find a misplaced comma or a misspelled word. He handed the sheet to Barney Epstein, who was a lawyer and could not find an error either. In the smooth they seemed proved already, as in effect they were. Ben felt a tug of pity for his ex-steward. He initialed the sheet in the margin and handed it back to Christy Lee. "Go down to the brig and serve him. And get our depositions today, to send to Pearl. One from everybody who was at mast, including yourself." The whole fiasco seemed a month ago: it was only six days.

Ben watched him leave the wardroom, typically carrying out the order before eating breakfast. He hadn't meant that, but screw him; let him starve. He was conscious that Epstein had sensed his loathing; probably he thought it was the simple jealousy of a mustang officer for an Academy man already touched somehow with stars.

He ordered breakfast, watching the wardroom fill with tired pilots in flight gear. Epstein began to probe at the Academy-constipated language of naval jurisprudence, comparing justice as applied by ex-law students to law as practiced by ex-midshipmen. Ben pretended to listen, toying with his eggs; Epstein did not realize that he was talking to an expert on Annapolis and midshipmen but he let him ramble on.

FOUR

Honeymoon over, dusty and tired, he had rumbled into Annapolis with Terry on a Saturday afternoon, bouncing over eighteenth-century bricks past teahouse signs swinging in the hot Chesapeake wind on Duke of Gloucester Street. A stream of midshipmen on liberty trickled steadily from the main gate, all starched white uniforms and high collars and glittering brass buttons. He felt a pang at what might have been. Terry squeezed his hand.

"Cheer up, Ben. You've got the only girl in sight."

"A great place," he agreed, "to open a whorehouse."

"We could check it out with my Uncle Nick."

They found a place to live on King George Street, where the town, like a feudal village, snuggled against the Academy wall. It was grimy and damp; in winter they had practically to live in the kitchen, the rest was so cold. The plumbing was horrible but the place was close to first class gate so that Ben could cut through the yard to catch the motor launch to the air station across the Severn and leave Terry the car for the day.

Their house was a firetrap, but long ago, perhaps in Admiral Dewey's day, it had earned Academy approval as fit lodging for a midshipman's weekend "drag." For two years Ben refused to let Terry rent the spare bedroom, although the money would have come in handy; he was damned if he'd have her cleaning up after Bryn Mawr girls or Baltimore debs. It was a dull two years: every other chief on the station was twenty years older than Ben and their social contacts with midshipmen were zero. It was so dreary a tour that out of boredom Ben picked up a high-school diploma through the Armed Forces Institute, in case he ever went up for warrant officer, and enrolled in college courses in engineering. But one November afternoon before the Army game Christy Lee, All-American hope of the fleet, stepped onto their creaky porch and everything changed.

He was regimental commander. Ben had read an article on him in the *Baltimore Sun* and seen his picture in *Time* and once paused to watch him in the flesh taking the weekly review on Worden Field, trim and broad-shouldered, adding stature that morning even to the bellhop jacket midshipmen had worn since Admiral Nelson's day. At close range on the porch he was still a picture-perfect midshipman, with a strong tanned face and lean firm jaw. He was as tall as Ben and his hair was curly blond and he had direct blue eyes and his co-ed fanmail, it was said, ran to five hundred letters a season. He had a strong grip and an easy smile and he wanted a room for his drag the weekend after the game.

Ben turned him down but asked him in for a beer. They sat with Terry at the kitchen table and talked football. "Navy by twenty-one points," Christy Lee promised of Saturday's game.

Terry studied him. "We can't get tickets," she murmured.

Ben's face flamed. "Jesus," he flared, "why don't we just hit him on the head and search his pockets?"

Christy Lee grinned. Somehow his teeth had been spared violence. He handed Ben two golden Army-game tickets as though he were passing a book of matches. "On the *forty?*" breathed Ben.

"They gave us six."

"What about your family?"

The blue eyes turned blank. "Just my dad. I sold the other three."

"Well, here," Ben said, tight on cash but cornered, "let me buy these!"

Christy Lee shook his head decisively, so they had to promise him the room, of course. Army-Navy Saturday they arose at dawn. Terry sleepily filled their thermos with bourbon and coffee and he backed the Ford from the garage. There was a tang of snow in the air and the cobbled streets were supercharged with tension. The overcoated ranks swinging from the yard toward the electric train punctuated the Navy songs with puffs of steam. A block from their house the Commodore, a doddering relic of the Class of '82, stood outside his screen door in a bathrobe waving a tiny flag of blue and gold.

"My God," marveled Ben, "look at that!"

"Crazy," yawned Terry. "The Commodore, the Academy, the whole silly game. But it's getting me out of that g.d. house."

In Philly they slid into their seats across the aisle from the massed blue regiment, which would stand throughout the game. They introduced themselves to Golden Boy's father. He was a tall lean oil-rigger with kind and lonely eyes and a palm of steel. All the first half he smiled down with radiant pride on his son. Golden Boy deserved it. He had hands like an angel and an eye like a hawk. His passes were beautiful floaters and looked so easy to handle that Ben longed to be on the field loping under them. He was as great a broken-field runner as the papers had said.

He had given Ben a locker-room pass and asked him to

bring his father down after the game. "He has to go back on the bus tonight, and I won't get to see him at all."

At half time, over Terry's steaming, dynamited coffee, Ben told Lee's father of the dressing-room pass. His face glowed. "Say, now, Ben! That's right thoughtful of him!" A stream of players burst back from the lockers and the regiment went wild but not before Ben heard Lee's father say, quite quietly, "I wish his mother could see him now. Or his sisters . . ."

Navy won, 14–7; Golden Boy averaged five yards a play and everyone knew that he had cinched a spot on anyone's All-American team. In the chaotic locker room Lee grabbed his father, hauled him up on a bench, and bellowed for silence. He introduced him to teammates too excited to listen, and the tall Texan grinned and waved his calloused hand lightly to a few offhanded cheers.

Golden Boy dressed and they met Terry outside and bucked a mass of Navy brass, midshipmen, and civilians who wanted to shake hands with Golden Boy Lee; finally they got the old man onto a bus and watched it go. When Lee turned back, his face was flushed and dreamy.

"That admiral shaking hands with me—the old man won't forget that in his whole life."

"And that's important," Terry said thoughtfully.

Golden Boy glanced at her. "Well, he *is* my dad. And *hey*, when that dolly wanted my autograph, did you see the *look* on his face?"

After that Christy Lee began to use the spare room almost every weekend for his drags, mostly a dull-eyed admiral's daughter from Washington to whom he finally gave a miniature. Ben would pick her up at the station because midshipmen weren't allowed in cars. When Christy wasn't dragging he brought his roommate Bottle Bailey and their friends. Terry was queen. Most of them were not much younger than she and the football men and regimental stripers who moved in Christy's wake were the top of the very select.

"All these guys," Ben warned her, "are horny as hoot owls. They make me nervous."

"Not me," Terry grinned.

"I noticed. I'm going to blast them loose."

"Not Christy," Terry said. "That isn't fair."

"Two tickets for the Army-Navy game don't mean we have to adopt him, for Christ's sake!"

"Damn!" she decided, studying him. "Jealous!"

He wasn't, of course; to prove it he dropped the subject. There was some reward: sitting in the moist kitchen drinking beer on weekends, he learned something of the kiln beyond the Academy wall in which the regular naval officer was fired. There was an honor system, but it stretched. You never lied and of course you never cheated, but the code under which a West Pointer was said to live—where you turned yourself in for breaking a rule—was not for the midshipman. Cheating in an exam was a little worse than turning in a classmate or shagging the admiral's wife, but it was all right to corral a midshipman who had just finished the exam and ask him what the questions were, especially if you played football together. Most of the conversation in their kitchen was of steam and bull—English—and of slashes, who studied too hard or buckets who studied not hard enough, or of starring in skinny or bilging juice.

But Ben found himself falling behind in his own self-imposed courses. He was becoming a middleman between the midshipmen and the local liquor store; he could hardly get off the squeaky back porch for the empty beer bottles. One night he came home from across the river to find Christy

Lee with his feet on the kitchen table alone with Terry, drinking beer; when he suggested that he needed the table to study, Terry glowered and Christy, although he moved quickly enough, looked hurt.

"Sure, Ben." He shrugged into his greatcoat. "Say, if you ever need any help on that stuff—"

"I can sweat it," Ben said stiffly. "I'm already up to the nine-times table."

When Christy left, Terry said, "You know, Ben, you can be an awful pain in the ass."

"Sorry. But he's using us. If he had any place else to go swill beer, we'd never see him again." He opened his book. "Well, he can start looking. He's got to go."

"Ben!"

"I mean it."

Later that night, serving him coffee, she asked, "Can he come to Christmas dinner?"

He looked up from his math. "Christy? Hell, they get Christmas leave! He'll take off like a bird!"

"To Port Arthur, Texas?" she demanded. "That's where he spent one Christmas. In his dad's hotel room, overlooking the Texaco refinery. They had Christmas dinner in a *diner* backed up against the Sabine River levee. Ham! No turkey!"

"How do you know?"

"It just slipped out."

"I hope that's all that slipped out," Ben said brutally.

"You're hilarious, you know? I think I liked you better when you were moaning around about losing your squadron." Her eyes went suddenly soft. "Ham for Christmas, Ben. Think of that. And us stuffed with turkey! Well, *can* he?"

"You're too damn young to be housemother to a bunch of

sex-starved midshipmen. Goddamn it, I'll get you a puppy, or a kitten, or—what about a baby?"

"A baby will do it," she promised. "But in the meanwhile . . . turkey . . . cranberry . . . drumsticks . . . and Christy in a *diner*, Ben?"

"Go ahead," he sighed. "Ask him."

"I already have," she murmured.

"I figured," he said.

Golden Boy gave them a set of dinner plates with Academy scenes delicately done in blue; they must have cost him a month's pay, and they ate Christmas dinner on them. The turkey was all that was advertised, and afterward they sat around the tiny tree in the dismal living room and drank egg nog and Golden Boy placed a call to his father in Port Arthur. By the time the call went through, Ben and he were both drunk, and there were actually tears in Golden Boy's eyes when he came out of the kitchen, where the phone was.

"Poor old bastard," he said. "I should have gone down."

"Thanks," said Terry dryly.

"I didn't mean that," said Golden Boy. He reached out and prodded a glittering red ball on their own tree. "Christmas is a bad time for him."

Terry relented. "Why, Christy?"

For a long while Lee studied his drink. "Because," he said finally, "he lost his whole damn family one Christmas. Everybody but me . . ." The blue eyes were glazed: Lee wiped his lips and spooned another egg nog from the bowl and changed his mind and poured it back into the bowl. He moved restlessly to the ancient piano and struck a note, tentatively, and plunked a one-fingered bar of "God Rest Ye Merry, Gentlemen." "Three days before Christmas of thirty. I was ten. He took me to a basketball game, a lousy tank-town high-school game, it wasn't even close. In fact . . ."

He struck discord. "In fact, he wanted to leave before the last quarter, but no, not me. I had to see it, all the way through. He says no, now, but I remember—I had to see it all the way through, I had to stay—"

Terry said gently, "Come on, Christy. It doesn't matter."

"No," he said tightly, "it doesn't." He struck discord again, louder. "And now, he comes all the way up here to see me play football? How's he do it? How's he forget?"

Terry said, "Whatever it is, *whatever* happened, he couldn't blame you for wanting to see the finish of a basketball game! And you can't blame yourself!"

Christy Lee looked up from the piano. His eyes were clear again. He smiled lopsidedly. "For what?"

"For wanting to see the end of the game!"

"For that? Christ no! That's funny, that's very funny."

"Well, what *happened*? What *do* you blame yourself for?"

"Nothing," Golden Boy said mildly. "Who said I did?" He was spending the night; he yawned. "Well, sack time. Good night, kind people. Good night . . ."

"Good night," Terry said softly. "*You* don't make sense, but the plates are lovely."

After the plates Ben could never bring himself to evict Golden Boy or, for that matter, any of his clique, and Lee seemed properly grateful. In April, while the Royal Navy tried to fend German troops off Norway and the midshipmen's hats bloomed white again, Golden Boy came through with two guest invitations to the Spring Hop, forcing Ben to rent a tux and inciting Terry to excitedly rework her satin wedding gown into a precarious formal. But the morning of the dance Washington called him at work across the river.

It was Mitch Langley, who had spent a year at the Navy Department and was leaving for a new air group in

Bremerton. Mitch wanted him at the Bureau of Aeronautics that day; something had come up. Ben unloaded his morning flight of midshipmen on a tolerant j.g. and signed out an N3N floatplane and within an hour he was standing before Mitch's desk in the deserted Navy Department.

"Ben, they're giving chief AP's temporary commissions, some of them. I want you first in line."

"*Commissions?*" Ben's heart jumped. "You mean *warrants?*"

"Commissions."

"Come on, Commander! They make ensigns out of Yale kids with a two-week ROTC cruise on the Delaware. But a CPO with ten years in and three thousand hours in the air? Hell no!"

"Now, Ben! You've seen mustangs from World War One."

"We're not at war yet. How about my deck court?"

"I'm going to introduce you to the senior member of the selection board. That ought to help."

They drove to Arlington and Ben met the captain who would head the board. He stopped at Mitch's home to say hello to Mitch's wife and over a drink Mitch promised to get his yeoman to work on the forms and letters Monday. "You're too old for ensign, we'll try for j.g." It suddenly struck home: temporary or not, a commission was a commission; he was going to make it after all. It was nearly dark and the N3N had an open cockpit so Mitch invited him to spend the night. He remembered that Terry did not know where he was; he slugged down another drink and phoned home and told her he'd be back tomorrow, saving the good news for when he could see her face. She was very cool, and in the background he could hear Bottle Bailey laughing and the chime of women's voices; the Saturday-night scene out of Hogarth was taking shape in his kitchen.

"Party time?" he asked. "Jesus, don't they ever quit?"

"Party time," she said acidly. "And you know what I'm wearing?"

"Not a smile, from your voice— No, what are you wearing?" he asked good-naturedly, swirling his drink.

"My new formal. I'm just wondering who'll take me to——"

Jesus, the hop! "Oh, hell! I'm sorry, Terry. But look, I had no choice, and by the time I could get to Anacostia and fly back and then get a launch across the river—"

"In other words, not you?"

He groped for her sense of humor. "Well, you might stuff that tux. We're paying for it."

"*You* stuff it," she flared. "And you just *may* pay for it."

"What do you mean by *that?*"

"Good-bye, Birdman."

Seething, he hung up. Here he was, changing their whole future, and she was bitching about a college dance. He had dinner at Mitch's and afterward, smoking cigars, they stepped to the back patio. It was a warm, clear night with a good moon; suddenly he wanted to get home to Terry, make up, tell her the news. He changed his mind about spending the night and Mitch drove him to the Naval air station at Anacostia and he flew singing home at fifty feet across the Patuxent and down the winding Severn, wings rocking in time to "Nancy Lee," scaring hell out of fishermen and froggers anchored off the banks.

He crossed the yard afoot and noticed that the lights in Dahlgren Hall were going out: the hop was over. His own house was dark. He crossed the creaking porch and stepped into the living room and stumbled over a midshipman and his drag clinched on the floor by the couch, and then onto another pair by the battered piano. "Jesus," he muttered.

He felt through the dining room, which reeked of spilled beer, to the lighted kitchen. Lee's roommate, Bottle, sat soddenly at the kitchen table, his full-dress jacket open. He was a big, black-haired Boston-Irish tackle. When his eyes focused on him an odd look crossed his face. He lurched to his feet.

"Where's Terry?" Ben asked tautly. An ache began in his chest; he found himself breathing hard.

"Now, Benny-boy, don't get your balls in an uproar――"

Ben shoved past him and moved through the house in long strides, racing up the stairs and into their bedroom. There was nobody there. He stepped down the hall and slammed a shoulder into the spare-bedroom door, not even checking to see if it was locked. It splintered open at the latch. He jerked on the light cord. There was a startled shriek of bedsprings and Golden Boy Lee, half-dressed, faced him, arms hanging loose. Terry, rumpled and red-eyed, glared at him as he moved in on Lee.

It was short and dirty; Ben knew that if he didn't finish it quickly he was licked. He feinted with a left, jolted a right into Lee's hard gut, and took an elbow in the neck, staggering him, as Lee lurched for the door. Ben leaped in close, risking the steely biceps, and brought his knee up hard into Lee's groin, once and then again. Lee went white and dropped to his knees. Ben swung a right from his ankles into the open face. He hit him again and kicked him as he toppled. He moved to the bed and looked down. Terry's golden eyes regarded him defiantly.

"You got here too soon," she murmured. "Nothing happened. *Next* time――"

"Why?" he demanded. "For Christ's sake, *why?*"

She got up, smoothing her crumpled formal. "Why Washington? On *business?* On a Saturday *afternoon?*"

He slammed into their bedroom and began to pack his gear. Downstairs he tossed Lee's stupid painted dishes one by one from the dining-room window. Then he picked up his bags and left.

FIVE

He was living in the chief's quarters on the *Reina Mercedes*, the barracks ship tied to the Academy dock, when he got his commission three weeks later. Terry still had the house; apparently she didn't want to go home, although he had brought the Ford back for her to make it easy for her to leave. He had a crazy surge of joy when he unfolded the cardboard tube and spread the parchment on the table in the chiefs' mess, forgetting for a moment that she would never see it. A lanky chief boatswain read it over his shoulder. " 'Reposing special trust—' Benny, you s'pose that's really Roosevelt's signature?" Ben passed a thumb across it and decided that it was stamped. He told the chief to pass the word that he'd throw a wetting-down party that night at the Legion Hall. He put the commission back into the tube for mailing to San Francisco; his mother could have it framed if she wanted. He wandered to the yard, vaguely aware that Monday he'd have to hit Robber's Row for uniforms, morose and discontent now that he had his desire and no one to tell.

The sudden roll of the Lone Drummer and the chant of male voices told him that the regiment was marching to chow. He found himself watching from the shadow of Tecumseh, Indian-chief god of the failing midshipman. The Navy's monolithic heart stood before him in blue and gold; rank upon rank of midshipmen, sheltered in the arms of

Bancroft Hall. Golden Boy Lee and his staff stood dead-center. The platoons in motion were singing. As the first units passed into Bancroft the chorus was hushed in the womb and there was silence. Then the company commander nearest him grated an order and the company wheeled and swung by in the easy Navy stride, picking up from some mysterious source, like a triggered school of fish, the song:

There's an aggregation known throughout the country
Always ready for a frolic or a fray. . . .

He knew that there were pot-bellies in the ranks and buck-teeth and an occasional pair of glasses, and yet the norm somehow hid them and they all looked exactly the same.

From their high and mighty station
They are known throughout the nation
As the boys from down in Crabtown on the Bay. . . .

His own commission might be cleverly stamped, but he knew suddenly that theirs would be signed by the President. Golden Boy Lee, who had not a visible sign left on his face from Ben's attack—Christ, he hadn't left even that mark on the endless ranks—muttered a quiet command to his staff and it wheeled and fell in between two battalions.

In the midst of scrap and scrimmage
You will find the busy image
Of the spoiled and pampered pets of Uncle Sam.

A penny-pinching congressman had coined the phrase and the complacent Academy had absorbed the "spoiled-and-pampered" image into its bloodstream, so that West Pointers from Hell-on-the-Hudson called Annapolis the Country Club on the Severn.

It was no country club, Ben knew. The classrooms were high-pressure boilers into which young men were tossed to survive or perish, and the survivors emerged a band of brothers like Nelson's, only more tightly knit. They might laugh at the old school tie in their songs, but threaten an Annapolis man and watch the ranks close.

Well, the hell with them. Let them remember their class-rooms and hazing and extra duty in the snow. He had a few memories himself: of holystoning decks barefoot in pre-dawn darkness and of hunger pangs in the Dago brig and of carrier launches in Force Seven seas.

Ben found that he was alone on the terrace save for the enlisted drummer beating himself frostily back to Santee Basin. It began to rain.

SIX

The naval hospital paged him that night at the Legion Hall in the midst of a stilted celebration. Somebody had spotted the Ford folded messily in two in a ditch off the Baltimore Road: they had called the state troopers, who had found Terry alone, unconscious and bleeding, and discov-ered Ben's name on the commissary pass in her pocketbook.

Ben borrowed a car from a chief and raced through the main gate and across College Creek to the Naval Academy Hospital. By the time he arrived he was cold sober. He found a sleepy j.g. doctor working on his wife.

Ten years from the first day they had mated, two years after their wedding, he discovered that he loved her. He dis-covered it in an instant, watching her slip away. He had loved the dirty chuckle all the time, and the twinkle in her amber eyes and the way she would tickle him to awaken him, fiercely, a matter of life and death in the winter unless she wanted to start the furnace herself.

He grabbed the j.g. and demanded the senior surgeon, *now*. Incredibly, he got him, at 0300, and he had been right, he knew it by the older man's concern. For almost twenty-four hours she lay balanced in a coma, on the edge. Once, the next morning—or maybe the next afternoon, it was all a head-splitting jumble—he saw the Catholic chaplain hovering innocently. He told him to get his ass out, he was doing his own praying, and hers. He was backing the prayers with a few threats and promises too and he wanted no interference from the Church. The Church, wounded, left.

She awakened after dusk, the second night. She saw Ben and the great eyes came alive. She touched the bandages on her face.

"Raggedy Ann?" he murmured. "Not for long."

"Raggedy Ann and Raggedy Andy," she recited, "jumped in the sack— Ben?" She looked scared. "I don't remember the rest."

"Good," he said. "We'll start all over."

SEVEN

Father Epstein stirred his coffee at the wardroom table, still rumbling about naval justice. "What the hell will that poor black bastard face, anyway? Defended by some trade-school idiot with a semester of naval justice? Before a Navy captain and a half-dozen commanders who think that anybody that *belches* at captain's mast is a goddamned traitor to his country, and they'll be judge and jury. And the appellate court will be an admiral who thinks the same!"

Ben felt the jarring in the soles of his feet, or perhaps

the seat of his pants or the pit of his stomach. He raised his hand, listening, and Epstein trailed off. Ben felt it again: it was a single twenty-millimeter gun firing from the eyes of the ship, transmitted aft along a tenth of a mile of steel deck. No one else noticed. Half down the table the two chaplains commiserated over their stolen altar; the gunnery officer, whom he would never again see alive, replaced his rolled napkin in its cubbyhole on the bulkhead and strolled toward the door. Laughter burst from the junior officers at the next table. His last fleeting flash of a life that would never be quite the same was of Chief Mario hesitating at the galley door with a stainless-steel milk pitcher, sensing something too. Ben put down his fork and said to Epstein, "Something's coming," as if he really knew. He was half out of his chair when a forty began to pound, much closer than the twenty. As he lurched for the door he felt through the balls of his feet three quick jolts—five-inch guns firing— and then the *kong . . . kong . . . kong . . .* began on the 1 MC speaker.

Instinctively he glanced at his watch: 10:16. For an instant before time ran wild, it froze: tanned aviators half rising from white tablecloths, a steward in a starched jacket stock-still against the wardroom green. Then he felt a deep, gut-jarring concussion and heard a clang as if someone had dropped a ten-ton steel piano from the flight deck to the hangar deck. The linoleum beneath him jerked mischievously sideways. He fell, twisting his knee; before he hit the deck the lights were out and the wardroom was black until a burst of orange flame from a sudden galley fire cast witch shadows on the bulkheads.

From somewhere forward and below there was a greater but more cushioned shock, and the deck rose ponderously, tossing him into the air so that he landed again on the twisted knee. He heard the chaplain cursing softly; the wardroom table had fallen on his foot, bruising his ankle.

Ben scrambled to his feet. The duty cook was putting out the galley fire with a broom, flinching as gobs of grease stung him back with every whack. Ben had to get to secondary conn: God knew what had happened topside. He groped along the bulkhead and found a portable battle lantern; when he stabbed it through the wreckage of the tables he saw that officers were climbing from the shambles. The wardroom was filling with smoke drawn in through the ventilators, which meant that there were breaks in the duct and a hangar deck fire—oh, Jesus, with half the planes below and fueled and armed—and a long chow line doubtless snaking between them, and the double hatch open to the messdeck below. He could not think of it, not now, or he would never get to his station.

He scrambled over broken crockery and out the wardroom door. The passageway was pitch-black except for his own light. He sensed bodies groping past, officers and stewards. He felt a hand on his arm and heard Epstein's quiet voice: "Ben?"

"Stay with me," he barked, for Epstein could not possibly know the ship. He felt the jar of quads again and cringed at another attack. She was badly hit already and seemed uneasy beneath his feet, as if she had broken her back. He shot his battle lamp around, oriented himself with a frame number, and with Epstein behind him dashed to a ladder to the hangar deck. He was halfway up when he noticed that the hatchway was framed in incandescent light. Suddenly a crawling figure blacked out the strange glow above, pulled at the combing, and snaked through the hatch. Ben felt the impact of the body on his shoulders and yelped a warning to Epstein below. For the first time in his life he whiffed burning human flesh as the man slithered past; then a bolt of heat from the hangar deck hit him and he was sliding back down himself. He disentangled Epstein from the man, who was jerking convulsively, a burned rag doll of charred clothing and blackened flesh. Ben touched him; a seared arm twitched, and in moments the man was dead.

"He's gone," he said. Smoke lay forward, so they started aft, looking for a ladder to the island. Once he tripped on a hatch combing and landed on hands and knees. The light clattered across the passageway and went out.

"Shit!" he exploded. The dark was black velvet. He felt for the lantern, shook it hopelessly. He had an instant of infant terror. Far up the passageway he saw an oval reddish glow. Together they stumbled toward it like moths to a flame. It was an open door, above the ladder to the brig, and suddenly a tall figure appeared in it and raced down the passageway toward them. Ben jumped aside but a sinewy shoulder caught him in the arm and whirled him against the bulkhead and the figure was lost in the darkness down the passageway and the glow had left the open door.

Then he heard the voice faintly, from far, far below. He heard it, wanting to reject it, for it could not be—the brig was emptied at the first clang of the general alarm—and besides, his place was topside, he could not spare the time. If the voice had been screaming for help he might have convinced himself that the man was dying, that it was too late. But it was deep and resonant and strong and angry; you knew when you listened to it that the man who was shouting was very much alive.

"Where is he?" murmured Epstein.

Ben swung through the open door and started down the ladder. "Brig," he said.

"Oh my God," groaned Epstein, but Ben heard his feet on the rungs above him and knew that he had followed.

EIGHT

Whoever had left the brig—and Ben promised him, with the ladder rungs searing his hands and the burned-hair smell again in his nose, that he would search him out and hang him from the highest yardarm in the fleet—whoever had left could have stayed another ten seconds and the fire would have passed. In the light of the flaming brig log-book he saw the warden sergeant dead. Ben shoved the book to the deck. It flared higher and Ben could see a rack of flashlights. He handed one to Epstein and kept one and stamped out the logbook fire and shone the light on the marine's body. His eyebrows were gone and his hair too and the skin on his face, though hardly charred, was bloated so that his eyes were narrowed and he looked Chinese. He had died of burned lungs, and it had been very quick. He jabbed the light around. In the dead marine's hand he saw a glitter. He snatched at it, tugged, and the single key, chained to a lacquered wooden plaque emblazoned with globe and anchor, came loose. He took a deep breath and slid down the remaining ladder, kicking at the flames playing in the paint at its base.

"Who is that?" bellowed Perry Watkins from the last cell. "Who's that come down?"

"Take it easy, Watkins," Ben said, lurching to the rear. He flicked the light at the huge Negro. His eyebrows were singed, his hair was sooty, the whites of his eyes were shot red. There was a huge burned spot across his dungaree shirt, and his chest oozed serum; his pants and belly were crisscrossed with the pattern of the lattice bars, stenciled by flame from his stomach to his knees.

"Why you here, Commander? I didn't yell for help!" He grinned wildly. "We gonna *drown*, man!"

"Who's alive?" Ben demanded, unlocking the cell.

"The Jap, he's alive, I think."

Ben turned, opened the prisoner's door, and shone his light inside. The kamikaze was lying on the deck but breathing, and breathing hard.

"Get him!" he told Watkins.

Ben checked the other cells: Rainey and the two other brig prisoners, closer to the ventilator above, must have breathed pure flame. Their staring eyeballs were scorched and the skin on their faces crisscrossed like grilled steak.

"Hurry up, dammit!" Ben said, starting up the ladder. As his face grew level with the marine's body, he paused. It was lying oddly. Its arms were stretched toward the ladder, as if in protest, or supplication; as if whoever had knocked Ben flying in the passageway had torn away violently. Again he felt the bitter anger and promised justice to the charred mummies below.

In the passageway he pointed Epstein and Watkins toward sick bay, hoping that it was still there. Then he dogged the door to the brig to confine the smell of burned flesh and began to wind through a labyrinth toward the island structure.

He worked his way forward and outboard. Somewhere along the route, stumbling over bodies of whimpering, dazed men; squeezing past rescue parties tugging toasted stick figures from ladders which had sucked flame like chimneys, as everyone except BUSHIPS had always said they would, he glanced at his watch. It read 10:22. It was his first hint that his mental clock had gone crazy. It was only six minutes since GQ had sounded, and he would have sworn that it had been an hour.

Dazzled, he stood blinking on the starboard catwalk, only a hundred feet from his battle station. He glanced along the flight deck and saw that the planes aft were enveloped in a furnace from which oily black smoke arose a thousand feet, corkscrewing as Mitch spun the ship. A Corsair, its pilot charred in the cockpit, sat miraculously still ticking over behind a wall of flame. The forward elevator, bent almost double, rested twenty yards from its shaft. The flight deck was smoking like a bride's waffle iron.

The destroyers had drawn in to strengthen the inner screen. Ben, trotting forward to his battle station, heard distant firing and glanced along the line of sight of his own gunners. He saw a row of giant periods appear slowly in the sky, terminated by an oily black comma trailing away from an explosion. He finally spotted the target, a shattered Betty gliding down toward the *Lex,* drawing hyphens of inky smoke across a white sky until it struck and sent up a flame-tipped crown of spray.

A lookout forward was yelling and pointing. Ben squinted at the white cloud base. He caught a glimpse of a second Betty, climbing for cover, and when it disappeared, it left a tiny spot. At first he thought they had torn off an engine, but a Betty did not climb on one engine, and then he saw that it was a bomb, but a bomb with a peculiar, dogged trajectory which did not change at all except in size, and now he saw that the bomb must have wings, and it did: short, stubby wings and a miniscule tail and sunlight glinting from a Plexiglas canopy, and the bomb had brains, and he knew that no matter how Mitch on the bridge twisted and turned the ship the bomb would turn too.

Now Ben could see three orange-red spots of rocket flame from the aft end of the tiny coffin. Hypnotized and slack-mouthed, the gun crews stared until a lone marine broke his trance and began to track, and squeezed out half a dozen tracers far too short and behind, but it pulled the cork and suddenly the whole port side, all the way aft to the flight deck, was firing, and still the *baka* came, headed straight at Ben and growing and growing—the end of it all, then, would be here—and then it passed over with a sonic boom and hit in the conflagration on the after flight deck. Ben was a football field away from the impact but it jolted him from his heels to his neck. It jarred the stubborn Corsair loose and it came bounding up the deck, burning at last, swerving first toward the island and then to port, trying to fly with a dead pilot and wings and tail afire. Ben watched it coming and ducked and looked over the side. It hit the water in a shower of sparks, flipped a wing at the sky, and scraped helplessly down the length of the hull before it dived in the wake. He felt the shaft RPM's fall off and glanced over the catwalk rail as he raced forward. He hoped that it was merely that Mitch was trying to starve the flames of wind passage, but deep down he knew they were losing steam.

The forecastle was crowded with air-group refugees. A little knot of airedales stood by the port anchor, dazed and silent and somehow sullen; Doc Scliris was tending a blackened, moaning row of men lying by the anchor chain, some in litters, some writhing on the steel deck and some very still. Markowitz spotted Ben, grabbed the XO helmet from the rack, and raced over, trailing a phone line. "Christ, Commander, am I glad to——"

"Magazines flooded?" Ben demanded, jamming on the helmet.

"They tried, sir. Ruptured lines." He recited the damage: a two-fifty-kilogram bomb at frame seventy-six, followed by the Kate that dropped it. The bomb had exploded between flight and hangar deck, wiping out the men in the mess line, tossing the forward elevator up its own shaft, and starting the hangar-deck fire. The engine of the bomber had penetrated the flight deck and started another hangar-deck fire among the eighteen aircraft, fueled and armed, waiting for the elevator. No one had survived long enough on the hangar deck to even break out foam. The fire had licked down the double hatch to the galley on the messdeck. Auxiliary pressure on the fire mains was barely keeping the flight deck from bursting into flame. There were red lights blinking on the magazine-temperature panel in damage-control central, and damage control itself was taking smoke through its ventilators and had most of its men in rescue breathing apparatus. The assessment hadn't even touched on the new *baka* damage.

"Call the bridge——" began Ben.

Markowitz shook his head. "The JW's out, sir. The only people I can talk to are damage-control central on the 1 JV."

Without communications the ship was spastic. If the men died in damage-control central, she could not even fight the fever in her guts; if the unflooded magazines blew, she was doomed with them all.

He grabbed a seaman, wandering haphazardly. "Get to communications," he said. "Bring me back a walkie-talkie." He might have been pronouncing a sentence of death, but he had to talk to the bridge.

Markowitz clapped his hands over his earphones to hear. "The snipes are abandoning the firerooms and the forward engine room."

"*Shit!*" When her steam was lost, they were through.

There was a mighty crash in the bow bulkhead aft of them and a comet screamed over their heads. The huge new Tiny Tims that they had been so glad to get, slung beneath the Corsairs' wings on the hangar deck, were cooking off. For the first time Ben faced it. They would have to leave her, if they survived long enough to get off.

He glanced at his watch. Eight minutes ago he had been eating eggs in the wardroom.

NINE

Later he wondered how they did it and even why they did it, but then he was too grateful to care. Some day he would discover that the skipper of the cruiser *Dallas*, which came crashing alongside despite *Shenandoah's* un-flooded magazines, was a classmate of Mitch's. She took aboard the wounded and the air group, too valuable to lose, and, it turned out, ninety-three unscratched deserters from the ship's company. The captain of the *Bangor* was a class-mate, too; he backed and filled ahead until he was a sitting duck for the next kamikaze or even a Tiny Tim hurtling from their own guts. The *Bangor* shot a messenger line to their forecastle in a gleaming blessed arc and began to pay her tow cable off the stern. Ben saw only one blinkered message from the *Dallas* and none at all from the *Bangor*, but the Academy had things well in hand; it was as if psychic channels lay between the skippers, or as if they had taken a special course in what to do when a flagship was burning fifteen air-minutes from an enemy shore and drifting in.

It was spectacular seamanship and it took guts to risk the *Dallas* and *Bangor* and their crews for another ship when you knew that her bomb-stowage magazines and the five-inch handling rooms were baking below and could see ready-ammo boxes smoking in the catwalk guntubs. The only trouble was that in this particular case it was utterly useless: the *Shenandoah*, with no steam for her winches forward, could no more pull the five-ton tow cable across the gap between her and the *Bangor* than keep pressure up in her fire mains.

Ben had to try, of course. He jumped like a Union Square orator to the starboard bollard, where they would drop the cable's loop if ever they got it, and formed a line of half the men milling uselessly about; there was only room on the forecastle for a hundred to pull at once. They began to haul on the messenger and the two-inch line which followed, and soon they had a three-inch manila hawser in hand and then a six-inch one and were straining and falling on the moist steel deck, gaining an inch and losing it and gaining it back as the impossible weight of the steel cable, sagging in the swell between the *Bangor*'s stern and their own bow, tugged back contemptuously. It was impossible in the most heartbreaking, blistering way, and they all knew it. The *Bangor* began finally to blink, and Ben read: REQUEST YOU EXPEDITE HAULING HAWSER AND CABLE. AM AFRAID OF FOULING MY SCREWS IN SLACK.

Well, the bridge would answer that. Ben swallowed his anger. You couldn't blame the *Bangor*'s skipper for worrying about his propellers. He moved forward to the hawsepipe and looked down along the gentle curve of the hawser to the point, two hundred feet away, where it joined the eye of the cable.

Their starboard list had grown greater and it was difficult

footing. He knew that Mitch must be counterflooding; he thought of millions of gallons of water sloshing through gutted compartments below, pumped aboard too by the destroyers said to be aft trying to help fight the hangar-deck fire. On the bilge water would be oil and on the oil a scum of aviation gasoline, but there was no use thinking of that.

Markowitz beckoned him from the tether of his phone line. "The starboard forward twenties want an officer! Catlett won't let anybody off the catwalks!"

"Oh, Christ," Ben said. He put a gnarled chief boatswain in charge of the hawser and stepped aft. Catlett, his cheek bandaged, had organized the gun crews and they were jettisoning ammunition from the ready-ammo boxes, flinging it to the water below. As Ben moved toward them, a great surge of flame roared from the hangar deck. The men squatted, coughing, behind splinter shields; Ben saw dim shapes scurry for shelter at the island structure. Catlett was the first on his feet when the flame retreated. "Come on, you bastards," he yelled, "get on it!"

They began to fling ammo again, juggling it because it was hot. It had to be jettisoned, but if they lost half the gun crews doing it, it was useless. Ben told Catlett to take them to the island structure and get rescue breathing apparatus for them. He was starting back for the forecastle when thick black smoke from the hangar deck enveloped him. He dropped to his knees, crawling for the lee of the splinter shield. He knew all at once that he would never make it, he had been an idiot to go back there without an RBA, and he would die for it, and the last thing he felt was a dizzying, buoyant lightness as a massive arm passed under his chest and he was raised and pulled out of the way and deposited by the catwalk rail, where a faint breeze blew. He

lay wheezing and retching for a moment and focused sting-
ing eyes.

Through swirling smoke, turned yellow now, he saw Catlett return to the guntub, followed by two of the gun crew,
strapping RBA's on their faces as they ran. They clambered
into the tub and went back to their jettisoning. Ben heard a
chuckle beside him. He turned. Watkins had squatted a
few feet away, waiting for him to regain consciousness. He
was grinning at Catlett with a secret mirth. He stood up and
moved fluidly toward the crew, shoulders swinging, hands
ready. Ben croaked a warning. Catlett bent over a ready-
ammo box and grasped a shell and heaved it overboard and
bent again. Watkins vaulted the splinter shield, swooped
down, and came up with a five-inch shell case. He raised it
high overhead. As the two gunners gaped, he brought it
down on Catlett's spine in a crashing, lethal arc.

Ben could hear the crack from twenty feet above the roar
of the hangar-deck flames. For an instant Watkins stood,
black against the sky, and then, disdainfully, he threw the
shell into the water and turned away. Ben lurched to the
guntub, climbed in, and knelt by Catlett.

"He's *dead*," Watkins grinned. "He's *dead*, Commander."

Ben felt his pulse. It was strong enough.

"Not yet, you son of a bitch," he grated. One of the seamen made a move to ease Catlett from his crumpled position
against the ammo locker.

"Don't move him!" Ben muttered. "I'll send a corpsman.
"You," he lashed at Watkins, "come with me."

He felt curiously weak and ineffectual as he said it, and
the huge Negro must have known it, too, but he came forward to the forecastle. Ben spotted a big air-group ensign who should have left the ship heaving on the hawser. "Mister!" he called.

The young man moved over. "Yes, sir?"

His face was oil-streaked and his shirt was torn, and when he rubbed his forehead with the back of his sleeve, Ben saw that his hands were shaking from exhaustion. "Take him aft. Tell the first marine you find to get a weapon. He's to be kept under guard."

"Aye, aye, sir," the ensign said.

The big Negro shook his head. "No, sir." He brushed the ensign off and moved toward a group of steward mates, sprawled from their last stint on a canvas tarp. Suddenly, as Ben and the ensign gaped, he began to lash out at them with his foot, jerking the Filipino chief to his feet, herding them toward the hawser. He yanked white sailors from the line and at each spot he shoved a steward. When there were thirty of them in place, he grabbed the line himself.

The miracle of the *Shenandoah* began. The young ensign tugged the brake handle off the steam winch and headed for him, but Ben grabbed his arm. "Wait, mister." A sensation of inevitability, as if they had done all they could, invaded him. "Let's see . . ."

Watkins was first in the line, a huge foot braced on the bollard, and his shirt was burned and the lattice stripes were ugly on his upper shoulders and the incredible muscles riffled under the black skin like currents in a pool of molten tar. With his foot levered on the bit, he was pulling twice his weight. Someone behind him, from the steward's choir, maybe, began to hum the *Shenandoah*'s favorite, and then, in time with the heaving, another, and another, and slowly, softly, the pulse of it passed from ebony body to white to chocolate to black, and the rhythm was chantey time but the words pure New Orleans.

When the *saints* go marching *in*,
Oh, when the *saints* go marching *in*. . . .

The hawser moved. Ben had his eye on a black, oil-stained strand on it, and he saw it jerk, reluctantly, around the bit, and emerge on the other side, and suddenly it was coming, snaking in a half foot at a time, now, as the rhythm traveled the line in a sinuous wave and the momentum of the manila itself seemed to speed it along its length.

> When the *saints* go marching *in*,
>
> Oh, when the *saints* go marching *in*

There was an explosion aft and Markowitz stepped to his side. "Five-inch magazine blew, aft of the island, sir. They're afraid of the forward ones. They want us to clear the fo'c'sle."

"We can't for Christ's sake clear the fo'c'sle," Ben said, "until the towline's fast!" He called the chief boatswain over. "How long?"

"Five, ten minutes, sir. If we don't get hit again. Question is, why? We ain't goin' no place."

"We'll get it on the bollard," Ben said savagely, "and let the skipper worry about that. O.K.?"

A groan behind him made him turn. Catlett, his body twisted strangely, was being littered to Doc Scliris. Ben noticed that more wounded had arrived to take the place of those sent to the *Dallas*. How the hell many did they have? He followed the litter. Catlett's shoulders shivered but his lower body was still.

"Put him here," said Scliris. He passed his hands gently along his neck and back. "Broken spine," he murmured to Ben. "Sedate him a little, is all I can do now." The chief was wide-awake, fighting pain, but when he saw Scliris take a syringe from an aid chest he croaked, "No!"

"Chief," Ben said, "let him help you."

It burst through the chief's clenched teeth: "Leave me alone! I don't want it!" He stared at Scliris, and there was burning hatred in the green eyes.

A speculative look passed the doctor's face. He leaned over Catlett, unbuttoned the khaki shirt sleeve, and drew it up the arm. Ben stared.

Along a swollen vein were dozens of little blue islands. Scissors flashed in the gloom of the forecastle and one leg lay bare. Another series of ugly black knots rose from the corded leg.

"You son of a bitch," murmured Scliris. Catlett grinned and spat. Slowly, with Catlett watching every move, Scliris filled the syringe. Catlett's arm began to beat a dance on the plates like a wrestler caught in a hammerlock fighting to hold down a scream.

"O.K., Chief," muttered Scliris. His Greek face had turned very dark. He held up the syringe. "We know now, so you want it?"

Sweat squeezed from Catlett's brow. But when he spoke none of the hate had left his voice. "No!"

Scliris smiled. He pressed his thumb and a tiny squirt of fluid arched in the shadow. "None at all, Catlett?"

Ben looked away. From somewhere Foghorn Bailey had appeared, hair tousled and bleary eyes shining like a child's. He had drunk gloriously from some last hidden cache, and now he was weaving down the line of chanting men, trombone tossed skyward, slide zooming in and out, New Orleans-funeral style; and the notes were as clear in the steel cavern as Ben remembered from the days on the *Lex* when Foghorn was steady enough, without help from the next man in the line, to sign his own pay chit.

When the saints go marching in . . .

The *Bangor* must think we've gone nuts, thought Ben, and maybe we have. He looked back at the chief. "One c.c.?" Scliris was asking, begging really: sweat was glistening on the doctor's own forehead; he was folding fast. "Two? Just *ask*, damn it!"

"*No!*" screamed Catlett.

Scliris quit with an angry grunt. He took Catlett's arm and injected it, and he did it with gentle competence. The chief's tremors died and he smiled fleetingly and closed his eyes and in a few moments his scarred jaw slacked and Ben could see the too-perfect teeth.

Scliris touched the massive scar, manipulated it curiously. "I bet," he muttered, to himself or Ben, "he never had a day free of pain, since that. I wonder how he got it?"

"The screw on a motor launch," said Ben, "a long time ago."

Scliris hurled the syringe away. It shattered on an anchor. "Well," he said, "the son of a bitch probably won't die until the sun goes down."

There was another crushing explosion aft. The world of the forecastle tilted crazily and returned to its normal starboard list. "Another magazine aft," Markowitz reported. Ben glanced at the line of men on the hawser. A few had fallen and were climbing back to their feet. Watkins was still erect, and the line had hardly faltered. The hawser jerked in and stopped and jerked again, Foghorn hit a clarion C, and the saints marched on.

Up *there* I'll see the *Sav*iour
Who re*deemed* my soul from *sin.* . . .

Markowitz turned ashen. He said something into the walkie-talkie, stared at Ben, and could not even seem to speak.

"What the hell's going on?" yelled Ben.

"They want you and the doc on the double!"

"Why?"

"Skipper's hit!"

Ben dived into the smoke.

TEN

There was no way aft to the island except topside along the flight deck. He sprinted over smoldering teak past the forward five-inch guns, tripping on limp hoses, brushing ghosts groping in the smoke. Abreast the structure he was suddenly among those wounded who had been brought topside since the *Dallas* had sheered off. There were wounded everywhere; vacant in shock, overstimulated and talking too much, unconscious on stretchers. He saw men with blackened faces and no hair, or hair and blackened cavities for noses, men who had died topside and men who had died below and been hauled above by those who did not know. Corpsmen were moving among the wounded, and Chaplain Schram was limping about.

Ben started up a ladder within the superstructure, but found a charred foot inches from his face. His way was blocked by bodies trapped in the thin steel shield encasing it; the shield had turned the ladder momentarily into a furnace. He gave up and went outside again, squeezing between two charred gear lockers and around the forward end of the island structure. He swung to steel rungs welded to the outside. The starboard list hung him far over the water, so that he had to cling very tightly. The rungs were oily with stack gas and very hot. His feet kept slipping. Before he had climbed twenty feet he was exhausted. Acrid smoke chewed at his lungs and tickled his throat; he stopped, convulsed and coughing. He heard firing from the screen, hooked an arm over a rung, and twisted to see.

Wispy clouds, very high and feathery, hid the targets of the moment, but suddenly a black pockmark appeared and another and another, and all at once the sky ahead to starboard was peppered with them: five-inch bursts from the ships in the screen and the other carriers in the inner ring. Now he could see tiny olive specks, Bettys, they were, two, three, half a dozen. . . . As he watched, he saw that this was the greatest raid of all. He could not count the planes; the combat air patrol above was swamped. A Corsair dove on the endless chain of bombers and a brief dash of smoke showed that he had scored, and then one, and two, and a third Jap plane were flaming and swerving, but the rest churned on through the black bursts ahead. The *Shenandoah*, dead in the water at the root of the flowering smoke, was their prey; there was no doubt about that. All at once he discovered, as ominous black dots began to drop from their bellies, that though her quads and twenties were hammering wildly she was not firing her main batteries to protect herself.

It was coming, it was coming fast, and where in the hell were their five-inch guns? He leaned back to find out. The five-inch director loomed above him, a steel turret without guns in which sat hidden the pointer, trainer, and rangefinder operator who controlled the mounts below. It was motionless when it should have been tracking: the bedspring radar antenna on top was pointed dead ahead. The lenses of the range finder stared from their steel ears projecting right and left directly at the *Bangor*. As always, Christy Lee sat out of sight of his crew on the slanting steel face outside. He was gaping at the oncoming planes through his binoculars.

"Lee!" screamed Ben. "Christy!"

Lee did not hear him above the pounding forties, but yelled suddenly into the director, "Commence tracking." Far too late, the director and all the five-inch mounts below swiveled, locked on, and began silently to track. The target was a *baka*, and the quads and twenties lashed out uselessly at it, too early, and still the five-inch were silent.

"Commence firing!" yelled Ben. Lee did not even seem to hear. Ben leaned back, craning to see what he was doing. Slack mouthed, Golden Boy checked the CO_2 cartridges in his inflatable yellow belt, ducked through the strap on his binoculars, and threw them far from the ship. He spun his helmet after the glasses. Then he took three teetering steps to the end of the starboard range-finder arm and jumped.

He plummeted past Ben close enough to touch, arms properly crossed, hands hugging shoulders, legs together, golden hair trailing, eyes blank. Ben had a crazy desire to reach out for him, and then he was gone into the smoke. Dizzily he looked down. Through lacy brown wisps he glimpsed him knifing into the water feetfirst. He disappeared and surfaced, jerking the lanyards on his jacket, and drifted slowly down the hull until he was obscured again by smoke.

Forward, Ben heard a last chorus—"When the saints go marching in"—and a crystal blare from Foghorn's trombone and a sudden burst of cheering, and for an instant he thought that the *baka* had been knocked down, but it was not that, for it was still coming, and the cheer must have been because they had slipped the eye of the cable over the bollard, and in an instant they would all be gone, someone should warn them, and still the *baka* came, and he saw a twenty-millimeter gunner firing at it when it was almost upon him and tried to press himself into the steel of the structure, to become part of the ship, to weld himself to the steel, and there was a mighty explosion at the starboard bow and a searing blast through which no man forward could have lived, and the cable tautened and twanged a mournful chord. Ben hugged the rungs while the blast shivered its way down the hull, did its best to shake him off and failed.

PART FOUR

Kamikaze Alley

CHAPTER ONE

He moved along a bridge slippery with blood, past a quartermaster's body that had not been moved, past Mitch's marine orderly sitting dazed with shock. When the after five-inch magazine had exploded, debris and shrapnel had shredded splinter shields, bulkheads, and flesh. Mitch was braced on the deck near his swivel seat. A junior ship's dentist was losening a tourniquet on his leg. "Hello, Skipper," said Ben.

"Hello, Ben." His face was white and his eyes glazed. "Towline hold?" he grunted.

Ben nodded. "I think so, sir."

"New wounded ready to go?"

"Any time, sir." Ben drew the dentist aside. He was a delicate scarecrow kid, new on the ship at Bremerton. "How bad?"

His lips were trembling. "I want to evacuate him, sir."

Ben shook his head. "For a leg? He won't go."

The dentist's face twitched. "His back, his chest! There's a wound in his *back*. I'm afraid to move him. Christ, I don't think there's a doctor left on the ship!"

"Scliris," Ben muttered. "If he got aft before that thing hit."

The dentist left for plasma and Ben knelt and talked to Mitch of counterflooding and casualties and of the hangar deck fire, which was under control, and the messdeck fire, which wasn't, and of a quarter million gallons of high-test gasoline sloshing in her bilges. Mitch's breath came in gurgles, as if he had phlegm. "Now Ben," he gasped finally, "get this straight: the flag will leave."

Well, that was normal. Howland had to have mobility. "I know that, sir."

"Before the rest of our wounded."

"*Before* the wounded? Jesus, Captain——"

"Our radios are out, our radar's out," Mitch insisted. "So accept it now."

Before you make an ass of yourself, thought Ben. "Aye, aye, sir." The navigator pulled Ben aside. He reminded him that the breeze had shifted and the *Bangor* was barely holding them against the onshore current. You could see the tip of Fuji from the bridge; if the wind freshened, the *Bangor* would never hold their bulk at all. "We're yawing now, and tugging her stern all over the ocean."

"Ease it with our own rudder?" Ben suggested.

"Rudder control's lost, sir," interrupted the officer of the deck. "I thought you knew. Steering aft's taking three minutes to shift the helm. They're trapped, too; I don't know how we'll get them out when we have to go."

"What do you mean, have to *go?*" Ben hissed. "Knock off that shit! You understand?"

The officer of the deck stiffened. "Aye, aye, sir." His junior watch officer returned from a trip forward, looking sick. "Fo'c'sle's a mess, Commander. The guys that got the cable on are dead, and it's popping strands and stretching like an old rubber band."

Mitch said something and Ben dropped to a knee to hear

him better. Mitch's eyes were full of grief. "She's not a virgin anymore," he whispered.

"She's been raped by experts," agreed Ben.

"But she's still afloat," murmured Mitch.

"That's right, sir. As Jones said, don't give up the ship."

"Lawrence," murmured Mitch. A spasm shadowed his face and he coughed weakly. He was choking now on his own blood: Ben straightened and looked around. Doc Scliris, thank God, burst onto the bridge. He dove for Mitch, whose mouth had begun to trickle red, and passed a hand gently around his back.

"Captain? Can you sit up?" Mitch shook his head. He grabbed Ben's wrist as if clutching for an anchor. "You're right, Ben," he whispered hoarsely. "Don't leave her. . . ." The eyes squeezed shut and the pressure went out of the grip on Ben's wrist. Tenderly, Scliris pressed his ear to his chest. For a long while he listened and then he turned to Ben. "Ben," he grated, "he's *gone!*"

Ben, numb with shock, could not believe it. "That dentist!" he exploded. "Where's that goddamn dentist?"

Scliris grabbed his arm. "Take it easy! He couldn't have done anything!"

Ben got stiffly from his knees. "O.K.," he said dully. "O.K., Al." He had Mitch's body removed to the sea cabin and told the boatswain of the watch to clear the ladders of dead and then a Kate broke through and got as far as the inner screen, heading for the *Shenandoah's* deadly plume of smoke, which must be visible from Yokosuka. The Kate lost a wing to a five-inch proximity fuse from the *Washington* and fluttered down to an orange crater of spray, but Ben saw no fighters at all this time, which meant that there was action somewhere farther out, between the group and the mainland

of Japan. Jesus, he would like another twenty miles, or
even ten!

Josh Lowery, the chief engineer, climbed to the bridge,
blinking in the sunlight. His lined face was streaked with
oil; he looked like a tall and aging scarecrow, and when
Ben told him of Mitch, his sloping shoulders sagged further;
they had been in the same company at Annapolis. But he
had other things on his mind. "Ben, I think I can get down
to the number-one fireroom through the ventilating duct,
maybe light her off!"

"How many men?"

"Ten, maybe twelve."

The duct passed under a bomb magazine. "Suppose it
blows?"

Josh shrugged. "We need steam, to steam." He nodded at
the *Bangor* tugging uselessly ahead. "If she can't pull us
off Japan, she can't pull us to Pearl."

"Suppose it blows *after* you get there, and traps you?"

Josh said nothing, very loudly. Ben moved to the rail
and thought. There was no escape now from decision, none
at all, and no one at all to ask. "Go ahead," he said finally.

Josh touched the visor of his greasy cap and his hand
flopped down. He was the only Academy man Ben knew who
saluted like a reserve. "Aye, aye, Captain." Their eyes met,
but neither spoke as Josh swung awkwardly down the ladder
and disappeared below.

"Bridge from flag plot, sir," a phone talker broke in.
"Signal the *Talcott* to come alongside and prepare to shift
the flag."

"Make the signal," Ben ordered the owl-faced signalman
whose name he could never remember. He noticed that
he was flipping the blinker with his left hand; his right was
bandaged and seeping blood. "I'm going to send wounded,"

he told him, "and when I do, you evacuate too. Understand?"

"Aye, aye, sir." Ben told the JA talker to get a damage report from damage-control central. Then he wandered into the captain's sea cabin.

CHAPTER TWO

They had drawn the blackout curtains over the ports; he drew them aside. Then he stepped to the bunk. The corpsmen had not wanted to put Mitch there, assuming that Ben would sleep there if they lasted until dusk, but Ben had insisted; he somehow wanted him on the bridge. Now he stood above the oddly shrunken body and looked for a moment into the drawn face; it seemed troubled, as in life it had never been. Worried at the last they might give her up too soon? Well, not yet. He reached for Mitch's hand and began to work his class ring off his finger to send his wife; the hand was pliant and the fingers still rubbery, so that it was no trouble at all.

"Attention on deck," he heard. There was a shadow in the doorway and Hammering Howie stood beside him. "How are we doing, Casco?"

"O.K., sir."

"You got things under control?"

"Yes, sir."

The admiral looked down at Mitch's body, shaking his head. "The little bastards really hurt us *there*."

If we'd been a hundred miles farther out, thought Ben, they wouldn't have. He kept silent, as Mitch would have wished. The admiral seemed truly saddened. "First time I saw him, I was a big-shot athlete and he was just a fresh-caught plebe. Quiet, not very big. We used to beat a lot of plebe ass in those days. But not his ass, we didn't, for some reason." He shrugged. "He'd have made admiral, you know. Someday maybe CINCUS."

"I'm sure he would have, sir," Ben said. There must have been a trace of bitterness in his voice, for the admiral's brows shot down angrily. "You never liked this operation, did you?"

"I think we got too close," said Ben.

"Well," said Howland, "you're wrong." They moved to the wing of the bridge. The *Talcott* was sliding toward their starboard beam, and Ben could see that she was rigged for a highline on her forecastle and aft. Howland cleared his throat. "I'm leaving with my staff."

"Yes, sir."

The admiral looked uncomfortable. Suddenly he said, "Send your wounded over first."

"Thank you, sir," Ben said impassively. Sweat it, you son of a bitch, he thought, you got us into this. He told his talker to inform the flight deck and have the litter patients tied in.

"You understand," said Howland, "that I *got* to shift? Hell, you're blind and deaf and dead in the water and God knows what else. I can't run a task group from——"

"I understand, Admiral," said Ben. They watched the *Talcott* slow to keep pace; Ben recognized her as the destroyer he had seen four days ago leaving Ulithi with the jaunty Japanese banner and arrow on her fantail. It was gone now, presumably swept off or stowed for the typhoon. She looked not nearly so chipper, and her bearded skipper seemed very nervous; he kept looking up at the sky, and

Ben could not blame him. The wounded, strapped into cage litters, began to swing sickeningly across, fore and aft. The Jap went last. When they had been transferred, the admiral's staff began to leave; Ben saw Epstein, clutching his briefcase, swinging over. Hammering Howie seemed reluctant to go; Ben wished he would get on with it to ease the strain on the bridge. Ben's talker stepped from the pilothouse. "Sir, I have your rundown from damage control."

Ben shook his head. "Later," he said swiftly.

"Wait a minute, son," said Howland. "I want to hear it."

The talker glanced at notes. "Damage-control officer says there are fires going in the galley. There are sporadic fires on the second deck and gasoline fires on the hangar deck aft of frame one-twenty. Fires forward of frame eighty on the hangar deck were contained but busted out again after the last attack. Hangar and gallery decks were completely cooked. No survivors from combat-information center, sir, captain's in-port stateroom, or JO's bunkroom forward."

"Jesus," breathed the admiral. "Go on."

The talker recited from his pad, and Ben groaned silently. Magazine temperatures in rocket stowage were still in the red; a five-inch powder magazine above it and a bomb-stowage magazine were intermittently in the danger zone. There were three men hanging on in main engine control, but the after engine room had been evacuated due to high temperatures in the antiaircraft magazine aft of it. There were fires in the storerooms under the messdeck. Sick bay had been destroyed in the first attack.

"What did gunnery say?" the admiral wanted to know.

"Gunnery," the talker repeated. "Two five-inch twin mounts destroyed by fire and blast when their upper handling rooms blew up. One five-inch twin mount damaged by blast and salt water, and two slightly damaged. Two five-inch single mounts destroyed by fire and blast, when ready-ammo blew up and bombs exploded near the mounts. Two five-inch single mounts damaged at the same time. One Mark thirty-seven director damaged by blast, fifteen forty-millimeter mounts damaged by fire, explosions, and salt water. Two forty-millimeter mounts damaged when the *Dallas* struck them, coming alongside. Thirty-nine twenty-millimeter guns destroyed by fire and salt water. All fire-control systems of the forward batteries destroyed or badly damaged; all ready-service ammunition on the port cat-walks jettisoned. All sound-powered gunnery circuits out of commission since the last attack."

"What the hell you got left?" the admiral asked Ben.

Ben had been keeping desolate track. He tried to sound optimistic. "Well, a couple of dozen twenty-millimeters, two or three quads, and a couple of five-inch thirty-eights. And manual control, Admiral. We'll do all right."

"Stability," the admiral muttered grimly. "What's the damage-control officer say about this goddamn list?"

"Look, sir, we can handle it," said Ben. "We're counter-flooding now———"

"Stability, talker," the admiral demanded again. "What's he say about free surface? Metacentric height?"

Academy terms, marine-engineering terms, Ben thought disconsolately: he understood stability only vaguely. He was stranded in quicksand.

"Well, sir," said the talker, "the starboard list has increased to twelve degrees. Present estimated metacentric height is five feet. Aviation-gasoline discharge valves burst, and the DCO's afraid to pump any more water into the forward voids. The watertight bulkheads burst forward of . . ."

He went on and on until Ben could not visualize it all. The technicalities of damage control were simply beyond him. He only knew that Mitch had thought she was all right, list or not, and if they could just get up steam they would be safe. The talker left the admiral horrified.

"A hulk!" he exclaimed. "She's a goddamn hulk, Casco!"

"When we get steam up, sir——" he began.

"Steam? You'll be lucky if you get off before she capsizes!"

"Mitch didn't think so!"

"He's dead, damn it! You don't have enough pressure in your mains to get the fires out! What are you going to do? Piss on them?"

"When we get steam we'll have pressure! Josh Lowery——"

"That graveyard commander? He's not going to lose *me* a ship with all hands. And neither are you." Hammering Howie moved to the wing of the bridge. He pointed to port. "You see that, Casco? You see that haze? You see the tip of that mountain?"

Ben nodded, sick. "Yes."

"That's Japan, Casco. *Japan!* You're setting toward it at half a knot right now, with the *Bangor* pulling her ass off! When I tell her to cast loose, what's going to happen? If you *don't* sink? You going to let them capture her? Or you going to repel boarders in Tokyo Bay?"

"We'll get out," Ben said stubbornly. "We'll get up steam."

A Tiny Tim rocket in the hangar deck went wooshing forward trailing flame. It passed within yards of the laboring *Bangor*.

"No, you won't," Hammering Howie said. "Because when the *Talcott's* full the *Mulvaney's* coming alongside and when she pulls away, if you haven't blown up by then, you better be on her, because she's going to back off and put a fish in your guts. And it's a long swim home!"

The *Talcott* was blinking. The owl-faced signalman, who should have left already, turned and said to Ben, "They're sending back Mr. Lee, sir. He was blown off in the last attack."

Ben grabbed his binoculars. At the destroyer's forward station a knot of men was gathered, holding the breeches buoy for Christy Lee. In the glasses his blue eyes shone clearly; Ben saw him smile at the boatswain in charge, test the shrouds, and nod. He was suddenly dangling over the tin can's rail as the men on the *Shenandoah*'s forward station heaved him aloft on the main fall. He began to jerk over the slowly swirling chop. Ben turned to the talker. "Avast hauling," he said. "Belay that!"

"What in the name of Christ," demanded Howland, "do you think you're doing?"

Ben grabbed the bullhorn from the navigator. Christy Lee stopped with a jolt, dangling halfway across. "Haul him back," Ben blared. "And keep him!"

The destroyer skipper looked up incredulously, the knot of officers on the wing of the *Talcott*'s bridge milled about for a moment, and there was utter silence on his own bridge. He saw Lee's face, white with shock, twist upward. For a sculptured instant, nothing happened. Then Lee began to roll inexorably back toward the destroyer in the canvas pantaloons, stiff with rage.

"Do you realize," Hammering Howie murmured, "What you've done?"

"He isn't coming back," Ben said softly. "Not now, not ever."

"Why not?"

"He jumped."

"I don't believe it."

"I *saw* him."

"Bullshit, Commander!"

"I saw him. The son of a bitch stays off my ship!"

The admiral looked deeply into his eyes. "Understand this," he said slowly. "Get it straight?"

"Yes, sir?"

"If the next senior officer on this ship was fit for command—if he was anybody but Josh Lowery—I'd relieve you. But I promise you one thing."

"Yes?"

"If you've ruined that young man's career, it's the last goddamn ship you'll ever have."

He turned on his heel and the next Ben saw of him he was swinging down from the gutted hangar deck on the forward breeches buoy, a stolid immutable lump. Within seconds after he thumped to the destroyer's deck, his flag lieutenant had the two stars fluttering from the tin can's halyard, and the can was knifing toward the *Ticonderoga*, where the pennant would rise to stay. But by that time Ben had enough troubles of his own without worrying about the admiral, because the *Bangor* flashed him a warning of bogies and in a moment the sky was full of pockmarks again. He glanced at his watch automatically to get the time of attack. It was impossible, his mind told him they had been there forever, but it was barely noon.

CHAPTER THREE

The noon attack failed; *Enterprise* fighters intercepted off the coast of Japan and the last bomber was hit before it could release its *baka*. It made a glorious sunburst on the southwestern horizon, and gunners cheered from the twenty-millimeter tub over the *Shenandoah's* bridge.

But Hammering Howie soon stopped the cheers. The *Ticonderoga*, from the moment he swung aboard off the destroyer's highline, began to blink balefully, winking assignments to cover the evacuation of the ship. With the *Shenandoah* Hammering Howie left a screen of a half-dozen destroyers. He left the cruiser *Bangor,* which was to keep her in tow for steerageway until Ben had transferred survivors to the destroyer *Mulvaney,* which was to put her to sleep with torpedoes when the *Bangor* had cast off. He left a combat air patrol which was to shelter the "rescue operation," as he called it. He left no capital ships at all except the *Bangor.*

Having made his assignments, Howland took his remaining ten destroyers, his other three cruisers, his three remaining carriers, and his five fast battleships and crept at economical rpm toward the replenishment rendezvous far over the eastern horizon. The group moved so slowly that it looked as if they were ashamed to leave, but nevertheless they were out of sight in forty minutes and Ben felt very much alone.

He had no choice now that the admiral had set up the plan, and Mitch would have been the first to admit it. He began to make preparations to abandon ship. He ordered topside all those not engaged in fire fighting, and evacuated what levels he could below the third deck, allowing water-tight doors to be opened for passage, and then resetting Condition Zebra when men were freed. It was a tedious process: a man twenty feet below the waterline and four decks down might have to dog and undog a dozen doors to get to the flight deck for muster.

He did not evacuate damage control or steering aft; he could not bring himself to do it yet any more than he could pass the word to abandon ship until he heard from Josh. He got a rough casualty estimate from the chief yeoman. From the corpsmen's count of bodies and the half-assed muster the shaken yeoman was able to make, it appeared that they had around three hundred and fifty dead, two hundred and fifty wounded and transferred, and six hundred missing.

The wan, bag-eyed chief yeoman seemed embarrassed. "Captain?"

"Yes?"

"I heard we lost a hundred men to the *Dallas*, when she came alongside."

"Wounded, you mean?"

The yeoman shook his head. "No, sir."

"I don't believe it!" And yet he did, down deep. If a regular naval officer would leave her, how could he expect kids to stick who a year ago were roaming the streets of Chicago or reciting in high-school classrooms? He was sick at the casualties, and sicker at the desertions, but he kept his face rigid, as became a commanding officer, and acted as if he had expected the dead and wounded and didn't credit the desertions at all.

He got word over the JV phone that Josh and his snipes had made it to the number-one fireroom but would have to actually reset bricks in the furnaces before they could even try to light off. Well, they could hardly have got closer to the heart of the matter than that; they had done everything they could. The words of an old sea chantey came to him: "Time for us to leave her. . . ."

He called for a signalman, and the owl-faced boy appeared, the one whose name he could never remember. "Dammit, sailor, I told you to leave!"

"I missed the boat, sir," the boy said solemnly.

"Well," said Ben sharply, "don't miss the next one."

The wide eyes shot up behind round spectacles. "Are we really going, sir?"

"Signal the *Mulvaney:* 'Make our starboard side.' We've had it."

The boy looked as if he were about to cry. Behind his round eyeglasses Ben saw glistening eyes, and more: a locker somewhere below with all he owned, with a girl's picture in it or perhaps a pinup; liberties with messmates in Bremerton or Pearl; happy hours in the Marianas sunsets with the *Shenandoah* chorus singing and the blare of Foghorn's slide trombone. "Come on, son," he said more kindly. "Send it off."

He was turning to his talker to tell Josh and his snipes to leave the fireroom when the greatest explosion of all convulsed the ship. He felt it from toe to scalp before he heard the sound of it, and felt afterward an initial shock wave, like the warning of an earthquake, a slow, convulsive heave and then, from somewhere aft, a searing wall of heat.

He found himself squatting behind the splinter shield,

covering his face. Then the main concussion hit him, and he sprawled backward, his helmet falling off, the sweat on his hands turning Mitch's blood sticky beneath them. There was a volcanic rumble from below. He groped for the helmet in darkness; the black smoke had obscured the sun.

He clamped it on his head, struggled to his feet too soon, and heard the whistle of jagged metal far too late to drop again and saw the owl-faced signalman staring at him, mouth open to speak. Suddenly the owl-face was gone as his bandaged hand flew up to protect it, and he remembered Pappy in the rear cockpit at Pearl Harbor and it was too damn much to see twice in one life; he looked down to see the boy's blood mixing with the caked dark matter that had once been Mitch's; it was too damn much, too damn much. . . . He found himself staring at the pelorus by Mitch's chair, and the pelorus, too, was gone save for a wire entrail waving stupidly.

The signalman had flown twenty feet forward and was crumbled by the splinter shield, and next to him rocked a piston from a Pratt and Whitney engine—how the hell its trajectory had brought it from the flight deck to the bridge he would never know, but it was there, all right, in the waterway, and covered with oil and blood. Ben could not bear to look and yelled into the chart room for a corpsman and turned away.

An overheated bomb-stowage locker had exploded below, and now the Tiny Tims began again, wailing as they went. There was plenty of damage topside, and plenty below, and when the racket began to subside, his talker told him that Commander Lowery wanted him on the phone. Ben took it and jammed one earpiece to his head. He heard hammering in the background. "Go ahead, Josh."

"What *was* that, Ben?"

Josh was an absentminded scientist crossing Times Square, a professor lecturing while the classroom burned, a commuter caught in crossfire on a subway. "That," Ben said, "was a compartment full of five-hundred-pound bombs. Why do you ask, my friend?"

"Because I think it folded up that ventilation duct. All we got down here is smoke."

"You mean," Ben asked tightly, "you're trapped?"

"Well, Captain," Josh observed mildly, "we weren't going anywhere anyway."

When Ben tried to talk further, Josh had left the phone. But before he gave it back, he heard a tremulous voice trying to sound brave, from steering aft, thirty feet below the waterline: Keeley, an eighteen-year-old quartermaster striker, was trapped there too, with three others. "You won't forget us, sir?"

"Hang on, Keeley," Ben said. If that weren't enough, he got word from damage control that they were cut off too. A dozen men with Josh, three with Keeley, and fourteen in damage-control central. Twenty-nine men trapped because he had waited too long. He heard firing from the *Bangor* and looked up. This time the Japs were full-bore, and the Bettys had escorts, which engaged the CAP, and there were diving, twisting planes all over the dome of the sky. Ben crouched again behind the splinter shield as a *baka* skimmed the five-inch mount below. He caught a flash of sunlight on Plexiglas twenty feet away and glimpsed the pilot, all teeth and eyeballs, with an old-fashioned helmet and no *hachi-maki* band at all; miraculously the *baka* missed the mount and the edge of the flight deck too and skidded into the water to port and went up in a scarlet blossom of spray and flame.

He handed the phones back to the talker, for the first time

truly frightened, not at the attack but at what he had done to Josh and Keeley and the rest. He glanced again at his watch. There was still half a day to the oblivion of darkness. He was so hungry and tired and confused that he could not remember if it would turn to moonlight or not; the navigator, who had been on the bridge for sixteen hours, turned reddened eyes on him and reported that he couldn't remember either, and when the quartermaster checked, it was full moon. Full moon! One night in thirty, and they faced moonlight if they managed even to survive until dark.

"After guntubs want to know if you're abandoning ship," the talker reported.

"Tell them no, goddamn it," said Ben, fighting for time.

"They're trapped on the fantail with a fire, sir. They can't hang on much longer."

"At least they're topside," growled Ben. To tell them to go might start an exodus, but he guessed it had to be done. "O.K.," he decided. "Tell them to drop lines first. And after guntubs *only!*"

They were rolling the signalman's body into a wire litter. A quartermaster handling his shoulders grimaced and rubbed blood off his hands onto the dead man's jumper. He learned quickly, apparently. Well, why soil his own? "Send a signalman up here," Ben yelled at the signal bridge. He noticed that the blinker lens was broken and asked for semaphore flags. The *Mulvaney* off their starboard quarter blinked frantically that they were picking survivors from their wake, and that if *Shenandoah* was ready she would come alongside before the next attack developed.

Ben sent back a negative: HAVE TWENTY-NINE MEN TRAPPED BELOW X NOT ABANDONING SHIP AT THIS TIME. Reluctantly the tin can moved back and the next wave came on, as predicted. This time the CAP picked off three Bettys before they dropped their *bakas,* the tin cans shot down one, and a *baka* bounced from the *Shenandoah* at a shallow angle in the fire aft and somehow failed to detonate. Ben thought they were very lucky, which they were, of course, until Keeley called from steering aft with a report that the impact had opened up a watertight hatch somewhere and they were ankle-deep in water in total darkness, and the water was rising too.

The *Bangor,* writhing at the end of her towline, demanded by semaphore that Ben abandon ship. Her skipper was the senior officer in the tiny unit, and there was only one way to handle that one, ignore it. She came back with blinker, suggesting that if the *Shenandoah* didn't transfer now, while they were under way, she might find herself at the end of a cable alone and without enough speed to transfer at all.

You couldn't blame her: she wanted to be able to maneuver, and she had done her part. Ben could see still the peak of Fuji on the horizon, but had it not been for the *Bangor,* he would have seen a lot more of Japan than that. He sent word that he expected no more help and saw the florid, gray-haired skipper of the *Bangor* stamp into his pilothouse, but the line remained where it was, maybe because he couldn't see losing his towline or maybe because he couldn't cast a classmate loose off the coast of Japan and didn't know that Mitch was dead. Whatever the reason, it did no good; the wind had veered and the monolithic bulk of the *Shenandoah* continued to toy with the cruiser's stern like a mischievous giant.

The hangar-deck fire was impossible to fight further without water pressure so Ben relieved a damage-control party to try to open up Josh's ventilating trunk. They returned, having been lost in the dark for twenty minutes and having then found the duct in a twisted knot and the hole no bigger around than a thigh. No one could get anywhere near damage-control central either, or steering aft.

CIC on the *Bangor* relayed him a message that the combat air patrol was running low of fuel; when the aircraft had to return to the ships over the horizon it would really be *sayonara*, for sure. The *Bangor*'s captain finally decided that *Shenandoah*'s smoke plume was sufficiently visible from the mainland anyway to justify his breaking radio silence. He contacted Hammering Howie fifty miles away and relayed Howie's answer by blinker: SHENANDOAH WILL REPEAT WILL TRANSFER ALL HANDS TO DD MULVANEY NOW REPEAT NOW.

It could hardly be clearer than that, but Ben decided that maybe the admiral should be told he had twenty-nine men trapped below. He made up a long and convoluted message to that effect and told the signalman to semaphore it to *Bangor* as slowly as possible, with lots of errors, and demanded that his talker get Josh on the phone.

Josh was no help, no help at all. "Goddamn it," Ben blurted finally. "I got to know how you're doing! Do I hang on or not?"

"Ben," Josh said softly, "you're the skipper. How should I know?"

Ben moved to the rail and sat in Mitch's chair. The wrecked pelorus waved its lone wire in the wind. Savagely he yanked at it, cutting his finger. His head ached and his eyes were burning; he wondered if Mitch had aspirin in his sea cabin, but he didn't want to go in himself and didn't want to send a messenger; they were all too busy cleaning up the mess on the bridge, as if anyone would care six-hundred fathoms below.

The destroyer *Mulvaney* began to blink, and he moved to the wing of the bridge to read the message. ORDERED BY CTG TO MAKE YOUR SIDE BEFORE NEXT ATTACK AND TAKE OFF ALL

HANDS X THEN TO SINK WITH TORPEDOS X THESE ORDERS NOT
DISCRETIONARY X INTEND TO COMPLY.

The *Mulvaney* had been talking to Hammering Howie
too. Ben's talker told him that steering aft, with water knee-
deep, wanted to know if help was coming. Ben took the
phone himself but could not bring himself to tell Keeley
that they had already tried and failed. Instead he said,
"Hang on, son. It won't be long."

"Long until *what*, Commander?" Keeley wanted to know.

Ben looked at the *Mulvaney*. She was knifing toward the
starboard side, a bone in her teeth. Fuck her, fuck the
Bangor, fuck Hammering Howie and the whole damn fleet.
He told the signalman to warn her to stand clear, and when
she came on anyway, he could see that she was rigged fore
and aft to pass highlines, and he saw a boatswain point a
line gun at his hangar deck and suddenly fire a white messenger line in a writhing curve across the water. He grabbed
the bullhorn and told his hangar deck to leave the line
where it was and swung up the ladder to the level above.
He shoved a twenty-millimeter gunner aside and shouldered
into the harness. "Tell 'em again," he yelled below. He
heard the flutter of flags and saw the skipper of the tin can
shake his head and could read, on the tin can's blinker:
ARE YOU READY TO RECEIVE ME?

"Tell him yes!" yelled Ben. He eased the twenty along the
tin can's waterline and moved the orange cross of its sight
forward of the great bow wave curling to its hawsepipes.
He slapped the safety off and squeezed the trigger and the
gun jolted and jarred and orange-white tracers lanced ahead
of the charging can, *pam, pam, pam, pam,* and sent show-
ers of spray seaward. The tin can's skipper, officer of the
deck, and quartermaster of the watch were three blobs with
angry, gaping mouths at the corner of his eye. An officer rid-

ing the face of their forward director almost fell off in excitement. The boatswain at the forward station dived for cover. Ben quit firing, let the gun slam skyward and stepped to the edge of the tub. He grabbed the horn and shouted down: "I got two five-inch guns forward! If you don't stand clear I'll blow you out of the water!"

The destroyer sheered off as if stung and passed in a roar of spray. The last impression Ben had was a grizzled torpedoman setting his fish amidships. He stopped what he was doing, tossed his wrench into his toolbox, and shut it with a snap. Then he looked up at the *Shenandoah*. He raised his hand to his grimy cap and flicked off a salty salute.

My God, thought Ben, win, lose, sink, or swim, she's a hero ship already.

"Commander Casco!" the navigator called from below. "Captain!"

"Yeah?"

"*Bangor* signals bogies on the screen. She's casting off."

Suddenly he was sick at what he had done. He looked down at the figures moving on the bridge, the long lines of men snaking limp hoses across the smoking hangar deck, the gun crews slumping on the catwalks. For twenty-nine men, for the beau geste, he had doomed hundreds to the sea; God knew how many of those topside would be lost, when he could have saved them all.

The JA talker looked up and yelled something. The *Bangor* began to fire, and the *Mulvaney* and then the *Scott* astern and he heard the whine of the quad back aft, slewing for the target. "Aircraft starboard quarter, forty degrees," he heard a lookout yell. "It's a *baka!*" The twenty behind him opened up, but Ben's eyes were on the talker. "What'd you say?" he yelled.

The boy's eyes shone with tears. "They lit off! They're getting steam, Captain! Steam!"

"Oh, Christ," Ben murmured. He groped down the ladder and lurched to Mitch's seat. The *baka* hit short of the starboard quarter but sprung plates with the concussion; the bomb on an SBD cooked off aft and started another fire below, and for a while it looked as if it had all happened too late, but in twenty minutes Josh had a boiler on the line and the hoses were firm in the fire fighters' hands and in an hour the flames were contained and they were pumping gasoline and fuel oil out of the bilges and were crawling east on two engines. Sometime during the afternoon the *Mulvaney* cut north, where she blew stacks to make a great plume of smoke and suck the next attack over the horizon, so that by the time the Japs saw that the target was a twisting tin can instead of a burning carrier they had already released their *bakas*. The *Mulvaney* escaped with half a dozen strafing casualties from a hysterical Betty and no *baka* hits at all. By dusk, when the *Shenandoah* got the snipes out of the engine room and the men from steering aft, you could not see Fugi at all.

Al Scliris arrived on the bridge after dark with a fifth of whiskey and they stepped into the navigator's sea cabin. Ben had had nothing but a horsecock sandwich since his half-eaten breakfast a hundred years ago, and the first swallow of bourbon almost felled him. He was afraid to take a second; there was too much to be done.

"There's a health problem," Scliris said. "We'll be in hot weather by tomorrow. And you got a morale problem too. There are bodies on that hangar deck you're going to have to scrape off with a putty knife."

So they started cleaning up by moonlight. Ben found that the reefers had survived, and it was unlikely that the ship would ever need her beer for Mogmog again, so he established a happy hour at 2000, every night until Guam, one can for every man, two for anyone who had worked on a burial party during the day. It failed to make the burial party popular, but gave them something to look forward to. A seaman apprentice cracked and attacked an ensign with a hammer, but Scliris shot him full of something and they transferred him to the *Mulvaney* next day. Chaplain Schram swore that he was going to write the chief of chaplains when he found men using GI cans as biers, but Ben shut him up by burying Mitch first, as an example, *sans* shroud, canvas, or flag, at sunrise the first morning and with only the briefest of services.

They slid him from the forward door of the gutted hangar deck; the starboard list, which he was told they could not further counter-flood without sinking the ship, made it easy. It established the burial ground for those who followed, making it simple for the angry chaplain, who should have appreciated it but didn't, and for the forklift operator on the hangar deck, who saved hundreds of man-hours by lumping charred flesh, molten engines, and tangled spars, driving forward along jumbled roads he had cleared, and shoving the mass over the side while the chaplain chanted. There was no choice; with air group, wounded, dead, and deserters gone, there were less than eight hundred men manning a ship that needed a thousand. The young Catholic chaplain was somewhere in the jumble, so Schram alternated last rites, one *pax vobiscum* for every three "rest in peaces" with a few Jewish services thrown in.

After Mitch's "funeral" Ben wandered forward, inspecting the carnage that the *baka* had wreaked on the forecastle gang at the towline. He noticed a gleam of gold in the blackened rubble and picked it up. It was Foghorn's slide trombone, and he wondered which of the charred, ballooned caricatures sprawled about was the musician.

He heard a footstep and looked up. Silhouetted against the door to the catwalk stood a stumpy chief gunner's mate,

Eddy Levine, captain of the number-one five-inch mount. He was a gargoyle with a bald head far too large for his body and bright blue eyes radiating lines etched too deeply and colored too brightly, like a Schwartzwald puppet carved from wood. He saluted casually when he saw Ben and shook his head at the damage.

"Christ," he said admiringly, "that son of a bitch really done it!"

"Yes," said Ben, "he did."

"Flew right down my barrel," said Levine. "Could have hit him with the slue sight. Nobody give me the word."

Ben said nothing, feeling the rage tight in his chest. Levine stooped and picked up a metallic object that may or may not have come from the flying bomb. He polished it with his forefinger and put it in his pocket. "Souvenir," he said. "Show it to my wife." He looked up, and his eyes were curious. "Why didn't we get 'commence firing?' " he asked.

"Because," Ben said tightly, "your control officer went over the side."

"Lee? Lieutenant Commander Lee?" The chief regarded him speculatively. "We *wondered* why you wouldn't let him back. You sure?"

"I saw him."

"Jesus . . ." For a long while he thought. "What you going to do?"

"Court-martial him," Ben said.

"Court-martial him," the chief repeated. "Ain't he the Navy football star?"

"Golden Boy," Ben said bitterly. "Yes, he was."

"Christ, you think it'll stick?"

"I hope so." Ben started for the door to the catwalk. The chief's voice resounded in the metal chamber. "Captain?"

"Yes?"

"Wasn't you a chief, once?"

Ben turned. "That's right. Why?"

Levine smiled with a certain admiration. "Well, sir, I'll save you a seat in the mess."

PART FIVE

Band of Brothers

CHAPTER ONE

ONE

The ruined *Shenandoah* had rattled eastward past Kawaikini Peak off Kauai, a twenty-knot bone in her teeth and less than four hours to go. She had stopped at Guam; in a few months she would leave for Philly, for the West Coast yards were too jammed with battle damage for so hopeless a cripple as she. Her list to starboard was long gone: the millions of gallons of seawater and oil and gasoline had been pumped from her guts en route to Agana. Ben, exhausted and fanciful, living on black coffee and hope, knew nevertheless that she would not sail again in this war. Her shot-up superstructure depressed him, so he tried to keep to the bridge, where he could not see the blistered paint and jagged holes, being above them; but he could not escape sight of the scorched flight deck or the elevator jammed in its shaft like a half-opened hatch or the crazy radar antenna at its rakish, mawkish angle.

But the worst was the feel of her, the awful, mushy spring to her deck when the seas were high, and the sickness deep in her marrow. Her vibrations were not like the old *No-Go Maru,* which shook constantly at certain rpm's so that you learned to count on it to tell you how many turns she was making. *Shenandoah* shivered sporadically as if she had malaria; when she convinced you that she had somehow cured herself, the trembling would return. Sitting on the wing of the bridge, in what he still thought of as Mitch's seat, he touched the rail and waited. The shiver was not noticeable but he knew that sooner or later it would begin again.

"Captain?"

He removed his hand, for he did not like to be caught feeling her brow, so to speak, and swiveled the chair. A radioman handed him a clipboard; on it was a single pink dispatch. It was printed in pencil because the typewriter in communications had somehow been jolted during the attack and all but one of those in the office spaces were melted hunks somewhere in the Marianas Deep.

SHENANDOAH V CINCPACFLEET: ASSIGNED TUGS CHUMAC AND NAVAHO X ASSIGNED DOCK 1010 STARBOARD SIDE TO.

That was all, as he had known it would be. Hammering Howie had successfully finished hacking out, in five days pounding the Tokyo-Yokohama complex, the Mount Rushmore image he coveted. He had taken his staff and returned to Pearl. The *Shenandoah* was an albatross flopping in his wake; if she had not been saved no one would ever have known that she could have been saved, but now she was a forty-thousand-ton indictment of his judgment, shackled to his career. The excuse for drawing the veil of obscurity would be security: kamikaze damage was never released on the theory that since the pilot died knowledge of his successes died with him—or perhaps that if no one talked about the Divine Wind it would blow itself out.

Ben initialed the dispatch and went to the sea cabin. He was working on his action report when Josh Lowery knocked. He stooped at the door, but as usual not far enough, and added a scrape-mark to the scars and scratches and dents just under his hairline. He did not even flinch. He looked utterly exhausted. Damn it, he should be taking it easy topside, instead of trying to be chief engineer and exec all at once. Ben showed him the recommendation he was forwarding for the Navy Cross. For a long moment Lowery was quiet. "I won't get it, Ben."

"Because I'm a mustang?"

"Because in nineteen twenty-six I didn't use a stopwatch on the Point Conception light."

"Well, you saved *this* ship. I'll get it for you if I have to see Nimitz myself! Now, as an expert on 'the spoiled and pampered pets of Uncle Sam,' will *this* hold up?"

He showed him the charge against Golden Boy, and Josh read it with growing distress. When he handed it back, he was shaking his head. "Howland won't believe it!"

"I'm going to court-martial him," said Ben. "If I have to write a letter to Ernie King!"

"There's a poem they teach you at Annapolis, that a British admiral wrote——"

" 'The Laws of the Navy,' " Ben said bitterly. "Lee used to recite it all the time. Well, one verse goes: 'On the strength of one link in the cable, Dependeth the might of the Chain.' He's a rusted link. I'm going to cut him out."

"There's another verse." Josh Lowery smiled.

" 'Dost think in a moment of anger
'Tis well with thy seniors to fight,
They prosper who burn in the morning,
The letters they wrote overnight.
So thou when thou nearest promotion——' "

"I'll never make captain and I don't give a damn! All I want to do is get her to Pearl, *get* that bastard, and fade back into the woodwork."

Josh Lowery regarded him for a long while. "No, I don't think so, Ben. I think you want to make captain. I think you want to take her to Philly."

Ben glanced at his washstand. His water glass was rattling in its rack and a bottle of Benzedrine was dancing in his medicine cabinet. The shiver passed. "Do you think she'll *make* it to Philly?" he asked.

"Yes. But not out again. She's bent, Ben. Keel, frame, shafts, maybe the rudderpost."

Ben said miserably, "They straighten shafts! They beef up keels!"

"Not this ship," said Josh. "Ben, I want you to take her all the way. Christy Lee's Mister Navy. Don't fight it too hard.

'Now these are the laws of the Navy
And many and mighty are they.
But the hull and the deck and the keel
And the truck of the law is—obey.' "

"If I'd obeyed Howland's *last* order where would you be?"

"In five hundred fathoms off Honshu," agreed Josh Lowery readily, "with a U.S. torpedo up my ass, but that was combat."

"What's this?" Ben wanted to know.

"Politics," shrugged Josh. "Public relations. The press."

The speaker on the bulkhead quacked, "Captain from conn. They're ready to jettison the last load, sir."

Ben had told them weeks ago that he wanted to see the last debris leave the hangar deck himself. He glanced at his watch. Only hours to Pearl, and they had finished the job, eight hundred men working twelve hours a day, seven days a week, for two weeks; quartermasters turned morticians, yeomen turned stretcher-bearers, storekeepers cutting metal, musicians driving tractors, crypto officers toughening pudgy palms on jagged aluminum. They had moved the mass of scorched and twisted metal from hangar deck and messing compartment and gradually, piece by piece, dropped it in a twenty-five-hundred-mile trail from Japan to the Hawaiian archipelago. The last bodies had come from the chiefs' mess, a week after the attack. Among them was Ape Gorman, who should have been in the wardroom instead. The last were, of course, the worst, from the tropic heat, and the growing fatigue of those who had to handle them.

Incredible, elastic crew, gathering with their nightly beer on the forecastle, where the worst of the havoc had been, for happy-hour with the four surviving bandsmen around the bass drum with the scorched skin. No real food, for no real galley: sandwiches, or sometimes hot soup, meal after meal. Two cans of beer a day for everyone, finally, not just the burial detail, and every night, for many of them, sleep on a steel deck. And not one case of combat fatigue once the threat of kamikazes was over and the one berserk seaman who had attacked the ensign was removed. Ben moved to the starboard side of the bridge. Half a fuselage and the twisted, melted engine of an F6F projected from the barn door.

"Let her go," he said to his talker. The carcass rolled through the opening, half turned in midair, and fell with a giant splash into the racing wake. Ben watched a great bubble break from its cockpit as it disappeared under his bridge. "Pass the word: Beer call. Except watch-standers and the special sea detail, six cans per man."

"Six?" The officer of the deck swallowed. "Four hours from Pearl, sir?"

"Why not, mister?" Ben growled. "Nobody *else* is going to celebrate."

TWO

A signalman noticed the cars first, peering through the telescope by the flag bag. Ben heard him exclaim and put his own glasses on Diamond Head. The road from Waikiki was black with parked automobiles. Animated, colorful specks clustered beside them. Ben squinted and saw fluttering handkerchiefs. He was sure that above the ring of *Shenandoah*'s engines he could hear a faint cacophony of horns.

Instinctively he turned to see if an Army transport was returning from Okinawa. There was not another ship in sight, except the Navy tug pounding out of the channel chop to greet them. He focused again on the tug. Her halyards, three to a yard, were decked with flags; as he watched, a puff of steam appeared and in a moment he heard a deep, resounding series of blasts.

Oh, God, he thought, the beer! He whirled and strode to the pilothouse door. "Mr. Turk!" he called.

The OOD stepped out. "Yes, sir?"

"Prepare for honors. Something's going on. Quarters entering the channel, I guess it'll have to be dungarees, divisions with less than five men to fall in with the other divisions."

"Quarters?" the OOD gaped. "My God, sir, half of them won't be able to *find* the flight deck, let alone——"

"Quarters," Ben said again. "Pass the word now, quarters at 1300."

"Aye, aye, sir," the young man said.

Ben cast an angry eye at CINCPACFLEET headquarters,

dazzling white in the Makalapa sun. Why the hell hadn't they sent a dispatch first? The tug swung in a wide arc and fell in on their starboard bow. In her fat-bellied midships, Ben saw aloha shirts on the first civilians he had seen in a year: press photographers, apparently. He wished they had come alongside to port, where the damage was less. When the harbor pilot came aboard, Barney Epstein was on his heels, a folded newspaper under his arm, a briefcase in hand. He climbed immediately to the bridge and Ben took him to his sea cabin and poured him a cup of coffee.

"You look," said Ben, glancing at the briefcase and paper, "like a Philadelphia lawyer off the Paoli Express."

"You look like they squeezed you through the turbines," said Epstein.

"I lost a few pounds." He jerked his head at the tug full of photographers. "How come they aren't sneaking us in like we got a dose?"

"Funny thing," said Epstein, "somebody leaked it." He handed Ben the *Honolulu Advertiser*. On the front page, in all her tattered glory, *Shenandoah* was limping into Agana Harbor in Guam. The photo was nightmarish: she had still had her starboard list and her flight deck was a shambles. He had been colossally insolent to try to bring her back at all.

"*You* leaked it," he decided. "Jesus, there's nothing like showing the Japs what they did!"

"The Japs thought they sunk her," Epstein said cheerfully. "This proves they didn't."

The column was a lead one: HAMMERING HOWIE HOWLAND'S FLAGSHIP TO RETURN. And it ended with immortal words from Howie: "The ship that won't be sunk, can't be sunk. And someday I hope to drop her hook in Tokyo Bay."

"Did *you* write that?" asked Ben.

Epstein smiled secretively. "You want your medals approved, for the men, don't you?"

"They've *got* to be. I'm recommending Josh Lowery for the Navy Cross. There aren't a dozen people left on the ship who don't rate the Bronze Star."

"What about you?" asked Father Epstein.

"I ought to get the Congressional Medal," Ben said modestly, "just for not wetting my pants. But I'll settle if Howland doesn't court-martial me."

"Would you settle for a Navy Cross?" Epstein asked quietly. His brown eyes were serious. "And a spot promotion to captain?"

Ben's pulse pounded. Captain? Josh was right: if he made captain he could take her to Philly. He was thinking of that when the ship's ague began again. The drumming started aft, and you sensed it before you felt it and you felt it before you heard it, but now, with channel water under them, some resonance made it worse, and the vibration of it swung open his locker door; he shut it absently because it was full of Mitch's clothes.

"Barney," he said, shaking his head, "there's nothing I can say."

"The pen," said Epstein, "is mightier than the sword. Have you cooled off on Golden Boy?"

"I seem to have been the only eyewitness," Ben said. "Can I make it stick?"

"I don't know. Don't write the charges yet, smooth. I've got one to add."

"To *add?*"

Epstein stirred his coffee. "Ben, who do you think left those poor bastards to cook in the brig? Who do you think went past us in that passageway?"

It seemed years ago. "Some marine?"

"What about Lee?"

"What would he be doing in the brig?"

"You sent him. At breakfast. With Watkins' charges."

"Christ," breathed Ben. "You're right! But maybe he'd left."

"Not according to the Jap."

"The Jap?"

"The Jap's at Base Hospital Eight." Epstein drew from his scratched briefcase a legal-size paper, and Ben could see that it was written in Japanese. "Deposition," said Epstein. "Or half a deposition." He began to read, " 'The lieutenant commander was between the cells talking to the black man when the ship was hit.' *Me:* 'How did you know he was a lieutenant commander?' *Yokawa:* 'The corporal had taught me the ranks. He wore golden leaves on his collar. He yelled something to the sergeant and I thought the sergeant would come down and let us out. All at once there was much flame and much smoke, and the officer ran away.' "

"My God," said Ben, "it was him!"

" 'I could see' " continued Epstein, " 'the sergeant lying by his little table on the landing up above. He tried to stop the officer and grabbed his trousers. Soon I could not breathe well any longer and so I became unconscious.' "

"We've *got* him!"

"Have we? I wonder. He can always claim it was more important to get to his station."

"My God, Barney, I was *exec*, and I stopped long enough!"

"That's true," conceded Epstein. "And it shows his state of mind. We'd need that, because, don't forget, he's got the Purple Heart, and he never panicked before. Well, this shows he panicked in the brig, so he could have jumped later."

"*Could* have? Christ, I saw him." The tiny doubt had been born then, the doubt he could never admit. Perhaps Epstein was dubious, too. Ben had after all forgotten sending Lee to the brig; from the moment the bomb hit time had been a hideous scramble; was he sure, really sure, Lee had jumped before the *baka*, or been shaken off afterward? Of course he had jumped. "I *saw* him go," he murmured again.

Epstein accepted it. "O.K. But there's one other thing. Who's responsible for seeing that nobody's locked in the brig of a ship in battle? Mitch or you?"

"Legally, it was Mitch's fault, or mine. Anyway, they *were* locked up, and it's already in the battle report, and I'm *still* charging him. If they want to hang me too, O.K."

THREE

Three men marched over the side backward from the flight deck when a chief yelled "Open-ranks" as the *Shenandoah* was nudged to Pier 1010 by her tugs. They caused screams from the University of Hawaii majorettes and the Army band missed a beat, but fortunately all could swim and the water sobered them and they were hauled cheering and waving aboard the nearest tug.

From the port wing of the bridge Ben spotted a seaman drinking beer through a straw from a can in his shirt pocket and had him removed from ranks. He heard the surviving *Shenandoah* tractor start, and saw it rumble down the greasy ranks, the driver red-eyed and intent, his passenger standing like Ben Hur at the rear, alighting at his place in ranks and sending his chauffeur back to the island with an imperious wave.

As she moved dockside a line of children from the base elementary school held a long cloth panel: *"Aloha Shenandoah."* Rain showered suddenly and three grass-skirted hula girls waited on steaming asphalt for the band to play again. A *Shenandoah* gunner's mate on the flight deck lurched toward them, fell into the catwalk, and was barely restrained from trying to jump forty feet to the pier by two of his buddies.

The *Shenandoah*'s surviving band, four strong, strove mightily from its station of honor forward, and "When the Saints Go Marching In" blared through the rain-washed air. The first bow-line messenger looped across and then the after lines and the springs. The special sea detail, which was supposed to have waited for its beer ration, lost a man between ship and dockside, and by the time he was fished out, Ben's last clean shirt was soaking with sweat.

The huge band on the pier, in brass and khaki and white-webbed belts, was suddenly silent as its conductor raised his baton. Unheeding, the little group forward blared on. Ben turned to the quartermaster and said, "Shift colors." The great battle flag, grimy with stack gases, began to ripple down from above as the signalman broke the halyards loose. The chocks squealed in the twisted main-truck, and the in-port flag rippled aft. Ashore, the bandleader's arm descended. From the dock the ponderous Navy dirge Ben had last heard at the Naval Academy thundered "For Those in Peril on the Sea."

The band of the *Shenandoah* punctuated the Navy hymn, blending a sour bagpipe skirl that almost made you blush. The OOD turned to the phone talker and said, "Pipe those idiots down!"

"Belay that," Ben called. "Let them play."

"As an impresario," sighed Father Epstein, "you make a good fighter pilot."

"It's our party," said Ben, "not theirs."

"Don't count on it," Father Epstein said.

CHAPTER TWO

ONE

Hammering Howie Howland, smiling all the while, slipped the Navy Cross over his head. Ben, smiling all the while, accepted it. Flashbulbs glittered—one, two, three. The two double-spaced lines of dungaree-clad men looked blearily on. A drunken metalsmith in a rear rank yelled "Hooray" and a fireman fainted from excess emotion or Schlitz. Ben stepped back, saluted, and passed the word to secure from quarters. Suddenly he saw Christy Lee talking to Chief Levine by a five-inch mount.

"Show the admiral the charge," he told Epstein. He crossed the splintered flight deck. Levine saw him coming, touched his hat in a faint salute, and seemed to disappear into the air. Golden Boy swung around without the slightset shadow of shame or fear in his clear blue eyes, and saluted mechanically.

"What the hell are *you* doing here?" Ben demanded.

"She's my ship too," Golden Boy pointed out. "Could I ask what's going on?"

"Follow me, Golden Boy," Ben said tightly. He led Lee through the hangar deck, down the labyrinth they had had to learn now that half the ship's ladders were cut away. They moved through deserted, sooty passageways still heavy with the odor of gasoline and oil and charred human flesh, and then they were at the dogged-down hatch to the brig.

"Open it," he ordered. Without hesitation Christy Lee lashed out at the heavy steel dogs as if he were a boxer punishing an opponent; he hit them with the heel of his hand, and the tremor ran back through his arm and quivered his shoulders all the way down the back muscles to his hips. The hatch opened and Ben led the way down the ladder. The bodies had been gone for over ten days, but it was one of the compartments that had been judged better to seal than to try to air, and the burned-pork smell was very strong. Ben felt nauseated, but he forced himself down to the cell level and into the narrow passageway between Watkins' cell and the kamikaze's.

"Come back here," he said. His voice rang metallically. Lee moved down the ladder and back between the cells. His nose wrinkled in disgust.

"Smell bad?" demanded Ben. "Lysol helps, and soap and water. You want to try?"

"Why me?"

"Because you put it here!"

Lee looked at him as if he were mad. "If you've got charges," he said, "make them!"

"Follow me," said Ben.

TWO

Hammering Howie Howland sat half sideway on a tall stool by the flag-plot table. He handed the charge sheet to Lee, who moved under a porthole to read it. Epstein, across the compartment, toyed absently with the hand crank of a search radar. A clock with a cracked face ticked loudly on the bulkhead. Hammering Howie was studying him.

"You know, Casco," he murmured with a tiny smile, "if you'd cost me a destroyer out there or had to abandon after dark and lost some men, or been hit the next day—I'd have had your ass on a silver platter."

"I had men trapped, sir."

"Because you waited too long!"

"Yes, sir," admitted Ben. "Are you going to approve the Navy Cross for Josh Lowery? He's the one who saved her."

"A hero ship," the admiral said, "has to have heroes, doesn't she? And your buddy here must have told you about our little surprise for you. . . ."

"Yes, sir."

"You can't have a hero ship," Hammering Howie said, "without a hero skipper."

Christy Lee moved from the port, gave the admiral back his charges, and said, "Could I ask, sir, what you intend?"

"It may depend," Hammering Howie said, "on what you have to say."

"I'm not going to even bother to reply."

Howland growled, "You better. And right now, I think."

Lee moved to the plastic plotting board on which the red-circled Kawanashi and the last kamikaze were plotted; there was no plot at all on the plane that had sneaked in and got them first.

"I was on my way topside when the first one hit," he said. "I'd left the brig thirty seconds, maybe a minute before. Maybe two."

"The Jap told Mr. Epstein you were still there when it hit," Hammering Howie said. "Why would he say that?"

"Lying, maybe. Confused as to time, maybe. Are you going to take a goddamn POW's word for it?"

"I'm going to take whoever's word I feel like, because I'm not trying a case, I'm deciding whether to convene a general court-martial."

The clock ticked. Through the open port the band on the dock blared faintly: Bless 'em all, bless 'em all, The long and the short and the tall. . . ." Ben saw Golden Boy, straight teeth gleaming, in their kitchen in Annapolis, singing. "There'll be no promotion this side of the ocean . . . So cheer up my lads, bless 'em all."

"If this can be decided now," Howland pointed out, "we just might save six months' worth of legal crap in thirty seconds. All right, forget the brig. You're charged with jumping from your battle station: 'deserting in the face of the enemy.' Your commanding officer says he saw you go."

"I was blown off when the *baka* hit," Lee said flatly.

"And you hadn't opened fire because why?"

"I'd have raked the topsides of the *North Carolina*," Lee said, "and I'd be facing some *real* charges, instead of these ass-hole things."

"You're pretty damn arrogant," Ben lashed out. "And if you don't change your attitude, you're about to get another charge. And the admiral *himself* is a witness."

"I'm arrogant, sir," Lee said coldly to the admiral, "because I'm mad." He even looked mad. Jesus, thought Ben, if he'd been a politician, he'd be president. "I'm mad," Golden Boy went on, "because I'm sitting on something that explains it all, and I won't be able to sit on it much longer. He hates my guts, Admiral. And if he doesn't tell you why, I will."

Ben's tongue felt thick. "Go ahead, it's your story."

Lee said hoarsely, "Sir, it's personal. I'd almost rather disprove the charges."

"That's up to you," Howland said. "My advice is to throw away your violin and try to get off the griddle."

Lee looked at Ben. "I'm sorry, Ben." He took a deep breath. "His wife. At Annapolis. When I was a midshipman."

Ben lunged across the room, fist cocked. With amazing swiftness, Epstein was behind him and his arms were locked.

Eyes blazing, Ben swung to face him. "Get your goddamn hands off me!"

The brown eyes were calm. "No," Epstein murmured. "It's what he wants. That's all you'd have to do."

Hammering Howie's eyelids had dropped, and an odd expression of relief lay on his face, the same sort of look Ben had seen in the '30's on the *Nevada*, when Howland worked out a star sight wrong and, checking, found the mistake.

Ben was all at once horribly tired and almost sick. He shrugged off Epstein and moved across the room and looked out the port. Another dark-bellied rain squall was approaching and the band was heading for cover.

Hammering Howie said suddenly: "I want to speak to Commander Casco." Lee and Epstein left. The admiral tapped a pencil on the charges. "Ben," he said suddenly, and it was the first time he had ever used his first name, "I don't really think you want me to convene a court."

"*Want* it? I demand it!"

"You'd never prove the charges."

"He'll know he's been in a fight. We can prove he deserted the brig, anyway."

"Leaving three prisoners," the admiral said thoughtfully, "who died because the ship had left them locked in during an attack?"

"I'll take my chances."

The admiral shrugged. "*You're* not taking any chances. Mitch Langley was still alive; it was his ship; it was his responsibility."

"I don't believe in ghosts, and if I did, there'd be a couple of hundred of them up there on that fo'c'sle cheering us on."

"But the only man who saw him jump was you."

"I'm enough," said Ben. "He panicked below, and he panicked topside. It's that simple."

"No, Ben, it isn't that simple. You've got a hero ship, or you haven't. You've got *your* Navy Cross, but if you think I'm going to approve specifications for Lowery's, and Silver Stars, and enough bronze ones to cast you a new propeller, for a ship where three men died locked in the brig and another hundred dropped off——"

"They were boots," Ben said. "Not a single petty officer left this ship! You don't try eighteen-year-old kids with three months' training for hitting the silk when they think the ship's going down! Not when a lieutenant commander from the goddamn canoe college went too!"

There was a long silence, and Ben saw another tumbler slip into place in Howland's mind. Canoe college, canoe college? Why had he said that? "Yes," Howland said softly. "It makes you wonder, doesn't it? I mean, this guy was five-striper at the 'canoe college,' as you put it. God knows how he got there from whatever the hell cow town he came from——"

"Port Arthur, Texas," Ben said dully.

"Port Arthur, Texas," marveled Howland. "Well, he went through plebe year and all the rest and every year he got out there against the best college football teams in the country and when he ached the worst they sent him to chapel whether he wanted to go or not, and at ten-thirty every night they turned off the lights and if he wanted to study after that he had to go sit in a cold crapper, and if he ever got into any trouble he worked it off on a commando course at five A.M. or lugging a rifle around Smoke Park at night, and when the rest of the college kids were going home for weekends he was passing in review, and when he was a plebe he was getting his ass beat and when he was a first classman he was standing watches when he wanted to be laying some girl in town."

"He jumped," said Ben.

"And so he got out to the fleet, and he was at Savo and the Battle of the Coral Sea and Midway and the Second Battle of the Philippines, where he was wounded——"

"By a sliver of AA! Which he wouldn't have got if he'd been sitting inside that director instead of outside ready to jump!"

"Where he was wounded, and nobody ever accused him of turning yellow before, and——"

"Maybe he had a bad day!" Ben blurted. "Maybe he'd never been trapped before! I don't know, but he jumped!"

"*I* think you're mistaken. A Navy court would, too." The admiral got to his feet and wandered to the port. "But there are some people who wouldn't. You know who?"

Ben didn't answer, and the admiral jerked a thumb out the port. "They'd believe it! The public. The press! The war's almost over, their asses are saved, they'd love it. Annapolis man deserted, football star? Eat it up! And if you think I'm going to set him up for the concerted attack that people like to make on the professional naval officer who's accused of something, *anything*, from seducing the mayor's daughter to misappropriation of funds, you're crazy as hell!"

"I'll go around you," Ben said thickly. "I'll go to CINC-PACFLEET."

"Go ahead," suggested Hammering Howie. "He'll convene it. But see what a court-martial does to your spot promotion."

"I don't care if I go back to *chief!* He jumped!"

"See what it does to Lowery's Navy Cross."

"It won't be the first time he's been screwed."

"See what it does to the unit citation. You've got a hero ship, or you've got a hulk with ninety-three deserters and a bunch of slobs who got the hell whacked out of them and came dragging their asses home."

"They know what they did. What the hell's a piece of ribbon?"

"See what being witness in a court-martial," Howland said softly, "does to your wife."

Ben's throat tightened. He saw Terry on the hospital bed at Annapolis, afraid enough of officer life without scars to mar her looks, waiting as they peeled the bandages from her forehead and cheek. He saw tears in her eyes as she faced the mirror he held up; not as bad as he had feared, but worse than she had hoped.

"Is that all, sir?" he asked dully.

"That's all, Commander," Hammering Howie said. "Or Captain, as the case may be."

He spun around and left, too tight with anger to think. In a haze he moved down ladders and across the hangar deck. Teams from Commander, Service Forces, had begun to move through the ship, clipboards and flashlights in hand, evaluating damage. They would search out her broken keel and twisted shafts and the ribs of her body knocked askew and gather like crows at the sites of her wounds and write her death warrants on their clipboards until everyone would know how badly she was hurt. Within the next few hours her own crew would be gone, to barracks ships or replacement pools; only a few of them would be back to take her to Philly for what was now euphemistically described as "rebuilding," but which might well someday mean scrapping instead.

A line of men, some with seabags and others with only a few skimpy possessions salvaged from the rot below, was forming at the gangway. The men were filthy, because there had been no laundry for three weeks. The chief yeoman was standing by the OOD, checking off names. As each man passed he would wait while the chief found his name, then step to the officer of the deck, salute, mutter, "Permission to go ashore, sir," move to the gangway landing, face aft toward the invisible flag, and salute again. And that was all, even for plank owners Ben had known for the past five years.

He moved down the gangway in their midst, shaking hands with a beery boatswain, a sweating gunner, a tired fireman. A gray Navy bus was loading with ragtag first-division men; with the key to Honolulu firmly in their grip once they could find dress whites, they were bulls on the scent of a herd of cows. But as the bus passed the foot of the gangway, word rippled through the length of the vehicle and every single hand snapped to the salute. They may have been saluting the ship, for all he knew, but he returned the salute anyway, and somebody yelled, "So long, Benny-boy," from the safety of the crowd. He had been aboard five years, and had no idea that the white hats called him that.

The bus rumbled down the wet asphalt dock, leaving a muddy tire track across the *"Aloha Shenandoah"* banner that the grammar-school kids had held. He had a sudden desire to stop everything for one last happy-hour on the flight deck and a last showing of *West of the Pecos*, but the cold blue light of a blowtorch was glaring there already.

A Red Cross mobile canteen, with an ancient mama-san behind the counter, was closing its panels. A radio cackled cheerfully of war production. In front of it, dunking a doughnut in a paper cup, stood Chief Gunner's Mate Levine, every smile-line on his face carved and eyes twinkling with anticipated joys along Hotel Street. Ben wandered over.

"Coffee, Skipper?" mumbled the chief, mouth full of doughnut. The mama-san poured it and the two of them looked up at the gray *Shenandoah* looming against full-bellied clouds, bursting with gold, sailing in from the west. Then the chief said, "They going to scrap her in Philly, sir?"

Ben wouldn't admit it. "Hell no. But I don't think she'll get back in this war."

"No," said the chief. "She won't. Almost over. Man, the air corps just bombed hell out of some town, really creamed it, just came over the news."

"What town?"

"I don't know, sir. Nothing I ever heard of."

The shrill scream of a boatswain's call sounded from the quarterdeck. Hammering Howie was leaving and Ben was not there to see him off. "Shouldn't you be up there, Captain?"

"I guess," Ben said, making not a move. He blew on his coffee.

"Should I save you that seat in the mess?" the chief wanted to know.

"It won't be necessary," Ben said thoughtfully. "As a matter of fact, Chief, I'm going to fold. No charges. So we all forget it happened."

They watched the admiral move to his sedan. He rolled off down the dock, fender flags whipping, in lonely majesty in the stern sheets.

"There's a rumor," the chief remarked, "they're going to spot-promote you to captain."

"That isn't why I'm folding," Ben flushed.

"I didn't figure it was," said the chief. "But take what you can get."

They looked up at the battered island structure. "Funny thing," reflected the chief. "I'm a plank owner, like you. There's something, when you're a plank owner."

"Yes," said Ben.

"Like you're hauling ass across the lagoon dead-drunk after Mogmog, or maybe staggering down the dock after that damn ferry ride from Seattle and you see her sitting there and she ain't a hunk of iron at all, man, she's home. And when she starts out the way this one did, with everybody bulkheading about what a pig she is, and we end up with a hero ship——" He snapped his fingers. "That's it!"

"That's what?"

"Hero ship! Hiroshima! That's the name of that town in Japan."

Ben had never heard of it. It began to rain in huge splatting blobs and the front of the Red Cross van slammed behind them and they sprinted across the dock, slipping and hurdling puddles, for their charred steel home.

The end of the war pulled the rug out from under Hammering Howie and he not only didn't get to fondle the Emperor's horse, but wasn't invited to the ceremonies on the *Missouri*. He retired as a vice admiral and for all Ben knew grew the finest geraniums in San Diego County. Six months later Ben, who got the spot-promotion but was transferred to Japan before the *Shenandoah* left Pearl, had a clipping from Philly. It read: "The USS *Shenandoah*, Pacific veteran, was towed from Philadelphia to the reserve fleet in Bayonne today. It is not known whether she will be repaired from extensive war damage or scrapped." Scrawled across the bottom, over the signature, "Levine," were the words: "Hero Ship."

CHAPTER THREE

He lay in his bed at the Marriott Motor Inn listening to the crunch of tires on Memorial Drive and the growl of snowplows working between the inn and the Pentagon. Gray frost behind the slats of the venetian blind reminded him of rime ice on the leading edge of an aircraft wing. He heard snow squeaking underfoot. The trunk of a car opened and slammed and a husband called impatiently for his wife. He lay still, reluctant to rise.

Usually he awakened confidently, but the confrontation he had promised himself with Admiral Christy Lee, and the lunch with Epstein's senator, loomed on the horizon and depressed him so that he wanted to sink back to sleep. But he got up and breakfasted and rumbled in the rented car a few hundred slushy yards to the Pentagon. He parked in the restricted zone he had used when he ran the helicopter desk during Korea, a thousand years ago. He trotted through falling snow to the basement arcade.

No particular military emergency loomed so the Pentagon was taut. Civilians and military men scurrying late to work showed the strain. When peace menaced, Pentagon administrators became Horatios armed with memo pads and pens at a thousand bridges: overworked, understaffed, threatened with the loss of bodies to State or Interior or Treasury. The cutbacks never came, but one never knew.

Ben climbed the ramps and drifted from frosted-glass slums to the paneled dignity of Chief of Naval Operations country. Christopher S. Lee, Admiral, USN, was already only four doors removed from the sacred foyer. Ben felt like a seaman passing through wardroom country; the deposition in his pocket seemed a poor talisman for what he intended to do.

Lee's outer office, carpeted in scarlet, was furnished with a desk for his marine orderly. Apparently the marine was on an errand. Ben opened a paneled door with Lee's name engraved on a brass plate. But he was not yet in the sanctum, merely in a secretary's office. A chubby WAVE j.g. looked up from a filing cabinet. Ben smiled at her, noting stacks of files ready for a move. Suddenly he wanted to catch Lee off balance behind the barricade of oak and brass.

"I'm Captain Casco," he told the girl, giving her a card. "I was his skipper once. I'll surprise him, if you don't mind."

She looked confused and he took advantage of it to open the last oaken door. She did not follow. He faced an empty desk beneath tall windows, flanked by a U.S. flag and the blue-and-gold standard of the Navy Department. In a place of honor hung an autographed photo of the President. On every other wall hung oils of naval battles by the Navy artist Shepler. The lush quiet inside was oddly disturbed by the snarl of an electric razor. The door to the private bathroom was open, and at the mirror stood Christy Lee, unsuspecting, apparently hurried at home and shaving on government time. Ben sank into a leather chair facing the bathroom and waited, studying him.

From the back he had not changed. Broad shoulders, narrow hips, thighs firm under blue uniform pants just a little too tight. The wiry blond hair seemed unthinned. Lee finished, blew his razor clean, and put it away. He turned and started for his desk. Ben saw that he was tanned as ever, with the outthrust jaw and the flaring nostrils that were supposed to denote physical courage. A perfect CNO, if you were casting for a movie.

"Hello," Ben murmured from the depths of the chair. "Hello, Admiral."

Christy Lee froze for an instant. Ben, watching for the tiniest flicker of fear to cross his face, could only be sure that he was startled. He recovered immediately. "What the hell are you doing here, and how'd you get in?" He called the WAVE on an intercom. "This gentleman wasn't announced, Lieutenant," he commented, putting faint quotes on the "gentleman."

The WAVE sounded stricken. "I'm sorry, sir."

"It wasn't her fault, Admiral," Ben remarked.

"I'm sure it wasn't," Lee commented. "What did you do? Crawl? All right, you've got five minutes. I'm going to a breakfast for the Thai Naval Mission." His eyes flicked to Ben's. "At the White House."

"Bully for you," commented Ben. He stood and moved to an oil painting of the USS *Washington*, crouched low at night off Savo Island, gushing flame from sixteen-inch batteries trained port and starboard. He glanced at the other oils. "No *Shenandoah?*" he prodded.

"Four minutes."

Ben faced him. "Resign."

"Sure. When?"

"Now. This week."

Lee said, "You had any psychiatric treatment lately?"

"Not lately, not ever."

The admiral ignored him. "Are you a Republican or a Democrat?"

Ben smiled softly. "It isn't politics, Golden Boy."

Lee flushed, but his voice was controlled. "You're talking to an admiral. Are you still on the retired list?"

"Yes," Ben smiled. "Are you going to call me to active duty and court-martial me?"

"No, but I may throw you out on your ass."

"Call your marine, then," Ben advised, "or you won't make that breakfast."

"I'll be there," Lee promised. He glanced at his watch. "Three minutes."

"I'll show you why you're going to resign." Ben took the Jap's statement from his pocket.

"You know," the admiral said, "I'm not very interested. You were already a captain, practically speaking, twenty years ago, with a new Navy Cross and a big fat carrier, and I was nothing but one more black-shoe lieutenant commander in a world full of aviators. You threw your best punch then. You sure as hell aren't going to frame me now."

"Frame you? No, I'm not." Ben tossed the deposition on the desk. "But I didn't throw my best punch. My best punch was this."

He watched Lee intently as the admiral scanned the deposition. Not a flutter of concern passed his face, only what appeared to be wonder. He read the heading again. "*Deposition?* This isn't a deposition! How can you have a deposition unless both parties question the witness?"

"The technicalities don't matter. I'm blackmailing you. Nothing legal. Just get the hell out or I'll light the fuse."

Lee seemed not to hear him. He tapped the sheet. "You mean you had this made up twenty years ago?"

"Made up? Epstein questioned the Jap, if that's what you mean."

"Where?" snorted the admiral.

"Base Hospital Eight. At Pearl."

"A scared, burned POW who probably thought if he lived you were going to hang him by the balls? If you *did* question him, I wonder what you promised him?"

Suddenly Ben realized the enormity of his mistake. Epstein was right: they'd had one advantage, surprise, and now he'd given it up. Lee crumpled the paper, looked toward his wastebasket, changed his mind, and smoothed it out. "I'm keeping it," he decided. "It's got all the legal weight of a butterfly in a hurricane, but what the hell." He jerked his head at the President's picture. "He might get a laugh himself, someday."

"He might, or he might not. He's got a Senate committee to get you through. *They* aren't going to laugh."

Comprehension dawned but no fear. The admiral looked relieved, if anything. "The Senate Armed Services Committee," he murmured. "I bet some of them are Epstein's clients. Mosk, that's for sure. You are indeed a shipmate. Will you be here for the show?"

"Maybe," said Ben.

"I hope so," Lee said. "It may distress you, though. A hero ship's being scrapped up in Jersey, and on top of that we learn that maybe she wasn't such a hero ship, since damn near a hundred men deserted her——"

"And one officer," spat Ben. "Don't forget him. Look, you're threatening a ship that's being scrapped. You can do better than that. What about my wife?"

Lee shrugged. "Well, she's your reason, isn't she? If I have to show your motive, she's it. If you're stupid enough to press it——"

"I am."

Lee regarded him strangely. He tapped the deposition. "Then why show me this ahead of time?"

He was on dangerous ground. "To give you a chance to keep it out of the papers," Ben said thickly.

"Because it makes the ship look bad? You didn't care about that at Pearl. No—something else. I wonder if you *do* think I jumped? Only you're not sure? I wonder if you want to see if some great remorse will come over me, and I'll sneak away in the night?"

"The Jap saw you leave the brig, *we* saw you in the passageway," Ben said softly, "and I *saw you jump!*"

Lee looked at his watch. "Five minutes is up." He looked deeply into Ben's eyes. Then he said, quite softly, "I left the brig before we were hit, Ben."

Ben got up, throat tight with anger, and moved to the door. He heard Lee say, "Ben?"

"Yeah?" He turned. The blue eyes regarded him unwaveringly.

"And I *was* blown over the side."

Something snapped. "*Bullshit!*" he yelled. He slammed out of the office, brushed by the startled girl, and drove back to the Marriott Inn. In his room he began viciously to pack. He had fired too soon, he had flushed the quarry, the bluff had failed where a surprise attack would have succeeded. He called Epstein and told him.

"Did he deny the facts?"

"He always has, hasn't he?"

"I mean again."

"Yes. He was very convincing. Like he believed himself."

"Anybody else with you?"

"Of course not."

"I wonder why he bothered. Ben?"

"Yes?"

"Let's not cancel that luncheon?"

He thought of home and fog-rinsed air and the sun ruddy over the Gate. "I'm leaving. The hell with it."

"He's going to be *CNO*, Ben! It's not much of a Navy sometimes, but it's the only one we got!"

"Oh, for Christ's sake," Ben sighed. "Two o'clock?"

"The Mayflower," said Epstein.

CHAPTER FOUR

ONE

Senator Mosk, elbow on the snow-white table-cloth and picking his teeth behind a hand, was watching him speculatively. He was a pleasant, silver-haired little gentleman with bright foxy eyes. "Captain Casco—or do you prefer 'mister'?"

"Mister," Ben said. "I'm very civil now."

"Well, sir, I'm surprised at you. And Barney!" he chided Epstein. "This schmuck should have been stopped twenty-three years ago!"

"Yes," agreed Father Epstein. "He should."

"Suppose, though," Mosk said, "I start to question him in committee and he's as cool as he was then? Or this morning?"

"He will be," Ben had to admit.

The senator spread his hands. "You see? He knows it's coming. If he could convince your Admiral Howland then, he can convince the committee on Friday. I've met him. He *looks* like he ought to be CNO."

"Will you have him appear, anyway?" Epstein begged.

"You haven't *got* anything, Barney," protested the senator. "An uncollaborated eyewitness won't do it, Mr. Casco, when there's the cause for enmity *you* have. Pardon me but that's true. And a one-sided deposition is no good either."

"But *will* you?" Barney insisted. "If I come up with more?"

Mosk shrugged. "All right."

That night, at dinner with Barney and his wife, Ben asked him what he had in mind, but Epstein wouldn't say.

TWO

Father Epstein's Nisei secretary was not at her desk, so Ben crossed the reception room and tapped lightly at the door. Epstein's shoes lay beside it side by side like sailboats rafted in a tidal stream. Epstein sat behind his cluttered desk, stockinged-feet up. He was dictating into a machine, but now he put the mike away, moved across the room, and pulled up a straight-backed chair.

"I want you to get the right feeling, from the beginning. You'll be sworn, first. You'll be asked your name, and give your rank, and be sure you don't forget the 'retired.' Don't give them anything extra. Keep it simple, but detailed. Now, to start with, tell me your whole story, from the moment you sent Golden Boy out of the wardroom to the brig with Watkins' charges."

Ben was halfway through his rehearsal when he heard the outer door open. Thinking it was Epstein's secretary, he went on, but Epstein put up his hand. There was a rap of a ring on the office door and Epstein, looking puzzled, opened it.

Christy Lee, wearing blues, his three narrow stripes gleaming above the broad one, regarded them coldly. "Well," he said, "isn't this chummy? This makes it simple."

"It's simple already," Epstein said. "If you have counsel, I'll talk to him. I'm not talking to you."

"Oh, I've got counsel," Lee said. "It's just that I like to have it out, man to man. Casco warned me, I got an invitation to appear Friday—never been done before, I found out— and now I'm warning you."

"Let your lawyer warn me."

"He'll warn you too. I'm suing you for slander. Both of you. You're trying to wreck my career, and I'm suing you jointly and separately for one million dollars each. How's that grab you?" he smiled at Ben.

Ben felt a sinking sensation. "If you win," he said, "I'll see if I can't dig it up."

"I'll win, all right," Lee said.

"You're bluffing, Golden Boy," said Epstein. "And you can tell your lawyer—if there is one—I said so. Now, leave, if you don't mind."

The outer door opened again and Epstein tensed. He called something out in Japanese, perhaps telling the girl that he was busy, but she must have missed it, because she appeared smiling at the door. Behind her was a short, squat Japanese. Ben stared at him. The hair was gray, the man wore a gray moustache and now he was overweight, but there was something in his stanch bearing that evoked a memory, a bad memory, of fear and fuel oil and smoke and burning flesh. The little Jap bowed stiffly at Epstein, and then Ben, and shot a glance at the admiral and bowed more deeply to him.

Ben watched Lee, his heart pounding, aware that Barney was tense as well. For a fleeting instant he caught the same glassy look he had seen in Golden Boy's eyes when he jumped; then it was gone and there was nothing in the admiral's tone to hint that he had ever seen him before. "Who's he?"

"A client," Epstein said. "In from Osaka. Would it be all right if I talked to him alone, or would you like a lesson in legal Japanese?"

Lee looked at them coldly, speculatively. "All right, gentlemen," he said. "I'll go. Sleep tight tonight."

He stalked through the door and slammed it. Ben watched the Japanese. He and Epstein were in animated conversation. Once the girl went to a filing closet and produced an Academy "Lucky Bag" yearbook and they looked up Lee's picture in the graduating class; later, she went to a file in the outer office and brought a glossy portrait of Lee as a commander, apparently from the files of the Public Information Office. Finally Epstein, face flaming, spoke to her in Japanese. Yokawa bowed again and followed her out.

"My God," Ben gasped. "Where did you *find* him?"

"He took me to dinner in Osaka last year," Epstein said quietly. "And I cabled him transportation."

"From Japan?"

Epstein shrugged. "I had the money, if he had the time. He's coming home for dinner tonight. Would you like to join us?"

"Sure!"

"Or would you rather go home to your goddamn choppers?"

Ben stared. Something was wrong, sour. "Go *home?* Hell no. Did you see that look on Lee's face? Christ, wild horses couldn't drag me away!"

"Go home, Ben," sighed Epstein. He crumpled the deposition and dropped it into his wastebasket. "An honest man, Okawa."

"What the hell are you getting at?"

"He isn't sure it was Golden Boy."

CHAPTER FIVE

He stood at the big bay window with a Scotch in his hand, waiting for Terry; they were going out to dinner at Fisherman's Wharf with his partner, a regular Thursday-night chore. He had slept all the way from Albuquerque west, and so could not honestly claim fatigue, but the prospect of dining out left him cold. A dead vacuum had settled at the pit of his stomach. Every time he read of a naval movement or deployment or an appropriation fight in Congress, every time he opened a retirement check, he would think of Christy Lee in the great JCS room in Washington, and he knew already how it would nag at his guts.

He glanced at his watch. Terry, as usual, was dragging her butt; so was his helicopter on the Oakland 6:15 commuter hop. He picked up a pair of binoculars from the coffee table and scanned the haze from the Bay Bridge to Alcatraz; finally he spotted his chopper, nose down and tail high, thrashing desperately toward the Ferry Building to make up time. It was already late; undoubtedly the fault of some steady rider who had presumed on the pilot's friendship. He tried to remember who had the 6:15 this month; the hell with it, let Operations worry about it.

"Come *on*, Ben, forget the schedule!" Terry said beside

him. "How do you think they got through the week? Zip me up."

He zipped her up and poured her a martini. He slid open the plate-glass door and together, as they liked to do for their evening drink, they stepped to the cement balcony overlooking Russian Hill. If he counted, he could see the gravel roof of his mother's house—in which, he'd heard, a Chinese family lived—and the peak of her father's false front, where her mother still reigned.

"Rough?" she asked of his trip. "You didn't pull any punches for me?"

"No," he said. She had made him promise before he left that he'd go all out for Lee, regardless of her reputation, damn the torpedos, full speed ahead. The threat of potential gossip was long past anyway; fifteen years ago, in Japan, it would have been an embarrassment to her at officers' wives luncheons; a few years later when he had commanded helicopter school, it would have been an irritation perhaps; even in Washington, before he retired, a minor annoyance. Now in civilian life it would have meant nothing. "He mentioned you again, but that isn't why I dropped it." He told her of the Jap. "Basically, though, it's because I warned him. If we'd hit him with it cold— Oh, the hell with it!"

"Why'd you warn him?" she wondered.

He had never told anyone of the tiny doubt, not even her, but now he did and suddenly he found that it was not a tiny doubt but a large one; that now that Lee had won he hoped his memory *had* lied.

"But you were sure at Pearl! You were sure when you *left* here!"

He found himself defending the doubt. "Off Tokyo everything was happening too fast and too slow. My time sense was screwed up. Why not my recollections, too? Memory lies, you know. Hatred distorts it. And I sure hated him enough."

"Yes," she smiled faintly. "I guess you did."

"Howland *could* have been right. Why would a guy like Lee panic? He'd been screened for panic a hundred times!"

"How do you screen men for panic?" she objected. "Have they got a machine, or what?"

"Well, for self-control, anyway. The whole Academy's a machine to screen out the kids with no self-control! Those P works they'd sweat, navigation against the clock? Plebe year's one screen, hazing's another screen, their stupid rules are screens. Football was a screen. He got through. Why would he lose control in the brig? That poor damn sergeant didn't! Watkins didn't!"

For a long while she looked out at the bay. "If he was in the brig," she murmured, "he lost control. He panicked. He damn near *died* of panic."

"But how do we know?"

She studied him. "You're an incurious bastard, Ben. You know that?"

"There was a time," he said carefully, "when it was just as well."

"There was a time," she admitted, "when it was almost essential." She grinned and pouted at the same time; when she did, she looked twenty. "Haven't you ever wondered what made Golden Boy tick? Didn't you ever try to guess what he was going to tell us that Christmas? His family dying, and the basketball game?"

"I kind of lost interest in his personal problems when I came charging through the door that night."

"Like a bull," she said, smiling. "Ben? I think he'd have been a lousy lay."

"I'm sure of it," he agreed, sure of nothing at all.

"He told *me* about his family," she said, "finally, the next week."

"I didn't know you saw him again," Ben muttered.

"You never asked me. You see what I mean? Incurious. Why do you think I stuck around Annapolis after you went charging *out?*"

"To wait for me to come home, I thought. But I see I was wrong."

She nodded. "You were wrong. I gave you hardly a thought, until the hospital. My entire affections were wrapped up in a poor twisted kid——"

"With five hundred letters from co-eds a season, and every admiral in the fleet aching to pat his butt and not one damn hurdle between himself and stars on his shoulders, as far as the eye could see? Jesus! How stupid can you *be?*"

"Pretty stupid, but that's the way I was. You knew that."

"Well," agreed Ben, thinking of Izzy Gomez, long dead, "I was warned."

"I know. I thought he needed me. *You* needed college algebra and psychology 1A. Psychology! God!"

"You thought he *needed* you? There's a line from a B movie! He was just trying to get into your pants!"

She looked up at him, and her eyes were suddenly amused. She nibbled on her thumb, speculatively. "Whereas you came over to play checkers."

Ben looked down at the old neighborhood. The vision of her silhouette in the window could still arouse him. "O.K.," he said impatiently. "What was bugging this poor, twisted kid who's going to be CNO? What was his bag, as our daughter would say?"

"Well, the night his family was wiped out, he kept his dad at the basketball game until the end——"

"And they got home and the levee had busted and flooded

the farm and all his little brothers and sisters were washed away, and he's never been able to sleep alone since?"

"Fire," she said quietly. "Not flood."

"O.K., fire." His mouth felt dry. He finished his drink, stepped inside, and poured another. He returned to the balcony and repeated, "Fire?"

"And not a farm. Just a frame house on a quiet street. Sisters, no brothers. And his mother."

"Well," said Ben, "maybe. It might have been a line of crap, too. Anyway, what's it prove?"

She ignored him and went on, "His father broke through the fire lines. And actually got upstairs, a wooden house, but his dad got upstairs."

"That's hard to believe, right there."

"Remember his dad?" she smiled. "I believe it. Anyway, Christy tried to follow. He got to the porch, and started in, and then he smelled it: burned pork, he said, and burned hair."

"Burned pork," Ben nodded. "O.K., suppose it happened. So what?"

"And he ran away from it. He couldn't stand it, the smell, and he ran off the porch, and he *hid!* His dad couldn't save anybody, but it was half an hour before they found Christy. In the neighbor's garage, hiding!"

The phone began to ring inside. He strode through the living room and answered it. It was Father Epstein from Washington.

"Ben, you watch the news tonight?"

"No."

Epstein cleared his throat. "You sitting down?"

"No. Go ahead, for Christ's sake! What happened?"

"Ben, he's dead."

"Who?"

"Golden Boy."

"Lee?"

"Hit an abutment on Memorial Drive."

"*Dead?*"

"They think he was doing around eighty-five, Ben."

"Jesus, you think——"

"Well, it's still snowing. *I* wouldn't drive thirty."

"Suicide?"

"It crossed my mind, so——"

"It *couldn't* be suicide!"

"Hang on, dammit! So I called the Navy. It's O.K., Ben. He was going to the airport to meet a plane. Maybe he was late."

Ben's knees trembled in relief. "To meet a plane," he murmured. "Thank Christ!"

"His dad," said Epstein. "Up from Texas to watch the Senate confirm him, and the ceremonies."

"His dad?" mumbled Ben.

"They were real close," said Epstein.

"Real close," Ben repeated. "Yes, they were." He said good-bye and put down the phone numbly and in a cold daze he crossed the living room and joined Terry on the balcony. He was shaking; he gripped the railing for a moment, eyes squeezed shut, until the weakness passed, and finally he told her and saw the shock and concern, and it was all for him. "Now, Ben, it wasn't your fault!"

"Terry, my God, suppose I was wrong?"

"He panicked," she said firmly, her eyes steady on his own. "He panicked in Texas, he panicked in the brig, he panicked and jumped off the ship. He panicked tonight."

"Tonight he was Golden Boy, with the President trusting him, and his wife and family proud of him and his *dad* meeting him. And tomorrow so far as he knew that Jap and

I were going to smash his whole life! Sure he panicked to-night! But suppose I was *wrong?*"

"Ben?"

Her eyes were full of misery. He laid his fingers against her cheek. He had been a coward to ask her to share the doubt, and he was sorry that he had. "Forget it, honey."

"No, Ben, listen!" She touched the scar above her fore-head, the one that stayed no matter how she powdered, the worst of all, and she said, "He panicked another time, before he ever saw the ship."

"Well," he said harshly, "caught by a pissed-off husband as big as him, I guess he did. What's *that* prove?"

"No. On the Baltimore Road."

"Annapolis?" He searched her face for deceit but she did not look away. "He was in that car? He *left* you? Bleeding?"

"He was, Ben," she said fiercely. "He *did!*"

"I didn't know it, though," he murmured, wondering if it were true. "I was still wrong, maybe—"

"Wrong to hate him?" Her eyes were very wise.

"As much as *I* did."

She looked away, over the darkening city. "That night you found us? You didn't believe me, did you?"

He found that he could not lie. "Not really, Terry, no."

"And it mattered?"

"It mattered," he said harshly, ashamed of his voice.

"You were right," she whispered. The fleeting light soft-ened her face. Far below a cablecar clanged. "I was lying."

Her gaze was steady enough to believe and full enough of love to doubt. "I see," he said, and his voice was worse.

"And Ben?"

"Yeah?"

"He *was* a lousy lay," she said and added, in the dirty chuckle she had not used for years, "No disrespect, of course."

He suspected that he would never really know, but the Hyde Street cable clattered on and the motorman shouted faintly, warning of the curve. He slipped his arm around her waist and for a moment hugged her close.

"We're late," he said. "Let's go."

ABOUT THE AUTHOR

Hank Searls was born in San Francisco in 1922. Throughout his boyhood he was fascinated with aviation. In 1940, six months before Pearl Harbor, he entered Annapolis. After graduation he spent a year on a battlewagon in the Pacific before starting flight training. During this service he saw the aircraft carrier U.S.S. *Franklin*, bombed and ablaze, survive off Tokyo Bay, and has been fascinated by the love of men for a ship ever since. Mr. Searls entered flight training but received his wings only after World War II was over. He continued to serve in the Navy through the Korean conflict, resigning in 1954. Thereafter he began free-lance writing. He is the author of four novels: *The Big X*, *The Crowded Sky, The Pilgrim Project*, and *The Hero Ship*.

Mr. Searls and his wife live in Malibu, California, where they sail a forty-foot ketch, skin dive, ski, and raise kids.

F   C.4

Searls

Hero ship